SO-FMH-822

THE
FOURTH
CODEX

ROBERT HOUSTON

THE FOURTH CODEX

Houghton Mifflin Company
BOSTON
1988

For information about permission to reproduce selections from this book,
write to Permissions, Houghton Mifflin Company, 2 Park Street,
Boston, Massachusetts 02108.

Library of Congress Cataloging-in-Publication Data

Houston, Robert, date.
The fourth codex / Robert Houston.
p.   cm.
ISBN 0-395-43097-6
I. Title.
PS3558.O873F6   1988
813'.54—dc19   87-37934
CIP

Printed in the United States of America

S 10 9 8 7 6 5 4 3 2 1

The author is grateful for permission to quote from the poem
"Mexico" by Richard Shelton. Reprinted by permission;
© 1976 The New Yorker Magazine, Inc.

TO LENA ROTH,
BERNIE AND HARRIET ROTH,
RICKY AND LISA SALBO,
AND MISSES JODY AND ROBYN SALBO

. . . and suddenly I know
everything I need is waiting for me
south of here in another country
and I have been walking through empty
rooms and talking to furniture

— *from "Mexico"*
by Richard Shelton

ACKNOWLEDGMENTS

The author would like to acknowledge the cooperation of William von Raab, U.S. Commissioner of Customs, in the research for this book, and to thank the many men and women of the U.S. Customs Service who generously shared their time and experiences with him. Among those are Special Agents Dale Brown, Duke Callahan, Mike McBride, Bill Laverty, Layne Peugh, Armando Ramirez, Richard Rivera, Don Wales, and Dan Walker; retired Special Agents Stewart Adams and Ray Medellin; Customs Patrol Officer Lambert Cross of the Tohono O'odahm Nation; and, most especially, Special Agent Skip Gerhart, gentleman and friend.

In Mexico, he would like to thank Anna Acuña and Teresa Camacho of the U.S. Embassy; Comandante Enrique Avalos Rodriquez, chief of the *resquardo aduanal*, Veracruz sector; and, for guidance, hospitality, and long friendship, Kevin and Leticia Giles of Mexico City.

In the preparation of the book itself, he would like to thank John Sterling of Houghton Mifflin for his great editorial forbearance, toughness, and insight, and Larry Cooper for his learning and care; Esther Newberg and Kathy Pohl of International Creative Management for their faith, and Maggie Curran for her good ideas; Boyd Nicholl, Laurie Kintzele, and Sara Nicholl for kindness and comfort; Greg Houston for his patience; and, most of all, always, Patricia Houston for her support, wisdom, and love.

THE
FOURTH
CODEX

ONE

WITH MALICE, Paz ignored the flat voice of the dispatcher from the radio under the pickup's dash and let his eyes follow Ethelbert Quivari, the Papago patrol officer, toward the mesquites of Mexico. Ethelbert, whose loose, sweat-mottled shirt hung like a circus tent over his global stomach, walked a few steps from the truck, stopped, carefully spread his legs, propped his hands on his knees, and bent over a footprint.

"This one's Bambi," he said. His soft, slightly accented voice broke the beats of silence that followed the radio's squawk.

Paz leaned out of the truck window. "The runner?"

"Yeah. We gonna lose him right over there." Ethelbert pointed past the obelisk of the boundary marker to what Paz could see even from the pickup was a well-worn path through the mesquites to a wash that ran beneath the border fence. "It's a highway there — wets, dope backpackers, Papagos going to visit across the line. That stuff, you know. But he crossed here."

"You sure it's him?"

Ethelbert paused before he answered to let Paz consider the stupidity of his question. "Yeah, I'm sure."

"Stake it, then. The army's got somebody coming to map the thing out today."

"That big a deal, huh?"

"If it was you and not your partner dead, you'd want a big deal, right?"

Ethelbert heaved himself upright and waddled to the truck to get a stake and a hammer. "If I was dead I wouldn't care. They didn't used to make such a big deal out of dead Indians." He grinned grimly, and what he had always reminded Paz of finally clicked into place: a jack-o'-lantern, with his missing front teeth and huge round face and heavy eyes, a gigantic, gentle jack-o'-lantern. The best tracker in the Customs Service, who had once taken eight rounds in all that fat from a guy driving a vanload of AR-15's into Mexico and had walked half a mile to his truck to radio for help, and he was a sweet jack-o'-lantern. Sweet, unless you tried to shorten his name a syllable, or to make fun of it. He wore it like war paint.

The radio spit and the dispatcher's clipped voice called Paz's code again. The dispatcher was a kid, an ex-rent-a-cop on the rise — he thought — and so afraid of screwing up he checked the Federal Code before he went to pee. He could wait; whatever it was could wait this Kodachrome desert morning. Ethelbert whacked the stake into the hard, sandy ground and said, "Quint? That's you, ain't it?"

"You take it for me. Tell them I've defected to the Mexicans," Paz said to him and thought, so I have.

The truck listed like a torpedoed ship as Ethelbert wedged himself behind the wheel. "You really going to quit?"

"Really going to." He leaned out of the way for Ethelbert to chuck his service revolver into the glove compartment. Like the rest of the Papago patrol officers, he always carried it stuck in his belt, Mexican-cop style. "Well, how do you make it?"

Ethelbert shrugged and cranked the truck. "Like I did this morning before everybody showed up and messed up the tracks. I make it there were two of them — backpacking dope in, I guess. Derek surprised them, the guy I call Cool Hand Luke took him down, then while Bambi took off running he got

Derek's pistol and gave him another one in his face to make sure. Then he drank his last beer and walked south to the line." His eyes stayed fixed on the steering wheel. "You going down to Hermosillo to talk to the Mexican cops?"

"Not me. They got a couple of hotshot cowboys from Houston region on the way down already."

"How come? You still chief of investigations, ain't you?"

The truck flattened a creosote bush as Ethelbert made a wide arc back to the washboard road that ran along the fence. "Lame duck. They only let me come out here today to keep me out of the coffee room." Paz smelled the bittersweet creosote, felt the dust building up in his nostrils like talc. He breathed deeply and remembered the deadening hiss of the air conditioning in his office, the insidious clicks of computer keyboards, the muffled, constant ringing of telephones from the secretarial pool. If begging was the only way he could have gotten out here away from the Monday morning routine of that office, he'd probably have done it. He felt embalmed in the place, had finally admitted to himself that he'd felt that way since he'd come back to the States five years ago.

"You leaving that soon?"

"Two weeks."

"Yeah. That's pretty soon."

They bucked along the ruts in silence. Paz waited for Ethelbert to go on. He didn't. "Going to work for my brother-in-law. Move to Mexico."

Ethelbert nodded. The radio called Paz again. They both ignored it.

"My divorce came through. *She* was the one who wanted to come back to the States. So why stay? My boy's in college year after next anyway."

Ethelbert nodded again.

Indians, Paz thought. He said, "I got my water-walking shoes twenty years ago last month — youngest special agent in the Customs Service then. Now I'm forty-five and I'm a dinosaur.

I get hives in front of a computer screen. Hell, I don't even like typewriters. The hotshots ask me if I knew Eliot Ness."

"They took our horses away from us," Ethelbert said sadly. "You know that? Gave them to the Border Patrol. I don't know if I want to do this without horses. I joined because they had horses."

Paz fought a smile and lost, then fought a laugh and lost that one, too. Ethelbert looked at him, sweet-faced and puzzled, as he shifted into four-wheel drive to ease through a wash.

"Horses!" Paz tried to explain. He thought of helicopters, computerized night-flying Lear jets, Blue Lightning intercept boats, great balloons dangling infrared cameras, of satellites, of whole suites of banked computers. Who the hell in Washington had finally discovered the Papago's horses? "Horses . . . goddamn, it's just . . . horses."

Ethelbert scowled, and Paz was almost grateful when the radio spat again. He answered this time. "Sierra 433, Alpha 4000."

"Report your location, Sierra 433," the dispatcher's toneless voice asked him.

"Papago reservation, Alpha 4000, approaching the Newfields gate. What's up?"

The dispatcher said something that the voice scrambler ate, and Paz asked for a repeat. As he did, Ethelbert slowed the truck by a place where the fence had been cut, all five strands of barbed wire, cut through and pulled back out of the way. Paz could see through the mesquites that the fence on the Mexican side, fifty feet away across the no man's land each country gave the other for elbow room, had been cut through, too. Ethelbert stopped the truck, rolled out of the seat, and braced himself over an invisible track again. Cattle thieves, Paz thought. Couldn't use the gate because of the cattle guard. Ethelbert was tracking — goddamn cutting sign on — small-time cattle rustlers while half the special agents in the Customs Service, plus the army, were roaring into his reservation to help him find some people who had blown his partner's face off last night. Indians.

The voice was clear this time. "Alpha 4000, Sierra 433. Report to special agent in charge's office at 1300 hours. Acknowledge."

Paz checked his watch: 11:18. An hour back to Tucson — after they got back to the reservation's Customs office and debriefed for half an hour. No lunch. What the hell was Harmon's hurry to see a man who had only two weeks to go? Nobody had yet needed him in a hurry in the four years he'd been in Tucson.

"What's up, Alpha 4000?"

"Acknowledge, Sierra 433."

Paz took a breath. Two weeks. "Ten-four, Alpha 4000."

Ethelbert performed his standing and bending engineering maneuvers to reach a track a few feet farther over.

"Ethelbert, let it go. You heard the man."

Ethelbert nodded and kept studying the track. "Two men on horses," he said. "They came through about three, four this morning, just after that little rain. They'll still be here. No tracks back out."

"Give it to the Border Patrol. Let's went."

Ethelbert moved to another track. "Maybe they seen somebody." He looked over his shoulder at Paz. "Derek's place, you know, is right up north about two miles. He keeps — kept — cattle. Nobody'll be watching them today. They got a medicine man in his house with him and everybody."

"I've got to move, Ethelbert."

Ethelbert used his hands like feet along his thighs to walk himself back upright. "You take the truck. You can send somebody back for me. Leave me my piece, OK?"

No better Customs cops in the service than the Papagos, the wisdom went. Just don't try to tell them how to do what they do. Or when to do it. Paz bowed to the wisdom and slid Ethelbert's revolver out of the glove box. Ethelbert moved into the shade of a mesquite in no man's land and waited for him.

"Don't hurry," he said as Paz handed over the revolver. "I got some beer stashed down by the gate." He smiled his grim grin again. "Mexican side. Indians can drink in Mexico. Am I going to see you again, Quint?"

"Can't say."

"How you feel about leaving?"

"It's tearing my guts out. To put it calmly."

"Well, I don't know. Maybe if they gave us our horses back, I'd feel different myself. You like horses?"

"Used to. Haven't met many in government work lately. At least not the front ends."

Ethelbert put out his hand to take Paz's — then froze, his hand poised, as stiff and unnatural as a mannequin's. Paz started to turn to see what Ethelbert did, but, at a wag of Ethelbert's index finger, froze, too. "You're about to," Ethelbert said softly, and now Paz picked up the sound, heavy things moving rapidly over the loose stones and dry sticks along the wash they'd just crossed. He backed silently away from Ethelbert until he had the cover of the pickup, raised his *guayabera* wedding shirt so his revolver was free, and unsnapped his holster. He motioned for Ethelbert to join him. Ethelbert shook his head and moved to the center of the cut in the fence, solid and still, the sweetness all driven from his face by concentration. Paz heard the voices now, rapid Mexican voices, whistling and yipping at something between breathless sentences.

The cattle broke into view first, four skinny, brown range cows loping ahead of the horsemen. Paz eased his pistol out, drew down across the hood of the pickup, and tensed. Four cows, he thought, four goddamn cows. Two weeks left, and it's going to happen to be because of four skinny cows.

The horsemen read the situation without losing stride. The lead *vaquero*, in chaps and sharp-toed boots and straw cowboy hat, spurred his horse and slapped at the nearest cow with his lariat. The cow bellowed and broke into a run; the others joined her. Their choice was the fence or up the side of the wash and into Ethelbert. They made the wrong one.

When they headed toward Ethelbert, he spread his arms, screamed something high-pitched and Papago, and fired his revolver upward, once. It was too much for the cows. They veered. One slammed the barbed wire before she got her footing and headed back north through the cactus and underbrush; Paz could see clearly the bits of blood and hide she left on the barbs.

The *vaqueros* didn't veer: the first one bore straight for Ethelbert. Paz whirled and aimed, but Ethelbert moved first. In a step as smooth as a dancer's, a nimble mountain moving, he avoided the horse, shot out a hand, and closed it around the *vaquero*'s wrist. Then he jerked. The *vaquero* flipped off his horse and splatted on the hard ground as easily as if he'd been a doll on a shelf. His companion reined hard to the right, just out of the reach of Ethelbert's other hand, and spurred through no man's land, through the rickety fence on the Mexican side, and off the edge of the world, into Mexico.

Ethelbert swore, Paz took it to be, in Papago and yanked the dazed *vaquero* to his feet. He was a kid, barely older than Paz's own boy. Paz tried to be easy with him as he began to handcuff him, then, when he felt the kid's broken arm dangling, let the cuffs go. Ethelbert slammed the kid up against a fence post and the kid howled.

"You come to steal a dead man's cows, you bastard. You maybe bring some dope in here for my kids, too. Huh? *Huh?*" he said, not giving a damn that the kid probably knew maybe three words of English. "You gonna grow up and come shoot me one night, too? *Huh?*" he scooped the kid up as if he were nine and not nineteen, lumbered to the truck, and pitched him into the bed. The kid howled again but Ethelbert ignored him and cuffed the kid's good arm to the tailgate latch. "You gonna goddamn stay off my reservation stealing dead men's cows now, *puta*. Hey? You gonna do that. *Sabes?*"

Ethelbert leaned on the truck, calming his breath. As he did, the anger drained from his face and the gentle sadness slowly took its place again. Paz holstered his revolver; Ethelbert rounded the truck and slipped his into the glove compartment. He glanced over the hood at Mexico. "I had me a horse, I'd have got the other bastard, too. You know?"

"Ethelbert," Paz said, and waited for Ethelbert to look at him. "Let it go. Derek's dead."

The hot June wind rippled Ethelbert's shirt; he pulled it away from his body to unstick it from the sweat so the wind could move through. "The medicine man," he said, "he told me this. He told me that if I slept on the place on the ground where Derek's blood was, I'd see everything. I'd dream everything that happened to Derek last night, see the faces of the guys, everything. You know? We could say who did it. Right now."

"You going to try it?"

"No."

"Why not?"

Ethelbert shook himself a little, like a bull with flies. "Because every night, all my life, I'd dream that dream. I'd die all over again, like Derek, every night. That's bad stuff."

Paz considered. "That's bad stuff."

Ethelbert looked beyond him to the struggling kid in the bed of the truck. "You not going to miss this shit, Quint."

There came times, Paz thought when he was alone with the air conditioning in the car — after the circling helicopters above the reservation had faded to the size of hawks behind him, then disappeared — times for summing up, résumés, neat biographies. This was that kind of time, had been for weeks, months, only it wouldn't get neat; he kept waiting for some kind of message about himself that wouldn't unscramble. Like, he thought, a snitty dispatcher's voice.

For example: had today's been his last bust? A nobody kid rustling Indian cattle in Arizona? A whimper, not a bang?

It was just that it had been *fun* for such a long time. Just goddamn . . . fun, Quintus Paz's definition of that boosterish word, and Noah Webster go hang. When he was a kid, hopping from embassy post to embassy post with the old man, learning to lie in half a dozen languages, it had been fun. You were always part of a place but not part of it, special, protected, a watcher, and that had been fun. When the other kids complained about wanting to go to a real school back in D.C., most of the time the idea had appealed to him like epilepsy. He had pictured drab, echoing green hallways in place of the sherry-fragrant, paneled study in the Jesuit school in Buenos Aires where he'd finally made sense out of Aquinas with Father Carnes, who secretly sent checks to the IRA. With a kind of horror, he'd imagined being trapped studying civics in Bethesda instead of Shakespeare at the British school in Lima. He'd seem himself cruising an Arlington drive-in on weekends, lost and bored, instead of heading for his Argentine grandfather's *estancia* ranch in the pampa to learn to hunt with the gauchos.

Not that he'd hated the American part of himself — there were those other times when he'd wanted desperately to know what it felt like to live for cruising drive-ins. To be normal, "civilized," as his mother put it, or to fall in love with somebody like Bess, his ex-wife, who was both. It had never occurred to him to want to *be* anything but American. It was just that he could be the other, too; he'd grown up believing he could be anybody.

And then, when his own Customs embassy posts and special assignments started coming — sometimes in places where the streets didn't even have names, and finally the attaché's job in Mexico City — he was good because he *could* be anybody. He could strike a deal for some under-the-table financial information with a banker in a bar in Bonn one year, then the next set up an Englishman for an arms-for-opium sting at the man's club in Hong Kong, and the next work the streets of New Orleans to bust up a plan for a mercenary attack on Aruba. He'd wake up in the morning and think, what else could I be doing that I'd like better than this? And the answer would be, always, nothing, nothing better.

It took him sixteen years of that to get it through his head that it had stopped being fun for Bess. Or maybe that it never had been. Craig in a different school in a different country every couple of years; himself not coming home for nights, sometimes weeks. And when he did come home, the .45 on the bed table — safety off — the unlisted phone numbers, Craig not able to walk to school in the morning like the other kids but being driven in by a father who wore a shoulder holster under his coat. The midnight threats from the emerald smugglers, the *esmeralderos*, that time in Colombia. The little black-leather fag bag he conspicuously laid on the table between himself and Bess in Bogotá restaurants after that, to show he was carrying his piece — always. The cocaine money launderer with a machine pistol the Marine guards took down five steps away from him as he left the embassy one rainy Friday evening in Mexico City.

Bess had thrown up after that one, had sat and not let Craig out of her sight for a day and a night, then in two more days was on a plane for Los Angeles. And, given her givens, he didn't blame her. They'd stayed at the party far too damned long.

Then the voluntary demotion he took to come back to the States, to Tucson, where nothing happened; a hoped-for miracle rebirth for a road-dead marriage. A wonder goat-gland cure, hair on a billiard ball. It is a marriage, O Lord, she quoted at him at last, one Sunday night when he was trying to sober up from the Friday before, so dead it stinketh.

His father had drunk himself to death in the clubhouses of half a dozen golf courses after *he* came back, in them and, at the very last, after his own divorce, among the shades of dead gauchos in his own father's great hulking gray house in Buenos Aires. Would taking a make-work job like head of Latin American security operations from your brother-in-law, who owned everything everywhere, stave that off? Would becoming a cliché become his salvation?

It had better, he thought, as along the highway the first trailer parks of Tucson uglied themselves in among the tall saguaro cacti, who watched with their arms held up in horror. It had better, Ethelbert, because yes, I am going to miss this shit.

The dispatcher's voice began, "Sierra 433," then faded into nonsense noises. He shut off the radio.

"I can't help you, Harmon," Paz said, his voice sharper than it needed to be. He let his eyes wander beyond the civil-service-contempo drabness of Harmon Blackstone's office, beyond the window, beyond the low skyscrapers of Tucson's glass-mad government complex, to the pure, sun-blued afternoon distances that surrounded the naked mountains. He wanted to hold on to that, not to Harmon's insistent voice. "I'm gone."

"Quint, it's a sop. What have you got here? Not the Papago case, no way. I looked at your file. Bogus Mickey Mouse watches from Taiwan, some piddling securities scam, two thousand — count 'em, two thousand — endangered lizards coming up from Sonora, for Christ's sake. You want to spend your last couple of weeks watching Fish and Wildlife count endangered lizards? You want to end it as a junior goddamned fish dick? How about we give you a couple of weeks temporary duty, a little TDY, in Mexico, for old times' sake, OK? Then so you have to extend a couple of more — who's it going to kill?"

"Me, maybe."

Harmon stood up. He did that when he talked, even on telephones. In the fifteen years Paz had known him, since the days they'd been Customs reps together at the embassy in Bogotá, he'd learned to be amazed that Harmon could sit still long enough to eat a meal with anybody. He didn't look much taller standing up than he did sitting down, but what he lacked in height he made up for in motion. And when he moved, he never simply walked: he paced, stalked, sidled, trotted, his head always in motion, taking in the street, people, dogs, doorways. His was a 360-degree world. Over the years, his round face's eternal flush had spread upward as his hair had moved farther and farther back. Paz had never been able to look at him without thinking of tomatoes; today, with his trunk swathed in the green leaves of a Hawaiian shirt, he was an entire plant.

"Yeah, I know that." Harmon paced to the door of his office, stuck his head out, yelled for Teri to bring in a couple of coffees, and paced back to his desk. "The woman's not there," he said. "You know she's yet to bring me a coffee when I ask?"

"She's not a secretary, Harmon. She carries a badge."

"Then how come when I ask for a secretary they send me a female Customs cop? You want to fall in love with her, be my guest. I think it's sweet. Just ask her to bring me a coffee sometime, OK? I thought Mexican women were supposed to *like* bringing men coffee."

Paz snuffed a flicker of anger. "Overeducation," he said, very evenly. "It's a killer."

"Quint, don't turn into a libber on me, too."

Paz started to get up. Harmon came to him, put his hands on his shoulders, and gently lowered him back to the couch. "OK, no more Teri stuff, promise. I can't help it — I was raised wrong. But you'll listen to me, right? You'll at least let me tell you about this thing?"

"Not unless I have to."

"Then you have to. That's an order."

"Harmon, Christ. Nobody's tried that on me since I was in uniform."

"Maybe they should have. You wouldn't be such a damn gaucho."

Paz paused a beat. "Like to explain that?"

"You didn't know? Nobody ever told you? Hey, Customs has got a shit pile of cowboys running around. But you're not a cowboy — you're a damn gaucho. You got more brains than any three other men I know, but if you hadn't had something like Customs around to give you a few regs to follow you'd be down tearing up the pampa somewhere still, eating live ostriches, whatever. It's that Argentine blood, you know? I been there. They try to live like a bunch of civilized Frenchmen, but they're all damn barbarian gauchos underneath. You were *made* for Customs. You *owe* Customs, no matter what kind of crapola you think you're about to pull with your brother-in-law. So listen."

Paz consciously sat very still. Strike two, Harmon, he thought, and then caught himself. No anger. Anger meant fire still smouldered somewhere in the ashes, which was what Harmon wanted to see. Just . . . stay dead, Paz told himself. Let it go out entirely. It will, eventually. Listen but don't feel anything, don't think anything, get out quick. "You're talking, Harmon."

"The Mexicans want you. By name. Special request through the Customs attaché's office in Mexico City. OK from Mexican customs, OK from Washington — deputy commissioner himself. Something about an art theft, and it's you, just you, they want to handle our end." Paz started to interrupt but Blackstone held up his hand like a traffic cop. "Don't ask. I don't know, and I never heard of a special agent ever being requested by name, either, much less getting an OK from the deputy commissioner. Maybe it has to do with your being such a hotshot while *you* were attaché down there. What's that war story about you tracing those Maya whatsits the guy from New Orleans was sneaking out of the jungle on his boat or something?"

"Stelae."

"Yeah. Ugly damn things. I think I'd steal velvet paintings first. Anyway, they got somebody from Mexico City calling to talk to you about it today, OK?"

He paused, waited for Paz to react, then, disappointed, went on.

"This is impressive, you know. They just don't do all this

crap when somebody rips off a plastic Jesus. *My* guess is that it's political — we're about to want something major from the Mexes. We're being nice to them."

"Are you working for the State Department now, Harmon?"

"Quintus, Quintus, Quintus. Look, I'm going to ask you. Talk to this individual when he calls, OK? Just if it's to give him some advice or whatever. Please?"

"Why waste the man's time, Harmon?"

Harmon paced to his desk and slumped against it. He picked up a long-dead cigarette lighter made in the shape of a 9 mm automatic, a Christmas present from his daughter one year, and fiddled with it. He pointed it at Paz and clicked it a couple of times. "Well, shit, then. You weren't always a bastard."

"No."

"Look, don't take the assignment, all right? Just talk to the man, damn it. One phone call!"

"And that'll be enough for you."

"Yeah. Then I can lie us out of the rest of it."

"You're lying now."

Harmon didn't answer him. Their eyes held each other's for a while. Harmon put down the pistol lighter, straightened his shoulders, and said quietly, "We're the oldest marines, buddy. You go, and then there was one. I told region I could at least get you to talk to the man. Don't leave me standing in shit."

Paz kept his eyes on Harmon's face and thought, no, I haven't always been a bastard. And he reminded himself that nothing was Harmon's fault, nothing. Not his own bollixed life, nor Harmon's three tomato-faced kids and Polish wife, who adored all four of them. Not the fact that Harmon's wife had toughed out the embassy hopping and so Harmon had made his promotion and showed up in Tucson two years ago as Paz's boss.

No, not Harmon's fault, not any of it. "Do you have a name on this guy?" he said.

Harmon reached behind him and dug through telexes. "Hell, some Kraut name. Von Hindenberg, something. I had it right . . ."

Paz watched him dig, letting the name sink in. And he thought, of course. Of course, given these two weeks and what he needed and, more important, didn't need, of course it would be that name. Who else's? The past was a Papago tracker.

"Don't bother," he told Harmon. "The name's von Hummel."

"Hey, you know the guy, then!" Harmon tried to hide his delight, but not much. "No problem to talk to him, right?"

Paz got to his feet. "I know him." At the door, he turned, "I'll take it in my office. Alone."

T W O

T ERI STILL WASN'T BACK at her desk when Paz left Harmon's
office. He stopped and scribbled her a note on a pink While
You Were Out form. "Need to do some research after Beloved
Sister's party tonight. Can you help?" She'd recognize the
code: can you stay over? His sister would short-circuit when
he showed up at the party with her — the party to announce
officially that he was "coming aboard." ("Quint, I don't care
that she's Mexican and trained to arrest people, you know I
don't. It's just that your divorce isn't even cold in the grave
yet, and Mother's coming.") Paz figured they'd both need some
comforting.

Beside the notepad lay the phony letter she and he had
concocted last night. It had been her idea; Harmon called it
harebrained, which was why Paz thought it might work, though
it would be one more bust he wouldn't be around to follow up
if it did. It was a love letter to a child-porn publisher in
Denmark, written out with lavender ink in her neat hand, the
latest in a half-dozen progressively more torrid ones they'd
exchanged. The Danes had been dragging their feet on bringing
the guy in for months, and Paz had decided the only way to
bust him was to get him on U.S. soil somehow. This letter
was the way. It was a steamy thing; he and Teri had both

broken up but gotten horny nonetheless inventing the exotic nonsense she could promise him if he came to visit her, one Louise Riddle, child-porn distributor and fan, of Tucson, Arizona. Teri's imagination had beat his, no contest. He tried to imagine Bess writing a letter like this one but couldn't. He picked it up, caught a whiff of Teri's perfume — a good touch — and felt last night start to come back to him again. He put it down. Wouldn't do, he thought — von Hummel and sex wouldn't mix.

Maybe *she* could make some sense out of von Hummel. Of all the army of archaeologists and anthropologists in Mexico, von Hummel should be the *last* that the Institute of Anthropology and History would have call him.

To hell with it. You let yourself wonder, Paz, you get the juices flowing again, you sucker yourself. You told Harmon, "I'm gone," then be gone.

In his own bare office he looked for something to keep him busy, anything to get his mind off von Hummel. Harmon had been right: his case file was deadly. A request from Interpol, for which Customs was liaison, for a routine background check on an international investments con man. An info copy of a memo to Fish and Wildlife about the two thousand endangered lizards. Two more border fence cuttings and eighteen cars rustled into Mexico from the San Rafael Valley. He'd already passed his best cases on: the boa constrictor that showed up in the Phoenix Zoo's air freight with its belly full of bags of coke, the Filipino guerrillas supposedly training in the Dragoon Mountains, the machine pistols that were being assembled for the *yakuza*, the Japanese mafia. He lingered awhile over a report that had just come in of an air interdiction of seventy kilos of crack on a private airfield. But it wasn't his district so he let it go, reluctantly.

Nothing was his district now. His eyes moved from his desk to the map of the world on his wall. King of the borders, he'd told himself he was, all the kinds of borders people could cross.

Von Hummel, he thought, was a man who'd never bothered with borders.

The light scent of Teri's perfume reached him before he noticed her standing in his doorway, cradling a Styrofoam cup of coffee in her hands as if it were a tiny animal that needed protecting. Her head was cocked slightly, as if she were trying to get a better angle on him, to figure out something about him. He smiled at her; she smiled back. And the phone rang.

He motioned her in as he answered it. "Mr. Quintus Paz, please," the overworked, slightly hostile Teléfonos de México operator voice on the other end asked. He said yes, the voice said, "I have a person-to-person call for Mr. Quintus Paz. Please hold the line," then the line promptly went dead.

"That the phone call?" Teri said.

"You in on it, too? Didn't they teach you about conspiracy laws?"

"Are you going?"

Paz shook his head.

"I would," she said. "You would have too, once."

"I took on three Libyans by myself once when I was sky marshaling, too. Once."

"Eggs and apples." She set her coffee down and took the chair beside his desk, still looking at him as if she were trying to figure out something about him.

"Do you *want* me to go?" he asked her.

She shook her hair away from her face, seeming to deliberately break off from whatever it was she'd been trying to get to. "I don't know," she said. "I honestly don't know. It's up to you."

The first day she'd walked into the office, the day after his divorce became final, he'd decided she was the only totally unplaceable woman he'd ever met. She was a blow to his pride: he was a card-carrying Treasury Department Customs Service special agent, a bona fide T-man; it was his *job* to be able to read people. He'd taken in the wide but slightly Oriental eyes — pale green eyes that seemed to make liars out of her almond skin and pure black hair — the slenderness that dress designers designed dresses for, the small bones and delicate fingers, and he thought, White Russian and Chinese? Filipino-American? Turkish, maybe, or, on a far chance, Oriental Jew. Or Tartar, and if he could think of something even more exotic than Tartar, maybe that.

That she turned out to be Teresa Sánchez from Las Cruces, New Mexico, was no diminishment: it only made her accessible. Neither was the fact that she was thirty-two and he was forty-five; he didn't see that he'd gotten a hell of a lot smarter in the thirteen years since he'd been thirty-two. She'd been smart enough to get out of her bad marriage — the guy was a back-up guitarist in a country-rock band — a great lot sooner than he had his. That she was a Customs inspector who'd gotten cabin fever in Gringo Pass, Arizona, and asked for a transfer to administration in Tucson was his good luck. That she wouldn't think of marrying him until she was sure he'd "recovered" from his divorce was his bad luck. Or maybe, given her wisdom, his good luck.

Or, he'd thought, maybe her way of lying to both of them.

"What does that mean, you don't know?" he said.

"It means what it means." She smiled and took a sip of coffee. "Harmon says you know the guy."

The hissing on the line changed pitch. He held up his hand to Teri and pushed the phone more tightly against his ear. "Go ahead," the accent at the far end of the hisses said.

"Baron von Hummel, how are you?" Paz said, trying to sound hearty.

"*Baron?*" Teri mouthed.

"Mr. Quintus Paz?" The voice was neither von Hummel's nor an operator's, and, as the line cleared, in the background Paz could make out several men's voices speaking in Spanish, some saying goodbye, as if there were a meeting breaking up. On the phone was a woman's voice, only slightly accented —

a trace of Spanish, a trace of British, maybe — and slower, deeper, more formal than the operator's. It sounded familiar to him, disturbingly familiar, but he wasn't sure. He glanced at Teri.

"Yes?"

"Mr. Paz, I believe we met when you were attaché here. I am Maritza de la Torre, an assistant director of the National Institute of Anthropology and History. You may remember me as Maritza Solans."

Dear God. This formal, official voice was Maritza's? No wonder he hadn't been able to be certain it was hers. The accent was the same, but not much else: six years ago, when Maritza had been sent to the embassy to help him identify the Maya stelae he'd helped recover, it had been the voice of an enthusiastic woman just finishing a doctorate in anthropology at the National University. Five and a half years ago it had been a hurt voice from the pillow beside him asking him why he wouldn't leave his wife and getting no good answer. Five years ago it had been a quiet, strained voice on the telephone asking him please not to try to contact her after he went back to the States. He felt a rush of blood, the same dry-mouthed rush he'd feel when he'd see her standing nervously waiting for him in the lobby of the Hotel Marie Isabel, next door to the embassy, when he'd leave the office in the evening. It was part excitement, part anticipation, part fear.

"I do remember." Teri gave him a questioning look. He shrugged.

"You are expecting a telephone call from Baron Frederick von Hummel. I believe you are his friend."

The voices kept up in the background. She was clearly playing for an audience — as he was. He felt a little absurd, more than a little traitorous. "He was my father's friend, yes."

"You are aware that the codex is missing, I assume."

Paz paused. "No, señorita — "

"Señora."

Your point, Paz thought. "No, I'm not. I haven't spoken to Baron von Hummel in over five years."

Now it was the voice's turn to pause. "But you did know he had found the codex."

"No, señora, I'm sorry. What codex might that be?"

"But because of your sister, I thought, I naturally thought . . ."

"My sister, señora?"

The voice paused again. "You are not being helpful, Mr. Paz. Isn't it true that you have a treaty obligation with my country to help in these cases?"

Don't, Maritza, he thought. Don't make us play it this way. "First of all, señora, *I* don't. My government has a mutual customs assistance treaty, but I'm not quite sure what you mean by 'these cases' just yet. Second of all, as I'll explain to the baron — "

"You cannot explain to the baron, Mr. Paz. If it were possible for you to explain to the baron, he would be speaking to you now, not me. I do not know where the baron is. No one does."

"I beg your pardon?"

"If you are coming here to Mexico City, please come as soon as you can — tomorrow — and we will talk better then."

Teri poised her fingers over the button for the speaker phone and raised her eyebrows, asking whether she could turn it on. He was trapped. He nodded. "I think we should talk now, señora."

A hand covered the mouthpiece on the other end and Maritza said something in impatient Spanish to someone else. Then, to Paz, "Mr. Paz, the codex has been missing nearly two full days. Now, since sometime last night, Baron von Hummel disappeared from his apartment here. The anthropologist we had assigned to work with him has been found dead. I don't know what to tell you about the baron, except that I am extremely worried."

"What do the police say?"

"They are investigating it as a kidnapping."

"Von Hummel?" The surprise in Paz's voice was genuine.

"Von Hummel's got to be well over eighty, señora. What in God's name would he — "

She cut him off, apparently still more conscious of her audience in Mexico City than anything else. There seemed to be almost a desperation in her need to appear in charge of the conversation. "Mr. Paz, all along he said that you were the only man he would trust to find the codex, that he trusted your intelligence, that you knew Mexico, that you would come . . ."

Paz didn't try hard to conceal his own impatience. "*What* codex, señora?" He searched his memory for what he knew about codices. Books, in a way — Maya were the rarest and most mysterious, but there were Aztec, too, maybe even Mixtec, Zapotec, Toltec — astrological texts, histories, myths. He'd seen them, had once known a hell of a lot more about them than he could make come back to him now. The Spanish conquerors had done a thorough job of trying to wipe them out, but some had managed to survive. They were valuable, but he didn't think they were *that* valuable; he remembered rumors of one or another of them being discovered with fair frequency in a church or village somewhere.

"Mr. Paz, will you accept for now that Baron von Hummel believed — and had begun to authenticate — that he had found a fourth Maya codex, and that it proved to be far, far older and more valuable than any of the other three that are known to exist in the world. *Pre*-Maya, actually. If you want dollar terms, I cannot give them to you. No one can, since the codex has never been sold. But if it were, I expect the bidding might well begin in the millions. In terms of what it means to the history of this hemisphere, well, we shall simply have to begin writing much of it all over again."

No, Paz thought, not the kind of thing you found with fair frequency — anywhere. And they wanted him, just him? More, *Maritza* wanted him. Once upon a time, when his ego was greener, he would have begged for something like this. Now, with two weeks — thirteen days beginning tomorrow — what could he do besides just the preliminary field work? As for doing anything about von Hummel, even if he had time enough, there was no chance in hell the Mexican cops would let him poke into a local kidnapping.

And Maritza? Who was this Maritza he was talking to, this married Maritza, with an official title? What a fool he'd be to jeopardize what he wanted to happen with Teri and himself by taking off to Mexico because of a memory and a rush of blood. No, he told himself, say no and forget it. It's just an act of will — easiest thing in the world.

"Why us, señora? If it's purely an internal Mexican affair so far, there's nothing in the treaty — "

"Please be realistic, Mr. Paz. Is the codex more likely to be bought by someone in, say, Honduras, than in the United States? And two of the three financial backers of Baron von Hummel are in the United States. I take it from our conversation that you are not aware that one of those backers is your sister."

"No," he said. "I regret to say I'm not," and thought, what reasonable cultures remain that allow the putting away of treacherous younger sisters? But the fact that his sister had known the baron as well as, maybe better than, he did let what Maritza was telling him make at least an oblique kind of sense.

"I'm sorry if that has embarrassed you, Mr. Paz. I thought you would have been aware that you are involved in a number of ways already." The men's voices in the background faded, and Paz heard a door being closed. In his own office, Teri clicked off the speaker phone, got up, and left the room. Paz tried to read her face as she did; he found nothing but a kind of efficient purposefulness.

"Maritza," Paz said when she was gone. "I'm no good to you. I'm sorry. I'm quitting in two weeks."

Maritza's voice was quieter now, softer. It was a voice he

recognized. "Please, Quintus. Please come. If it's only for two weeks, I don't care. Don't think about what used to be — come because of now. If it weren't as important as I say it is, do you think I could have made myself call you? After making myself *not* call you for five years?"

"Maritza," Paz began, then stopped as he heard the hiss on the line grow louder, then turn into a series of clicks, then a final ringing clink just before the dial tone hummed at him. Teléfonos de México strikes again, he thought. He held the receiver in front of him, staring at it as if it were itself some sort of incomprehensible artifact from the past.

When Teri came back into the room, she was smiling, smiling and writing something on a notepad. Paz hung up the phone and leaned toward her to see the notepad when she sat again. He read:

1. *Salvoconducto* permission card to carry weapon.
2. Driver's license, cover passport, tourist visa, credit cards, etc., issued in name of . . . ?
3. Official passport and visa.
4. TDY orders.
5. Cash from impress fund in amount of . . . ? Pesos? Dollars?

It was a standard list of things he would need to operate outside the United States, under cover if necessary. He knew he could take a day or so, look at his motives, make a couple of plans, "examine his options," as the radio talk shows told him to. And then not go. But his blood wouldn't stop rushing — though for what one thing now he couldn't say, unless it was escape itself. I am surrounded, he thought, and let go.

"I've known him all my life," he told Teri on the way to the library at a little after four. "He and my father met when my father was just starting out in the foreign service, his first tour in Mexico, before the war. Von Hummel was something in the cultural attaché's office of the German embassy, and my father was in our cultural attaché's office. They got to be friends of a sort, and then, when Hitler tore off into Czechoslovakia, von Hummel pitched it in. He was in line to be a baron, the real thing, and he couldn't abide Hitler's bunch. So he walked out of the embassy and never went back. Stayed in Mexico and got involved in pre-Columbian archaeology. Whenever my father was posted somewhere in South America — Peru, Colombia, Ecuador, it didn't matter — von Hummel would show up for a while, chasing down some pet theory about the Indians. A little frail man, even then, like he was made out of sticks. But Christ, I can't think of a place anywhere in South America without seeing him in it."

"So he's pretty important."

"No — and that's the reason I can't figure why everybody's taking him so seriously now. The powers always thought he was a crackpot. I didn't keep up with it all, but I know he worked with another German named von Wuthenau for a while who *was* pretty important — something about tracing prehistoric migrations into Mexico from China, Africa, the Middle East. Then apparently von Hummel kept going off on wild tangents, and even von Wuthenau gave him the boot. I tried to use him as an expert witness once and came close to getting laughed out of the country."

"What kinds of tangents?"

"I don't know. I was in Hong Kong by then."

"What about you — did you think he was a crackpot?"

A moment came back to him. Von Hummel, as delighted as a child on an Easter egg hunt, was forcing the unhappy owner of a hole-in-the-wall antiques shop in Quito to dig through a dusty pile of Indian wood carvings forgotten in a corner, then paying the man easily triple what his, to Paz, unimpressive find had been worth. The carving had been of a boat, so crudely done that it could have been anything from an ancient galley to an Indian reed canoe.

"If he was, he was a harmless one. And am I concerned that something's happened to him? Yes. He had time for me when I was a kid. I liked him."

"Surely your sister knew about him, didn't she — about all those tangents?"

He winked at her. "That, madam, is what I intend to find out tonight."

By five o'clock, he'd been to the Mexican consulate for his official visa and picked Teri up at the resort hotel the university called a library. He took the armload of books on pre-Columbian codices she struggled out with, then drove her home to dress for the party. He winced when she told him the earliest flight she could book him on was the Aeroméxico milk run at eight in the morning. Back at the office, he resurrected his old file of Mexican informants he'd used when he'd been attaché. Which one was dead, which in jail, which in the States for safekeeping, which ones had been turned and weren't reliable anymore, he didn't know. But he coded a couple of phone numbers into his notebook and replaced the file. The CIA probably wouldn't think much of his coding system — only initials of names, reversed, and phone numbers written with the last four digits first — but at least he didn't need a computer to "access" it. Ethelbert had taught it to him.

At six-fifteen he called Craig to say goodbye. He was conscious of his relief when Bess didn't answer, then just as conscious of his flood of guilt and tenderness when he pictured Craig, in his forever-cockeyed glasses, hanging over the back of a chair in his room — the room Paz and Bess, in their last joint act, had picked new furniture for less than a month before they'd separated. They'd argued over even that. A lonely kid in a lonely room in a lonely house. "I thought you were all done with that stuff, Dad," Craig said.

"Almost."

"Can you tell me where this time?"

"No. It's one of those. I'm sorry."

Craig was silent, then said, "We were supposed to see each other this weekend. The Toros are playing Hawaii." It wasn't a reproach, just a flat statement, with a kind of resignation behind it. It made the distance between them heartbreakingly obvious to Paz. Each divorce, he'd read somewhere, was the death of a small civilization. Was Craig a refugee, somebody who would become a semi-stranger to him in a few years?

"When I'm back we'll see each other. First day."

"When's that?"

"Craig. Don't, son. Please."

Another silence. "I just thought it was over, that's all."

"I'm sorry, old kid. Soon."

"Yeah. Want me to tell Mom anything?"

"Tell her I said goodbye. Tell her I'll say hello to the baron for her. She'll know what that means."

"I do, too. I remember, you know."

"I guess you do. I love you, old kid."

A final silence. "Yeah, me too."

When Paz hung up, his hand, the one that had held the receiver, was shaking.

He remembered sitting with a book spread under the yellow light of a desk lamp at his grandfather's in Buenos Aires. He must have been about Craig's age, maybe a little younger. He was in the library, a dim cavern of a room in the mountain of a Victorian house in Palermo, the part of town where his Argentine grandfather and American grandmother and the other Best People lived. His father and mother had deposited his sister and him there for a school vacation while the old man went somewhere to dry out, and he remembered it was cold, that people were passing by the barred windows in topcoats. From somewhere deep in the house a man's voice was shouting over a radio; he knew the man was named Perón, but nothing else about him, except that his grandfather said Perón rhymed with *cabrón*, bastard.

The book was in an old Spanish he had trouble with, but

he'd made it through to the end. He didn't remember the scene exactly now, but Don Quixote was on his deathbed, and Sancho, probably, came in with news that there was one last villain left somewhere. Don Quixote threw off the bedclothes, shoved the priest aside, yelled at his family to get out of his way, and called for his shield and lance. Paz remembered very clearly, if not the scene, thinking as he read it, yes, that's right. That's how you do it. Get them out of your way. What else are they good for?

That had been Don Quixote's death scene. Paz slammed his hand down on his desk, hard, to stop its shaking, and, while it was tingling still, opened his locked file drawer to check the .45 he would take.

The musicians had followed Paz's sister, Mary Margaret, and her checkbook everywhere since the party had begun, apparently hoping that by sheer volume of noise they could magically increase their fee. But after Paz closed the door of the helicopter bubble around himself and Mary Margaret, the music, a blaring mariachi version of "Ay, Jalisco!" came to them as blessedly muffled as if they were under water. They were in a big fishbowl that smelled faintly of electrical instruments and motor oil, and beyond the bowl people peered from various angles at his brother-in-law Stanley's other airplanes, or lingered around tables for more conversation, or gathered in schools around the governor and the mayor and the half a dozen lesser politicians. His sister balanced a plate of carne asada and frijoles on her lap and, through her bright hostess's smile, tried to eat. Now and then someone would come close, start to look inside the helicopter, see them, then back away embarrassed, as if he'd caught somebody in a bathtub.

"I haven't had a minute to eat all evening," his sister said, cramming in a spoonful of frijoles. "I'm starving to death right here in front of the governor and everybody."

"Eat, Mary Margaret," Paz said. "But talk, too."

"Quint, if it's about Teri, we don't need to hide like this. She's here, and that's that. It should be Bess over there with Mother, but I'm not responsible for you. Not for the next two weeks, anyway." She swallowed. "Maybe it's her name. I mean I *know* that there are probably ten million Latin women whose name is Teresa, and that they all shorten it to Teri. But if you *don't* know any Spanish, it just sounds so . . . yuppie. Doesn't it?"

"It's not about Teri. It's about Baron von Hummel."

She took her time swallowing the frijoles, scanning the crowd as if she were looking for help. Paz had discovered when he'd arrived that he was really only a warm-up act. They were going to announce his new job, yes, but the main attraction, the reason for the whole thing being held here in Stanley's hangar, for the silly South of the Border motif — sombreros dangling from the ceiling, strolling mariachis, consuls, and, it was rumored, a surprise appearance by Cantinflas himself later on — was to announce Stanley's new airline to Mexico. His marketing wisemen were calling it Fiesta Airlines, which it wasn't. It was a no-frills outfit — bring your own tacos and maybe pigs and chickens in the overheads — that he was convinced would put an American tourist on every street corner from Mérida to Tijuana. *That* was why Stanley wanted to show off his new security-chief-in-residence here tonight: no hijackings with a T-man in charge.

Mary Margaret managed to get her frijoles down. Paz wondered briefly whether frijoles could be kosher. When she was a girl, Mary Margaret had loved religion the way other girls loved make-up; when she married Stanley Loeb, she kept loving religion. She'd seemed to make the switch from Catholicism to Judaism as easily as changing shoes, and had attacked poor Stanley with an Orthodoxy that was as alien to him as Taoism. He'd borne it well. His cross, Paz thought.

"I was afraid they'd get to you with that," she said.

"You know the codex is missing."

"The baron phoned us last week."

"Did he phone today to say *he's* missing?"

She slowly set her plate down on the cockpit floor. "Oh, God," she said. "When? How?"

Paz told her what he knew. When he was done, she said, "I suppose it's pointless to say I feel responsible."

"Why?"

"If I hadn't talked Stanley into letting me back him when he asked us . . ."

"How did he know to ask? Were you in touch?"

"Oh, just Christmas cards with notes in them, that sort of thing. I never mentioned it to you, did I? I suppose I didn't think you'd be interested. You've always been so . . . unsentimental. But he knew I'd married Stanley and I told him I'd converted, so I suppose that's why he came to us."

"What's that got to do with it?"

The grinning mariachi band set up a serenade outside the helicopter; Mary Margaret scowled and waved them away. She kept looking at them as they moved off into the crowd. "Because the plumed serpent was Jewish."

"The what was *what?*"

"Do you wonder that I didn't say anything to you? Truly, Quint, what would you have thought if I'd told you that?"

"What I think now, I suppose." The plumed serpent, Quetzalcoatl, probably the most powerful god of all — Paz remembered that much. He'd been fascinated by him as a boy when they'd lived in Mexico, and then, when he'd had time for fascination, again during his own last assignment there. The god who had been a man, too, who had opposed human sacrifice, who had never quite fit the rest of the Indian mythology, with his unlikely conical hat and light beard. Who had been the morning and evening star, lord of the dawn and the wind, the lawgiver, the teacher, the builder, the bringer of corn and of writing. Who had been pursued and tricked by sorcerers all his life because of his piety and his gentleness. Who had returned to Mexico on the very day of the year he was predicted to — except he'd been a Spaniard named Hernán Cortés, who wasn't very pious *or* gentle to the Aztecs he conquered.

Who one "researcher" or another for almost five hundred years had decided was either the Apostle Thomas or a pilgrim from China or Ireland or Scandinavia or, God forbid, Atlantis.

And now he was Jewish. Paz knew a couple of rabbis who would be bowled over. The plumed serpent, bringer of matzo to Mexico.

"The baron had *proof*." Mary Margaret turned back to face him, angry now. "I saw it — it was the codex."

"OK," Paz said. "Convince me."

"Oh . . . Quint! Listen to me. Before there was a Quetzalcoatl, he was called Kukulkan by the Mayas. And before that, Votan. He came from across the sea to the east, from a place where people had tried to build a tower to heaven but couldn't because of a 'confusion of tongues,' the legend says. And when the baron was working with von Wuthenau, von Wuthenau found a stone with a ship and a star of David carved on it. But everybody said maybe, maybe it meant something, maybe it was coincidence, maybe this, maybe that — everybody except the baron. He believed it, and ever since the war had been trying to prove it. He had it all worked out — Phoenician sailors and Jewish traders who came and taught the Indians everything. Didn't you ever listen to him telling Daddy about it? No, you wouldn't have. You never took him seriously, did you?"

"I must not have. Why did he believe it?"

"Because it was true."

"Aha."

"And because of what the Germans did to the Jews. Don't you see? He said he *owed* it to us. And then three years ago he knew he'd found proof — or where the proof was. That's when he came to us."

"And to the others."

"There were other backers, yes, but I don't know who they were. He never would tell us."

"Why not?"

"I don't know."

"Didn't that strike you as strange?"

Mary Margaret laughed. "No stranger than the rest of it."

"Touché. How was he when you saw him?"

"Old, Quint. He's older than Daddy would be now. He has to use a walking stick to get around, and he shakes. But, oh, Quint, you should have seen how excited he was. It was just the way it was when he would show up at our house in the old days. You remember how he always had some new project he'd get Daddy excited about?"

"I remember," Paz said, not recalling the projects so much as the way his father had almost succeeded in sobering up while the baron was visiting. Those were among the few times outside work his father had seemed to focus, to take a real interest in anything you couldn't buy in a bottle. Paz had been grateful to the baron for those times. *That* was what he had taken seriously.

"He asked all about you, Quint — wanted to know if you were still in Customs, how you and Bess and Craig were."

"Did you tell him?"

"I told him that you were fine," Mary Margaret said and looked away. Yes, Paz thought, you would tell him that — and would want desperately to believe it.

"And he's the one who explained everything about the codex to you?"

"Yes, he and another archaeologist and a woman from the institute of anthropology. They *all* agreed on it. And I do read, Quint. I've read everything I could get my hands on about what I'm telling you. Will you ever believe I'm not still eight?"

Paz decided to leave that one alone. "Where did he find the codex? Yucatán? Chiapas? Quintana Roo?"

"No, and that's what explains why it took him so long to

get support. He'd found it in the state of Veracruz, in the mountains near the coast. There was a temple mound near the town of Papantla, he said, that nobody had excavated yet. Nobody had thought it was important enough to. And it was really too far north for anything Maya. But the Indians in the village next to it told him that from the time of the first coming of the Spaniards, they'd known their priests had buried something there to hide it. They said it was a book, a book that had been so old even when the Spaniards came that a special temple had been built for it. A temple to Votan, Quint — to the oldest name of the plumed serpent. And they said their legends told them that the book had come from the people who had been there even before their own. From the Olmecs, you know the ones who left those giant stone heads everywhere? They're the ones all those other civilizations started from — writing, all of it. So the baron *knew* that if his proof was anywhere, it was there."

"So he excavated. And, lo and behold . . ."

"I *saw* it, damn you, Quint. Stanley and I went to Veracruz and he showed it to us. He even sent part of it to have the ink and the parchment tested, sent it to Mexico City *and* to this country. Quint, listen. It might be as old as three thousand years. Do you know how old that is?"

"Close to three thousand years, I suppose," he said, and wished he hadn't. How many times in a single day did he want to be a bastard to somebody he cared about? He finished his drink and realized it ought to be his last one. Everything he'd ever disliked about himself and Mary Margaret was right there, too close to the surface, sharpened by his anger at her involvement in this whole damned situation. One more drink and he'd slide over the line from flip to truly nasty. Neither of them needed that tonight.

"It was all there — dates, drawings of the ship, teachings, even a few Hebrew letters the Olmecs had remembered."

"And what about his other backers? Did they see it, too?"

"Yes. All of us separately."

"Any idea how many people all told knew about it?"

"No."

"What did he plan to do with it?"

"When he'd finished deciphering it — he'd only done parts of it — he was going to make sure the museum in Mexico City got it. He said the whole thing could take him years, because it was in an old language called Mixe Zoque that nobody knew very well."

"What did Stanley think about that?"

"And what's that supposed to mean?"

"Oh, Stanley collects things — airplanes, yachts, politicians, art, money. How did he feel about just giving the thing away after he'd let you put what I guess was a fair chunk of money into it? Have any regrets or maybe second thoughts about wanting to hold on to it?"

"My God, he's your *brother-in-law*, Quint. Have they trained you to suspect your own brother-in-law of something like that?"

"Yep." He reached for the door handle of the bubble. Across the hangar, his gold-rimmed glasses glinting, Stanley was hulking over Teri and his mother, who were obviously grateful for somebody to look at besides each other. In his dark three-piece suits and silent sobriety, Stanley always reminded Paz of a huge raven. Paz liked what he knew of him well enough, but when they were around each other, they seldom got much past the hello-good-to-see-you stage of conversation. You could be in a room alone with Stanley and almost forget he was there unless you asked him a direct question; it was like being with a computer. Even his offer of this job had taken no more than five minutes of personal contact on the phone. The details had all been worked out by subordinates — and by Mary Margaret. "He wouldn't have hired me if they hadn't."

"How about your sister, then?"

Paz leaned over and kissed her on the cheek. "Look. Do me

a favor. Stanley's busy tonight. Beg off for me, will you, when you can get him alone. Explain to him. I've got an early flight in the morning. Oh, and tell him to hold off on that job announcement for a week or so, OK?"

"Quintus, you're not going — "

"It has to do with bangs and whimpers, baby sister. And maybe with thinking more of Baron von H. than you give me credit for." He lifted the door. As he did, the governor, looking every inch the frumpy car dealer he was, stepped up from the rear of the helicopter with the pilot, who was giving him the ten-cent tour. Paz held out his hand to the governor and smiled. "Here, Guv. Give an old man a hand down, will you?"

Teri's other shoe finally dropped as she leaned across the bed to show Paz a passage she'd found in a dull, diagram-filled monograph on ancient Mesoamerican languages he'd given up on an hour ago. The shoe was a slipper, and, fascinated, Paz had watched her balance it like an unconscious juggler as she read. She was excited. "Look at this part, Quint. If it's true that what he found could be three thousand years old, my Lord, that means that it's just at the very *beginning* of writing. See? This part: 'It is believed that writing may have been introduced into Mesoamerica as early as 900 B.C., somewhere in the area of Olmec (Mixe Zoque language group) influence located in the La Venta area of the present state of Vera Cruz.' It fits, Quint. It all checks out! Do you realize what that codex is probably worth? Your woman from Mexico wasn't exaggerating."

"I never thought she was." His woman from Mexico. Paz felt another shot of guilt, then shook it off. If this was a time of résumés, of reordering his life, then Maritza had to be part of the process of finishing unfinished business, too. Just that, he told himself, just that.

He knew now that codices were up to sixteen feet long, folded like screens, were made out of agave paper or deerskin, and that of the Maya variety, there were indeed only three: one in Paris, one somewhere else called the Tro-Cortisianus, for God knew what reason, and another in Dresden. He also knew he had to get up to catch a plane in five hours, and that his eyes wouldn't focus. "I think von Hummel was from Dresden. You know that?"

"No. If you believed her from the beginning, why are you acting toward everybody like you don't believe any of it?"

"Because it ought to be unbelievable. It's out of some forties movie."

"So were the Dead Sea scrolls. This one seems pretty ironclad."

"I know."

"Is it because it was von Hummel who found it? Or because your sister is involved with it?"

On the TV, David Letterman watched two armadillos race each other across the stage. The audience was approaching hysteria. Paz took his glasses off and rubbed the heels of his hands into his eyes, hard. Teri pulled them away. "That's the wrong way to do it," she said and put down her monograph to massage his eyelids gently. He thought a minute. "Von Hummel may have been a crackpot, but he wasn't a con man. Nor was he a crook — he didn't need to be, with his income. If he found the thing, he found it. And he didn't skip with it. And Mary Margaret may have her tangents, too, but she's not stupid. Especially when it comes to spending Stanley's money."

"So even though you don't think it ought to be believable, you believe it, verdad?"

"I can't not believe it."

Teri thought a moment. "That's reasonable."

"Why else would one man be dead because he found the thing, and von Hummel be missing? I have to believe Harmon has left me standing in shit."

"And you're still not glad you're going?"

"You seem to be glad I am."

She thought again. "It was your decision."

"But you're still pleased."

"OK, yes."

"Why?"

"Because I'm pretty sure I'm in love with you. And because it was your decision, not theirs."

"Who's 'theirs'?"

"Your family's. I don't know, Quint — I don't know where this is going. But I do know that what I love in you is what they don't."

"Meaning?"

"Meaning that they're desperate to have you safe at home as a mini-Stanley. You know, I actually think that it's not just *me* who's an embarrassment to them. And meaning because they want that, they'll never in hell forgive me for not being Bess — or for being too much like you. Listen, what do you think you've failed at anyway, *mano*? What are you trying to make up for? That marriage? I'd have turned into a lump of mud a long time ago in something like that. You stuck it out twenty years."

"Which leaves me forty-five, and I'm still tearing off to Mexico. What's to show for that?"

"Stanley's fifty and he's rich. What's to show for that?" she said.

"I can operate in Stanley's world if I have to. And survive it." It sounded odd to hear himself say aloud what he'd said to himself so often these past weeks, and to hear it come out with, he thought, such smooth conviction.

"Yeah, you're the guy who can be anybody, you used to tell me. You want to be a Stanley forever now, and tell me you won't turn into a full-time lump of mud? Things didn't work with Bess, so you're going to fix it by getting civilized *all* the time? Maybe I should just fall in love with Stanley and simplify my life."

"He's married."

"Paz, you're a mess right now. You know that?"

"It's crossed my mind." No more thinking, he thought. No more thinking tonight. It was too dangerous. He'd think tomorrow when he'd have something to think about besides himself, a subject he was thoroughly weary of lately. He reached for her. "Never been to Veracruz, have you?"

"No. No farther south than Juárez."

"If they'd elected me God at the right time, that's where I would have set up the garden of Eden. Up there in the mountains, where vanilla beans grow from the orchids and the orchids grow wild in the mango trees and the ceiba trees and the banyans. If you have to be a peasant, do it there."

"I'll get there one day," she said as she slid under his arm and her face vanished under the dark sheen of her hair.

"Be a reverse wetback, eh?"

"If that's what it takes."

Ten years ago he would have tried to make love to her once more tonight. Now, he silently blessed her breath for growing slow, for slipping into the rhythm of sleep. He checked to see if the safety was off the .45 and turned out the light. David Letterman's guests, now that the armadillos were gone, were better than Valium.

THREE

HARMON HAD SCRIBBLED a note on the bottom of Paz's TDY orders. "For the record, Quint, since you know this as damn well as I do. No gaucho crap. You're investigating an art theft. If it involves this country somehow, that's your business. But you get involved with local kidnapping, murders, whatever unrelated non-treaty stuff, and you're on your own. The Mexes can fry you. Go out in style, not in a goddamn Mexican jail. But I do appreciate this — I want you to know that. Good luck. As ever, *abrazos*, Harmon Blackstone, Special Agent in Charge."

CYA, Harmon, Cover Your Ass, Paz thought as he ripped the moronic note off the orders, tore it into small pieces, and let the wind skitter them away across the rain-slick tarmac of the Mexico City airport. He remembered Ethelbert standing in the great hole in the border fence yesterday morning, snatching one *vaquero* off his horse and raging because he couldn't chase the other one all the way here to Mexico City if he had to. Style, Harmon? Ethelbert was doing his *job*, which might wind up being the closest he — or you or me — ever gets to any kind of salvation. That's style, he thought as he flashed his red Official passport and shoved his way through the envious crowd of waiting tourists in the customs area, shoved as if each one of them were a subspecies of Harmon.

Paz's life had unraveled like a sliced rope these last months, and Harmon was writing him nitwit notes about style? The salvation interested him more.

He slipped into the loud concourse, glad to be invisible in the crowds. He'd been careful not to let the Customs attaché, Gallagher, know he was taking the early flight. If he had, he'd have been met here, briefed, then assigned a keeper from Mexican customs to work with. He didn't want that, not yet: with less than two weeks, he didn't want to start tripping over his own players until he had to.

At a pay phone he thumbed through his notebook to the coded numbers and out of habit started to drop a twenty-centavo piece into the slot. But a cleaning lady beside the phone wagged her finger at him, the universal Spanish "no." "It's free, señor," she said, smiling like somebody sharing a good secret. "Since the earthquake, they're all free." He smiled back, left the coin on the phone for her, then, while he was waiting for the phone to be answered, put another hundred pesos with it. An offering, he told himself, to the Mexican gods of tricky habit.

A woman with a hacking cough answered the phone. He identified himself, asked for Manolo, and took down an address the woman gave him. She didn't seem pleased to hear from him.

Outside the labyrinth of the Dallas-shiny new airport terminal — new, that was, in everything but its blissful Mexican chaos — he was hit with a quick wave of nostalgia for the vanished clamor of shuddering, ancient Chevy taxis that once had jockeyed for a chance to haggle you to your destination. Now, as he bought his prepaid taxi ticket from the bored clerk and faced the great line of patient, take-your-turn, bright yellow official Volkswagen beetle taxis at the official taxi stand, he considered how much Stanley's tourists from Syracuse would appreciate such order. The address the woman had given him was a church in the Churubusco section, near the movie studios. Not a good part of Churubusco; no arching eucalyptus here, only pharmacies and cheap shoe stores and record shops, and the old stone church squeezed in among them like a forgotten piece of a movie set. It was as out of place as Paz felt when he went inside, his suit bag draped over his shoulder and the weight of his .45 pressing against his side. The sweetish odor of candles and the faintly subterranean smell of mildewed, damp plaster mixed with the sharper scent of fresh paint in the watery light. He crossed himself — habit again — and his eyes found the church's other occupant high on a makeshift scaffolding, leaning close to the wall and dabbing at something with an artist's brush in the glare from a mechanic's work lamp.

His voice echoed in the mine shaft of a nave. "Manolo, *qué tal?*"

Manolo, thin, graying, with Coke-bottle glasses that rode a scythe of a nose, squinted down into the dimness at Paz. When he recognized him he showed no more surprise than if Paz had been gone only a week. What did four years mean when you'd spent forty working in places like this? "Señor Paz," he said in a nasal, joyless voice.

He hiked his paint-stained pants and squatted on his scaffolding but didn't come down as Paz approached. Paz said, "I talked to your wife. She sounds good."

"She has emphysema. Smoking."

Festive Mexico, Paz thought. Glad to be back. "I'm sorry."

"If not the smoking, the smog. No difference. I'll be next."

Paz tried to think of something else sympathetic to say. "I'm sorry," he said again.

"You've been away."

"I've been away. Still in the business, Manolo?"

Manolo glanced over his shoulders at the covey of ancient angels he'd been restoring. "Frescoes pay less, since it's government work. But I like it. You can't steal them, you can't sell them. I can go back and see them whenever I like, no?

Next month, I go to work on an Orozco that the earthquake damaged. Thank God for earthquakes."

Paz wagged his finger. "The other business, Manolo." With Manolo he was never sure whether he was being jacked around or whether Manolo was truly a little east of things: he was a man with a middling talent and cursed by being smart enough to know it was middling. God only knew what dodges he'd invented to deal with that.

Manolo shrugged. "Frescoes don't pay much."

Paz scanned the church. Nothing moved but the wavering flames of a few votive candles on the altar. "All by ourselves, Manolo?"

"Just us, Señor Paz."

"If you had a codex, then, a Maya codex, one of a kind. Worth maybe as much as a drawer full of Picassos. Where would you take it?"

"Who are you asking for?"

"I'm here by myself, Manolo. No Mexican customs people." Paz spread his arms, as if to show he wasn't hiding anybody under them, and immediately felt foolish. "*Ves?* I just want to talk, not put anybody out of business."

Manolo studied him a moment, then said, "I don't care what you do to him. What I pick up in places like this is too small for him to buy. Just don't involve me, you understand?"

"Manolo, *por favor.*"

"Collosini, then. Nobody else. Nobody else in Mexico could do it but him."

"Why?"

"You can trust him to get it out, and to the right dealers. Collosini builds theatre sets — for the ballet, the folk dancers, everybody who goes on tour from Mexico."

Paz waited for him to go on. "And?"

Manolo clicked his tongue, as if he were impatient that Paz had missed something obvious. "You want to get a painting to France? The next show that goes to France has a painting as part of the set. If he can't make it fit *that* set, then the next one. What does the customs inspector see? A cheap stage prop. He's not going to look carefully to see what's underneath the canvas of the prop, is he? In France somebody is waiting, he goes backstage, the stage manager knows what's happening, and *ya*, it's done."

"That's no good for a thing like a codex, Manolo."

"I told you, he has the contacts. People trust him. If that way doesn't work, he'll find another. Nobody but Collosini."

"Where can I find him?"

"Calzado Morelos, just off Fray Servando. Ask."

Paz dug into his pocket for the two ten-thousand-peso notes he had ready — he knew what Manolo was worth, adjusted for inflation — and laid them on the scaffolding above him. "Fifteen years ago, I knew a man who got a deal on a car for a thousand pesos."

Manolo picked up the bills and stood. "That buys one taco now, Señor Paz." He bent over, mimed wiping himself with the bills, then turned back to his angels.

Outside, the rain had picked up, a drizzle that silently sliced the yellow smog but didn't wash it away, that sizzled under tires and made puddles that splashed more gray onto the gray concrete, gray streets, gray people. Sky, smog, buildings merged into a world like an old photograph whose images were blurring and losing their shapes, a city seen through a glass grayly.

But then in the taxi, the bright red fringe above the windshield and the plastic, glow-in-the-dark Virgin of Guadalupe who hung from the mirror comforted him like a familiar night light. In spite of the gloom, his spirits slipped up a notch. Even somebody who might have known Eliot Ness remembered a few rocks he could kick over and find an informant still wiggling beneath. Bless me, Lady, he thought: a hit, first try.

On both sides of the Hotel Fremont, earthquake-ruined buildings hulked like skeletons from some grotesque Day of the

Dead festival. But the Fremont, clean yet cheap enough so he could pocket decent leftovers from his seventy-dollar per diem allowance, hung on like a memory in its narrow street behind the soaring Old Lottery Building. He'd stayed here on his first TDY to Mexico, before Craig had been born, and Bess had flown down for a weekend with him. He'd been what, twenty-eight, twenty-nine? Dear God. He remembered the room number, 315; they hadn't left it except for a night of tequila and mariachi music at Garibaldi Square. He asked the desk clerk for a room on any floor but the third.

In his room he dumped the suit bag and found a loose edge of the carpeting to slip his Official passport and ID under. He hesitated over the *salvoconducto* pass for his .45, then pulled up the inner sole of his shoe and slid the pass beneath it. It was a chance worth taking: it might buy him time with the Mexican cops if he needed it. His clothes had U.S. labels in them, but the name on his false ID's was Spanish, Quintero. It was a good cover; he could move any way he wanted with it.

He stretched out on the bed for ten minutes to put his cover story together for *el maestro* Collosini. This was a part he liked, telling himself stories, becoming somebody else for a while, making pieces fit. Becoming one of *them*, crossing another kind of border into *their* world, the way he'd been able to lose himself in books in that great dim study in Buenos Aires. It was there he'd first read Stanislavski's *An Actor Prepares*. Best training manual he'd ever had for this kind of work, though the Customs Service hadn't seen it that way when he tried to get them to add it to their trainees' reading list.

When he got up, his watch had a few minutes past two o'clock. If he hadn't shown at the embassy after the 12:30 flight from Tucson, Gallagher would be expecting him on the 4:00. He had time to get to Collosini's and back to the embassy by five.

The patient yellow Volkswagen fought the piraña traffic well, and Paz let the chorus of horns relax him. He closed his eyes against the burning smog and diesel fumes. Something was different about this place he'd loved for most of his life, something he didn't like. He'd been here less than two hours and he sensed it. Not just the earthquake ruins that littered the city, nor the rusting "temporary" corrugated tin shanty-towns the government had thrown up in vacant lots for the survivors, nor even the fact that beggars had reappeared in force on the streets. It was nothing he could see as clearly as those things. The earthquake had just focused it. *It* was something he felt, had begun to feel as the plane had broken through the rainy-season clouds and he'd seen the endlessness of the city, the huts that seemed to cover the entire huge valley of Mexico now. He saw it in people's closed faces, heard it in voices that were as cold as the damp air. It had to do with scale, he thought, with the lack of any center. When you put nearly twenty million people in one place, and made them every day poorer, what you created in them was, above all else, fear. And fear was unpredictable, dangerous. More than once this place had been home to him. Now he rode with a tight wariness, a feeling new to him here, one that said, Don't relax, don't believe habit, you're a stranger in this place.

His eyes opened as he felt the taxi swerve off the boulevard onto a side street. In front of him a sign rose three stories high up the corner of a building. *Partos*, it read. Births. Sure, he thought. Just the ticket.

The taxi driver got the right directions to Collosini's on the third try. From the street, the place was a mottled, cracked stucco wall, no different from the other walls along the street. They all joined to make an unbroken landscape of walls to mask body shops, mechanics' shops, and other nameless, small, noisy businesses, a landscape whose only color came from peeling advertisements for bullfights, concerts, movies, dem-onstrations, political parties. An open steel gate in Collosini's wall, wide enough to drive a truck through, led Paz into a large dirt patio littered with sheets of tin, sawhorses, piles of graying lumber, oil drums, trash. Under lean-to roofs nailed to the walls of the patio, he made out stacks of canvas flats, of stage lights, of boxes and trunks and platforms. The whole workyard had the air of a place unnaturally abandoned, like something from an old black-and-white sci-fi movie. He maneuvered through the debris uneasily, with dark, shallow mud sucking at his shoes.

Near a door into an adjoining low building, a squat man was welding together what looked like a spotlight housing. He raised his mask when Paz approached, so that Paz could see his round, flat face. It was flecked with the white burn marks, like smallpox scars, that gave away the fact that he'd learned his trade in a place too cheap to provide him with more than goggles. Paz worked a smile for him.

"*El maestro Collosini, por favor,*" he said, hitting the Italian lilt and "zhh" sounds of an Argentine accent harder than he needed to.

The man motioned toward the door. "*Allá, señor,*" he said. He kept his mask lifted, watching, as Paz entered the building.

Off the short hallway, only one door was open. Music, a scratchy recording of an aria from *Pagliacci*, curled from the door. Caruso, Paz guessed — it was close enough to the version he'd heard so many times from his grandfather's study. He approached the door quietly, so that he saw Collosini before Collosini noticed him.

Collosini sat behind a desk mounded with papers and folders and empty coffee cups; on top of the stack nearest him a plate, apparently recently emptied, balanced. He was holding his dentures in front of him, scraping earnestly at them with the corner of a matchbook. Paz guessed him at pushing sixty-five, though his thinning hair was still perfectly black and was slicked back like a forties tango dancer's. He was nearly as huge as Ethelbert, but his fat was slack, settled like water in a balloon. What Paz could see of his wrinkled blue suit — was the thing actually serge? — looked as if he'd picked it out that morning from the jumble of fading stage costumes that hung from nails around the office or covered what might have been a couch. The music, Paz saw, came from a fancy tape deck that shared the top of a file cabinet with a cage in which something with a long snout crouched and chittered along with Caruso.

Collosini started when he looked up and saw Paz, then looked down again at his dentures as if Paz had caught him shoplifting them. His eyes were not kind as he worked them back into place.

"Señor Collosini," Paz said, easing the Argentine accent down to a more natural level.

"Collosini, yes. And you, señor?" There was no mere lilt of Italian in his wheezy voice: it was the real thing.

"Adolfo Quintero, your servant."

Collosini took the hand Paz held out. His hand had the onionskin texture of an old man's hand, but was too soft, a hand used to baby oil. "In what might I serve you, señor? Have we met? Corresponded? My memory . . ."

"No, señor. I only know your work."

Collosini grunted, suddenly a grunting public man used to such intrusions. "You are Argentine, I take it. The Festival Mexicano I sent there last year."

"I was in the United States last year, señor. I live there now. To my knowledge, I've never seen one of your productions."

Collosini rose, lumbered to the tape deck, and lowered the volume. The thing with a snout stopped chittering and turned back to the depths of its cage. "Then, Señor Quintero, I think I am confused."

Fine, Paz thought. My point. He gave Collosini the story he'd worked out, trying to read him at each new lie to see if he'd lost him. He was indeed Argentine, looking after another, rich Argentine's business interests in the States. The Argentine he worked for was a collector and lived in England. The man knew a fabulous pre-Maya codex had recently been found, but none of his regular dealers in the States could help him with it. So he'd sent Paz to Collosini, the one man in Mexico the Northamerican dealers said might be able to tell him whether this codex was on the market. He wasn't at liberty to divulge the names of those dealers, of course, as Señor Collosini would surely understand, but if Señor Collosini would be kind enough to help him locate the codex, Paz's employer would be pleased to pay the dealer's commission directly to Señor Collosini himself, and everyone would be infinitely grateful.

Collosini listened, noncommittal, nodding at appropriate moments and keeping his eyes steadily on Paz as if Paz were an auditioning actor.

When Paz was done, Collosini sank back into his chair again. "And how does your employer know about this fabulous codex, Señor Quintero?" he asked, his voice as noncommittal as his eyes.

"He was one of the backers of the expedition that found it, señor. He would simply like to get his property back."

Paz watched Collosini adding up things. After a time, Collosini opened a drawer and dropped his used dinner plate into it. It clattered against other, older plates. "Señor Quintero, forgive me a moment," he said. "A man walks into my office from nowhere, claiming to know about my business. Who is this man? Argentine, from his accent. But could that be a disguise for somebody from Mexican customs or the Federal Police? No. If I have stayed in business this long, I know they are all safely . . . invested in. Northamerican Customs? Why would they send a man to do something like this? If they know about me, they could simply stop my shipments at the border and try to embarrass the Mexican attorney general into indicting me, which he would probably do to save face. Then, whoever this man is, he has nothing to do with the police, which means a possible business arrangement for me. And an Argentine in England? Europe is full of Argentines with suitcases full of money and odd tastes. I know. I have dealt with them. What you are telling me is plausible, señor, just sufficiently plausible."

Collosini leaned an elbow on his desk and regarded Paz out of the corner of his eye a moment, then said, "So I wish I could help you. But I cannot."

"Then you don't have the codex."

"I do not. I had offers from two potential sellers at least a month ago. I have not heard from either of them again. Since you tell me the piece is on the market, and I do not have it, then the likelihood is that I *will* not have it."

"Two sellers, *maestro?*" Paz's attention sharpened. A gift horse, he thought, a gift horse in a blue serge suit.

"Two sellers, both of whom I had good reason to believe could obtain the codex for me." He opened another desk drawer, took a marshmallow out, and heaved to his feet again. "You will not, of course, wish to cause any awkwardness between us by asking me who those two persons were, señor, since I would have to refuse you. To tell you that they exist hurts no one, and inclines you to accept that I am being open with you. But to go further, ah! That breaches professional confidentiality."

The snouted thing chittered as he shoved the marshmallow through the mesh of its cage; the snout appeared briefly, grabbed the marshmallow, and disappeared again. Collosini turned back to Paz. "What I cannot understand, Señor Quintero, is why a man would go to the trouble to construct such a plausible story and then tell such a bad lie. Of course I accept that you did not know I had two offers to sell the piece, and that both persons I spoke with mentioned no Argentine backer. At my request, one of them, in fact, kindly furnished me with the backers' names. Two Northamericans and one Mexican, Señor Quintero. No Argentines. I'm sorry. Since the best lie is the one nearest the truth, you should have researched your facts more carefully."

For a moment, Paz was twelve again, caught in a stupid lie,

fearful and angry and frustrated as he tried to come up with a bigger lie to cancel the last one. "There were intermediaries, señor."

Collosini held up both hands, puffy as inflated surgical gloves, in a weary "spare me" gesture. "Please, Señor Quintero. I have been open with you, and would appreciate the same from you. If for some reason you indeed wish to buy something from me, simply ask. I truly do not care who you are. On the other hand, if you are trying to find out if I have the codex for some other reason, I have told you that I do not, and good afternoon to you, señor. Or if perhaps *you* have information that could lead either of us to the codex and have chosen this bizarre way of exploring me first, then please have a seat and I will send out for a whiskey. Which is it, señor? My guess is that your reasons involve the last of those."

Still angry — at himself first — Paz thought, cut your losses. He quickly checked the door behind him, ready to move if he had to, and said, "My apologies, señor. I've taken your time."

Collosini studied him a long moment in the Caruso-laced silence. Then he reached inside his coat pocket; instinctively, irrationally, Paz stepped back and tensed. Thirteen days, he thought, and would this be any better place to go down than a Papago reservation? His tension held even when Collosini pulled out a business card and extended it to him. "Perhaps you haven't," Collosini said. He gave Paz an indulgent smile, partly, Paz knew, to acknowledge that he'd seen him go tense. Bastard. "I would be pleased to do business with you when you've had time to reconsider. I have no desire to embarrass you, you understand." Paz took the card.

Collosini turned to the file cabinet and twisted the volume of the music back up. "The first concert I staged in Mexico was Caruso's, señor. He gave me the original records I made these tapes from. Mexico owes Western culture something in return for all she has received from it, no?" He made no effort to face Paz as Paz reached the door. "If I can be of help to you in something else, the National Workers' Theatre goes to England in the fall."

The sidewalk outside Collosini's was still wet, though the rain had stopped for the moment. Paz checked his watch: not even three yet. His best bet for finding a taxi was on Fray Servando, then there should even be time to go back to the hotel to shower and put his pride back together before he made his entrance at the embassy. He wove his way around the cars, children, and trash barrels that clogged the sidewalk and tried to assess just what making a fool of himself with Collosini had been worth.

First, he believed Collosini. Why should he lie? He had nothing to gain by lying, and maybe a customer or a codex to lose. He didn't even have to be afraid of a rip-off: he only brokered things. He had no money in them.

So, another try, another hit. *Two* people had offered Collosini the codex; there'd been two separate plans to make it disappear. Both of the plans had to come from people who knew the codex existed and, according to Collosini, had a reasonable chance of getting hold of it. That meant somebody connected with the expedition. Not, Paz thought, the kind of patient archaeologists you expected to read about in *Scientific American*: the baron's judgement about people had apparently not gotten much better than it had been when he joined the German foreign office in the thirties.

But the start was good. Gallagher, at the embassy, could take the information to Mexican customs, and they'd *have* to make Collosini come up with the two names. And Collosini would, gladly; he was smart enough to give up any possibility of brokering the codex for the chance to stay in business. Which he'd do, though it might cost him a little more each month.

So maybe not so bad a return after all, considering the investment. He'd spent weeks on stakeouts before and had gotten less. He caught a wild soccer ball that bounded off a wall at him and butted it back to the ragtag bunch of kids waiting for it in the street. Not a bad butt, either, by damn, for an old man. He felt better than he had in months — or longer.

The obvious problem was this: if neither of the two who'd offered the codex to Collosini had actually come up with it, what did that mean?

It could mean any of a dozen things, a hundred things. For the moment, he'd settle for his starting point and harbor the undoubtedly temporary illusion that after twenty years he was owed an easy one.

When he reached Fray Servando, on an impulse he turned onto it and kept walking. A reward, he thought, for not getting himself blown away in that overstuffed office back there. A ten-minute treat to enjoy the luxury of being alive and alone and invisible in Mexico City, of no one's knowing he was here yet. And, after the drabness of the side streets, to enjoy even the rush of traffic, the shops, the crowded sidewalks. This was the Mexico he'd loved most back B.T., Before Tucson, working-class Mexico, Mexico not sanitized for the tourists. When he'd lived here, he'd lose himself on streets like this for hours at a time. Working for Stanley, he could do it again, he knew. But not the same way, not feeling this way he felt after Collosini's office.

He would miss this shit.

Then, as he stopped to check the street for taxis, he remembered: don't believe habit.

The spark-pocked man who had been welding at Collosini's shop was less than a block behind. He made no attempt to stop or to step out of sight when Paz spotted him. Nor did the two men with him.

Already they were close enough for Paz to get a decent make on them. So much, Paz thought, for invisibility. Collosini must have had them on him before he was well out of the workyard.

Collosini had *told* him he thought he knew more about the codex than he'd come across with. And Paz had ignored that, had gotten so full of what he'd learned from Collosini that he had taken the smile and the business card and never looked back. Only somebody pitifully rusty would have let that happen.

One of the men, probably the honcho, was tall and wore a well-cut tan business suit. His face was much more lean and European than either the welder's or the other man's. That one was a *chino*, an Indian with eyes so slanted he could easily have been Oriental. He had a boxer's build and cocky walk, and the crowd on the sidewalk parted before him like fish in a school as he sliced through it.

They'd picked up on his stopping to check for taxis, Paz guessed; they were in the open because they knew that if they didn't catch up with him now, they wouldn't. He stepped out into the street. Only one taxi showed in the stampede of cars and smoking trucks that bore down on him from the just-changed light. He flagged it, and the passenger in it gave him a bored look as it accelerated past.

He ran his eyes along the shops nearby. They could be cages; taking the chance he'd find a back door to one could kill him. And before the next wave of cars broke along Fray Servando, a crippled burro could catch up to him from less than a block away. He could run, but hell, the *chino* looked half his age. He ducked around a parked car to lose himself for a pair of seconds. As he came up, he saw at the end of the row of shops the distinctive, long, low cinder-block building that he knew had to surround a marketplace. And marketplaces had doors, lots of doors.

He sprinted. At the arched entrance to the market he dance-stepped past a gaggle of Indian women who squatted beside what looked like piles of dead leaves scattered on blankets, and was inside before he recognized the place. Ahead of him an echoing, block-long expanse of counters, stalls, booths, and blankets spread the smell, sharp and sweet at once, of a thousand herbs and potions. On a counter just beside him what looked at first like little umbrellas poked up from a shallow basket. As his eyes adjusted to the light, he saw they were dried dog feet.

Fray Servando — of course, yes, the witches' market! Give a curse, take away a curse, create love, cure cancer, make madness, get rid of stomach gas — all here. And escape, too. Invisibility again? Paz plunged down an aisle to his left, just a second too late. The three men — the suited man in the lead — skidded into the archway behind him.

The place was a maze, but not a blind enough maze. As he ducked behind scarred counters, zigzagging from aisle to aisle, customers and vendors alike took sides. He was a diversion, a greased pig. People either pointed the way out to him or tried to tackle him, and, as he saw when he risked stopping once to get his bearings, the ones who'd tried to tackle him made themselves into a fan club to show the three men behind him where he'd gone. They could Keystone cop him until the three-to-one odds caught up with him. He was better off in the open.

He scuttled to the center aisle and headed for the daylight beyond the archway at the rear. He'd take the chance he could lose himself quicker in the small streets there than on Fray Servando. He sprinted again now, scattering herbs from blankets, stiff-arming instead of sidestepping. Just at the door, a serious little man with a wisp of a beard and the eyes of a fundamentalist preacher stepped out in front of him and held up a wooden hex sign like a shield. Paz drove his shoulder into him and broke past into the soggy daylight.

Ahead of him was a weedy vacant lot. On both sides ran narrow side streets like Collosini's, walled streets as impossible to get off of as prison walkways. Beyond, across the lot, the shell of an apartment building with one wall and the top floors missing rose like something left behind after a bombing run. A hell of a choice. At least the streets might offer a friendly doorway, a few seconds to think. He started left, toward the nearer of them. He'd gone only a couple of yards when the welder rounded the corner of the market, directly in front of him. He hesitated, turned back. From the other end of the market the *chino* eased into a run toward him. The bastards had spread out. In seconds, he knew, the suited man would be in the archway behind him. He broke for the ruined apartment building.

He had no time to plan, to read the building before he leapt over the scree of rubble that surrounded it. If he could get *through* it somehow, onto the streets . . .

But as he got closer, he saw through the jagged holes in the building's skin that what hadn't been destroyed was the wall, the high cinder-block wall that had once guarded it from the street. He skidded down a wet, tiled hallway through the building, then dodged hunks of fallen concrete and smashed furniture across the service yard to the gate. It was as high as the wall, a good twelve feet, and was a solid sheet of rusting steel. He shoved it. It clattered open an inch and then jarred to a stop; through the open crack he could see the heavy lock hasp that held it. Locked, still locked more than two years after the earthquake.

He was inside the building again in time to see the suited man waving a revolver at the small crowd who'd followed him outside from the market. They scrambled away from him, back through the arches. Whatever the scumbag wanted with him, he wanted it with no witnesses. He felt for his own gun. Useless as tits on a boar hog, he heard Harmon's voice say. Use it and get to know the inside of a Mexican jail. But what else was there, where else? He shoved at the panic that crowded in on him. Where, goddamn it, *where?*

Only one corner of the building seemed to be reasonably intact, a corner on the street side to his right. If he could hide for just enough time to let them get past him and into the service yard, he could double back, make the streets. If. He ducked into a hole that had been an apartment wall.

Through an empty doorway, through another ruined wall, and he saw it, saw the concrete shell of what had probably been a utilities room. It was a bunker, maybe the only thing in the building that had survived. He pushed away a cobweb of dangling wires and scrambled for it. He tripped, felt blood running from the heel of his hand, kept scrambling.

He saw the eyes just as he stepped through the doorway, spots of white that seemed to suck up the little light that spilled in from behind him. Then, as his own eyes adjusted to the room's darkness, he made out the forms that surrounded those other eyes. There were at least five of them, three men and two women, that he could see. A clay charcoal brazier glowed dully from the center of the room; around it, flattened cardboard boxes were scattered for beds. A couple of the men held two-by-fours cocked like clubs, ready for him. Their hair was as long as the women's, and tangled like stray dogs'. Things that might once have been shirts and dresses seemed to have been shredded by claws. They were people and not people, almost simian. Scavengers, Paz thought, heirs to the earthquake's ruins. He took a step backward and stopped. No, he couldn't go that way, either.

He smelled the stale urine smell from the room in front of him, heard the water dripping down through the smashed nest of girders and wires behind him. He heard his own heavy breathing over that of the people in front of him and could think of nothing else but that he was afraid.

Then he thought, this is the dream, Ethelbert. He stepped backward one more step, reached inside his coat for his .45, and turned.

He was hit halfway through the turn. The *chino* caught him in the stomach; he lost his breath, doubled over, and fought the ringing fuzziness that told him he was blacking out. He lost. The edges of things went soft, and the world broke up and came back together, broke up and came together, each time in a different place, as if he were stumbling down a long strobe-lit hallway. Then, when he was able to blink it all back together, he was on his back on the broken tiles of the hallway, the welder was straddling his legs, the *chino* was grinding his knees into his shoulders, and the suited man with the pistol was standing over him, pointing the front sight at his face. Paz struggled to get his breath back, struggled to keep the barrel of the pistol focused, struggled to let the pain of the sharp edges of the broken tiles under his back keep the ringing fuzziness away.

"*Bueno*, Argentine," the suited man said, his own breath labored. "How did you know about the codex? Quick. Where do I find it?"

Paz had to try twice before his lungs found a rhythm that would allow words. "I work for a man — "

"You're lying, *pendejo*."

"This man works through — "

The *chino* drove his knees harder into Paz's shoulders. He laid the barrel of Paz's .45 along Paz's nose; Paz smelled the gun oil, saw the blurred, dark hole at the end of the barrel an inch from his eye.

"Do *you* have it?" the suited man said. He squatted and put his face so close to Paz's that the overpowering smell of his sweet cologne blotted out the gun oil. His voice became calm, reasonable. "I work for somebody, too. *Comprendes?* We both have jobs, no? We can talk like businessmen. You want to talk like businessmen? You know where that thing is? Eh?"

Time, Paz thought, buy time. "How much?" He forced himself to become aware of more than the pain in his shoulders, the fog that was still trying to burn itself off in his head. What were the real chances this bastard would kill for something as weak as the fact he had hold of a man who might not know any more about where the codex was than he himself did? Good enough — damn certain, in fact, after he'd gotten what information he thought Paz had. There was no panic now. His choices were gone, and so was the panic. He shifted his weight as best he could. It would have to be his legs first, he'd have to get his legs loose first.

He blinked so his eyes wouldn't telegraph anything and, as he did, looked down to check the welder.

The welder was holding a shoe, Paz's shoe.

Paz felt the cold that seeped through his sock now. His left shoe was missing — he must have lost the goddamn thing when he went down. Mother of God, which shoe had he put the *salvoconducto* pass in?

"How much? You know where it is, then?"

"*Carajo*," the welder swore. "Look at this."

The suited man took Paz's *salvoconducto* pass from the welder. He scanned it, then his eyes met the welder's. His voice stayed calm, reasonable. "Collosini," he said. "That *cabrón*, that stupid ass Collosini."

Paz jerked his legs up, hard. The welder lurched but held on. He locked his hands in a double fist and raised them above Paz's balls, raised them just as the two-by-four hissed down on him.

The scavenger got his blow in solidly. The welder slumped forward and to the side. But the two who went for the *chino* and the suited man got in each other's way. The suited man caught a glancing blow off his shoulder and twisted quickly enough to be ready for the second one. He fired once, the scavenger looked surprised, backed away, and Paz lost him. It was the *chino* who saved Paz. The first blow shocked him, and by the time he raised the .45, it was too late: the two-by-four was already coming down again. As he pitched forward, he took the scavenger's third blow, too, which Paz knew was intended for himself. And Paz had the .45.

He fired it up into the twisted basket of girders and wires and pipes above him, and rolled. The noise bought him a piece of a second. His back found a solid hunk of wall out of range of the two-by-fours, and he shoved himself against it as a light rain of plaster sifted down from the path of the bullet. For a long moment he and the suited man and the two scavengers didn't move, like staring cats waiting for the first to look away. Then slowly, very slowly, Paz got to his feet.

He motioned with his free hand for the two scavengers to back off. They did, moving as slowly as Paz had. The suited man still held his revolver, pointed now at the floor. The jackass hadn't thought quickly enough to cover Paz after he'd shot the scavenger. Paz kept the .45 steadily on him. Thank God for amateurs, he thought.

"Who offered to sell the codex?" Paz said. With a blown cover, he might as well go for what he could get. "I want that first."

"I don't know," the suited man said. "Collosini wouldn't say."

Paz accepted that. "Then put the pistol down and kick it toward me. We'll go see Collosini."

The man eased the pistol onto the ground and stood. And as he did, the Mexican standoff cracked apart. With a low grunt, the scavenger who'd been shot slumped out of the door of the utilities room and collapsed on the tiles like a stringless puppet. Behind him, a woman shrieked and threw herself through the door and on top of him. One of the other scavengers moved toward her, Paz instinctively swung the pistol toward him, and the suited man bolted.

Paz took a step after him, then let him go. Screw him. He could get to Collosini on his own. Screw covers. Screw the Mexican cops. Collosini owed *him* now, owed him two names. He hurt, he'd had the piss scared out of him, and he'd almost been killed. He'd get to Collosini, and the Mexican cops wouldn't touch him now. No matter what kinds of "investments" Collosini was paying, the noise that would come from his setting up a gringo Customs cop would drown out everything else — for the moment, anyway, for thirteen days. And if the embassy sent him home, well, he'd go back to Tucson with at least a better taste in his mouth than he'd left the reservation with yesterday.

As he stepped through the hole in the wall, juggling his shoe, the .45, and the *salvoconducto* pass the suited man had dropped, the two scavengers went to work stripping the welder and the *chino*. The other woman came out of the utilities room and stood sullenly watching her friend cry over the dead man. She made no move to comfort her. By the time the cops that Paz would call got here, they'd have all disappeared into the pit that was twenty million people. The dead scavenger, and whichever of the two men who were being stripped might be dead, too, would be the only ones waiting for the cops. In a week, two weeks, the scavengers would move back in. It was too good an address to give up.

He tied his shoe in the vacant lot while from the archway the little man with the whiskers made a sign to ward off the evil eye. Paz winked at him. He was in no hurry. He'd call the cops from Collosini's. Collosini wouldn't mind.

Collosini didn't mind.

Paz knew he wasn't going to when he spotted the suited man leaving the workshop. He was two blocks away when he saw him, but the way the man stopped to compose himself, then checked carefully but casually to see who was watching him before he walked away told Paz what he needed to know, told him who had been the final fool, *maestro*. He knew the man must have seen him, too. But when Paz didn't speed up, didn't make any attempt to stop him, he walked away nonchalantly. Why shouldn't he? Collosini was the only one who knew who he was. Which was why, of course, he had come back to see Collosini.

Caruso was still singing when Paz walked into the office. Verdi this time, Paz guessed as he hit the stop button on the tape deck. From there, he had to step over Collosini's body to get to his desk drawers; it covered nearly the whole space between the desk and the file cabinet. As far as Paz could tell, since there was no exit wound, the suited man had used a knife — probably what he'd been more used to before he'd found somebody like Collosini to front him the money to buy a suit and a gun. But Collosini was face down; all Paz could be sure of was that from somewhere beneath him blood was draining and puddling on the mottled yellow tiles. Careful to keep from stepping into the blood, he bent to check Collosini's pulse.

As he did, he heard a noise in the hallway, barely louder than the scuttling of an animal's feet. He hushed his breath to be sure. The thing in the cage heard it, too, and ran a trill of uncertain chitters, almost as if it were speaking to the sound. Paz slowly stood.

"*Quién vive!*" he said steadily.

Nothing answered him.

He took a step toward the door, gently unholstering the .45. But not gently enough. He lost his balance for a moment maneuvering over Collosini's body. As he did, the pistol clunked against the desk and a stack of Collosini's dirty cups shifted, slid, and smashed on the floor tiles. Paz ducked beside the desk and drew down on the doorway.

A figure — it might have been a child — darted past the doorway, too fast for anything about it to register. Paz leapt to the doorway, quick-checked the hallway with a flick of his head. The figure was a single frame in a film, barely seen as it vanished out of his vision into the workyard. Paz shoved himself off the door frame and followed.

Habit, good habit this time, stopped him at the outside doorway for a final scan of the workyard. No child waited for him, but a man hardly bigger than one — Craig's size when he'd been in junior high school, Paz guessed. He wore a frayed checked suit coat too large for him, khaki pants, and scuffed brogans, and he *was* waiting. He stood with legs apart, a broadsword held poised in two hands like a baseball bat. The sword was clearly a stage prop, with a painted wooden hilt. The man would have been ridiculous, Paz thought, except for two things: the blade of the sword was steel, and the man's eyes were invisible. His face was thin as a skull, the skin drawn so tightly over it that it was impossible to tell if he was thirty or fifty, and in the gray daylight his eyes seemed sunk so deeply into that skull that they were circles of shadow, no more. It was an Indian's face: Totonac or Mixtec, Paz guessed, a sharp-boned, beakish mountain face, the face of a hawk, *un halcón*, scoured of the saving beauty of feathers.

Paz eased into the workyard, the .45 conspicuously held in front of him. "I don't want you," Paz said quietly. "You've got nothing I want. Just get the hell away from here. You didn't see me, I didn't see you. *Entiende?*"

The man lunged, as if the .45 were no more than a rock Paz held. Paz sidestepped: the man was quick, moving without telegraphing his intentions or direction, but the sword was too heavy for him. He couldn't find his balance with it. He stepped back, considered, then raised the sword above his head. "Look," Paz said. "I don't give a damn if you killed Collosini or not. If I did, why haven't I used this thing?" He held the gun out again, like a kid doing a show and tell. "You speak Spanish? Just *lárgate*, go!"

With no warning, no sign from those dark eye sockets, the man dropped into a crouch. As he did, he turned the downward motion into a forward one, too, so that he launched the sword at Paz as if it were an ax. This time Paz couldn't settle for a sidestep. He flung himself flat on his stomach, hard, and rolled to the side. The sword smashed through a window behind the space he'd occupied a half second before. And the man, with a balance as perfect as a swooping bird rising, spun as he sprang from his crouch and was outside the workyard and onto the street before Paz was even on his feet again.

Paz stood for a full minute until the shaking stopped, until he was sure the little man was truly gone. Another one of Collosini's "employees"? he wondered. Not damned likely, not with that outfit he'd been wearing, inherited from a corpse or borrowed. Or was he just a well-dressed scavenger, on his way to rags but a few weeks away yet? Had he been here before the suited man had come back? Had he gotten to Collosini first? A local matter, Paz thought, tasting his own irony, another local matter. Collosini was dead. Paz had thought the tan-suited man had killed him. Now he didn't know. Either way, for what he wanted, it didn't matter.

Back inside, nothing in Collosini's desk drawers was any use to him. If there had been an address book, it was gone now, more likely into the suited man's pocket than the hawk-faced one's. Paz figured it ought to be good for at least a decade's worth of blackmail. In a drawer full of dirty dishes with a fuzz of mold on them, Paz found the bag of marshmallows. While he was waiting for the cops to answer their phone, he leaned over Collosini's body and stuffed one of them through the mesh of the cage on the file cabinet. The thing with a snout snatched it and began to rake at it with small, sharp claws, tearing it into smaller pieces.

In his Argentine accent, Paz gave the police dispatcher both locations, here and behind the witches' market, and hung up. He wasn't involved. He knew because Harmon said so.

He made one more phone call. It still wasn't four, but he told Gallagher that the plane had come in early. And yes, he knew he could get to the embassy before five if he came straight there, yes, Gallagher, but he wanted to get a couple of things in order first, already feeling the hot shower back in the hotel room, hearing Teri's voice from the clean, well-lighted office in Tucson, a connection to sanity. Yes, he could be free by six, and yes, he could find a place called the Prince of Wales bar on Dolores Street. What else? No, Gallagher, he was going to see Maritza de la Torre in her office in the morning, there was no need to bring her tonight. No, none at all. Hell, Gallagher, why hadn't he been checked with before she was already on her way across the city?

He left Gallagher in midsentence. He knew he mumbled goodbye, but he wasn't sure whether Gallagher was still talking or not; his attention was already fixed on the piece of notebook paper partly buried by a stained accounts ledger beside the phone. He saw first "Fiesta Airlines," written in an old-fashioned, curlicued European hand — a hand Collosini would use — half a dozen times, the way someone who was trying to puzzle out something about the words might turn them into abstract doodles. In two weeks he would be chief of security for Fiesta Airlines. He pulled the paper the rest of the way from under the ledger. Across from the haphazard column of repeated "Fiesta Airlines," the same hand had written "Stanley Loeb."

He scattered cups and papers, found bills and invoices and notes with other names and dates and places that meant nothing to him. He tried the file cabinet, which was locked, and scanned the cluttered room. Other surfaces were as heaped with papers as the desk. Maybe ten minutes to break into the file cabinet, he thought, and God knew how much time to search it and to sift those piles of papers. Then where might more files be stored in other rooms of this warren of a building? He'd need a platoon.

He stuffed the paper into his coat pocket. Even it wouldn't be any good to him if he wasn't gone by the time the cops got here. He quickly found a half-finished letter in Collosini's handwriting to take with him so he could compare it with the script on the note paper, to be sure. But he saw there was no need; the hands were identical.

The thing with a snout chittered at him as he left. He turned back, took out the bag of marshmallows, opened the top of the cage, and dumped the whole bagful in. The thing watched him warily as he did. Its black eyes were blank and empty as stone, the way those of the man in the workyard had been, and Paz smelled its feral odor even above the sweetness of the marshmallows. He closed the cage sharply, more sharply than he needed to. In a frenzy, the thing ripped open one marshmallow, then another, then another.

FOUR

SHIRTLESS, PAZ FELT like a preening circus performer as he sat on his bed at the Fremont, craning to check for the yellowish marks on his chest and shoulders that would darken into bruises by tomorrow. He was waiting both for the shower water to run hot and for his call to Teri to go through — no ordinary wait, given that the water had to make its way up from some geriatric boiler floors below, and that the Fremont's switchboard was placing his call.

If he could, he'd wash the afternoon off along with the sweat and mud. Satisfied he'd be mostly bruises tomorrow, he picked up the sheet of note paper from the night table and smoothed it over the table's edge. "Fiesta Airlines," in that florid hand-writing, then the quickly jotted "Stanley Loeb" beside it. Alive, Collosini had given him the beginning of a solution to a mystery. Dead, he'd given him an even greater mystery.

The notation could be nothing but a reminder to make a reservation — if Stanley's name hadn't been beside it. The name obviously changed it, but how? And now what? Should he claim a conflict of interest after all, and leave Stanley to the mercies of the next special agent? No. Not yet. The notation could *still* add up to nothing. If Paz was going to keep on being Mary Margaret's brother, and was about to take over security for Fiesta Airlines to boot, he wouldn't leave Stanley to anybody's mercies but his own yet. If the time came when he did have to — hell, truthfully he didn't know *what* he'd do. For right now, it was one more skewed piece, one more thing to put to the side until he could hack some of the bushes out of the way. And one more reason that he had to keep the attaché's office out of this, that he was on his own here.

In one afternoon, two men had tried to kill him, and he wasn't sure why one of them had. One of the two *had* killed an almost institutional fence named Collosini, but he didn't know which one of them had. Then Stanley's name turned up on the dead fence's desk. In twenty years in Customs, he'd come reasonably close to death just five times before this, and only once — when he'd been in internal affairs — had he investigated somebody he knew. He was worried, he was vaguely angry, and he was feeling more than a little conned. It was no way to work an investigation.

A change in the tone of the water's hum in the pipes told him the hot water had arrived at last, and he got up, feeling already the first twinges of tomorrow's stiffness. Keep this pace up, he told himself, and he'd be back down to his best weight in a week, beer wings furled. Or he'd be dead of a coronary.

The phone caught him before he made it to the shower; the switchboard downstairs had timed its fit of unexpected efficiency for this, he knew. He sprinted to the shower, cut the water off, turned back to the room, dove for the phone, knocked it off the night table, fumbled, snatched up the handset, and yelled hello at it.

"Quint?"

"Yes!" he shouted

"You OK?" It was Teri.

He took a slow breath. "I'm OK. I'm just in Mexico."

"No, you're not OK. What's going wrong?"

Paz considered for a moment. "I don't know yet. Can I get some help?"

"It's half an hour before quitting time here. More help than that?"

He explained to her briefly who Collosini was — leaving out the story of the killing — what his business was, and enough about Collosini's scam to let her know what he was looking for. "See if the computer's got anything on him. If it doesn't, get Harmon to authorize putting something on it to stop any pending or in-progress shipments under Collosini's name or of any major Mexican theatrical company. There shouldn't be that many. And get something on the Interpol wire. See if we can turn up any art dealers he's shipped to, and any regular theatre contacts. Look for currency transfers and for business contacts with individuals. Especially that last one."

With resigned sarcasm, Teri said, "Any particular limits? In the next thirty minutes, you want everything since 1890, like that? And don't you want to talk to Harmon about it?"

"I actively *don't* want to talk to Harmon about it, *lindita*, any more than I want to talk to the attaché's office here. I don't want to explain anything right now. There's no case to blow since Collosini's dead, so don't let that get in your way. And yes, there are particular limits. I need everything on his shipments since the baron began this current dig, which should be for about the past year and a half, I'm guessing. I'll change that if I find out more. And I need to know if the name Stanley Loeb turns up anywhere. *I* need to know that last part — nobody else does. Please."

The phone hissed a silence. "I see. Since when has he been dead?"

"This afternoon."

"I see."

"No, you don't yet, any more than I do. But trust me for a while."

"Where can I reach you? You know it'll be tomorrow on some of this."

He gave her the hotel's number. "I probably won't be here. I'll call you back."

"Fine." The phone hissed some more. "So how's the motherland these days?" she said at last, formally and without much real interest.

"Different. Different from before." He was not ready to explain that, either.

"Places always are. You trying to go home again, Quintus?" She tried to make her voice light. But he heard the edge of anger in it and knew she was feeling shut out.

"Look," he said. "I *will* explain everything when I know what to explain. And when there's more time. And when we don't have to worry about international hookups. I'm not being coy."

The silence hissed again. "I know." Her voice was still distant, but the edge was gone. "I'll get back to you."

"Thanks."

"Quint?"

"I'm here."

"Go easy, OK?"

When he hung up he was confused for a moment. Teri had been here with him, but now somebody else was. Teri had gone back *there*, to the other end of those thousands of miles of wire, in that keyboard-clicking office. Bess was here, where he was sure the aging RCA black-and-white TV was the same as the one that had sat on the dresser in the room on the third floor when he had last stayed here with her, back in the seventies, the weekend of that first TDY. This was *her* place, not Teri's. Bess had bought one of those embroidered cotton huipil shifts in the Zona Rosa, which she tried on for him in the room one night, her hair stylishly long and straight, a quiet blond not yet streaked with gray. Then he thought, no, not Bess, but the woman who used to be Bess was here with the man who used to be him, the man who'd been full of possibilities; Bessandquint, one word then, two people who talked about the future because there had been a future.

Unless you're an utter ass, he thought, no matter how bad

things have gotten, you don't just walk away intact. She had his whole youth, and he had hers.

He folded the paper with Stanley's name on it into a tight square no bigger than a postage stamp and slipped it under the piece of loose carpet with his other papers.

Going home again, Teri had said. Customs was home, Harmon had said. How could you go back home, Paz wondered, when you'd never been sure just where home was? And then you come to find out that home isn't a place, but something you do.

Now he was going to meet Maritza de la Torre at a bar on Calle Dolores, the Street of Sorrows, the street where she and he had said goodbye the last night they'd been together. He'd planned to put off seeing her until he had the protection of the impersonality of her office, of secretaries, of morning. Then why hadn't he just refused to see her when Gallagher said he was bringing her tonight? Because, he thought, I didn't want to.

It was no way to work an investigation.

He went back into the bathroom. When he turned the shower on, the water was cold again.

When Gallagher walked in with Maritza, Paz knew why he had brought her. In this businessman's bar, where she was the only woman, Gallagher held her arm as if to succor her through a crocodile wallow, and his eyes touched her almost tangibly as they maneuvered among the tables. Maritza, for her part, looked a little embarrassed by him and kept her eyes front, scanning the dimly lit, false-beamed room for, Paz assumed, himself. From Gallagher's nervous hovering as they approached his table, Paz guessed that if Maritza had said she wanted to see the Taj Mahal tonight instead of Quintus Paz, Gallagher would have arranged that, too. Fighting a slash of unjustifiable — he had left *her* — jealousy, Paz knew he didn't blame him.

She had changed but not aged, at least so far as the light in the fake-leather-chaired bar would let him see. She had traded her grad-student jeans for a gray tweed, double-breasted business suit with long lapels that reminded Paz vaguely of Russian commissars or a heavy from a Bogart film, and her hair was short, no nonsense. But if five years ago she'd looked a little older than she was, now, in spite of the power suit, she looked a little younger. She was in her thirties, but because of her tallness and the right bone structure, he knew that she would seem all of her life to age more slowly than most women. With her Indian-dark hair and unexpected blue-gray eyes, she'd always looked black Irish to him. She spotted him now, gave him a quick, nervous smile, and he saw with a kind of relief that those eyes still had no crow's feet clutching for them. He smiled back, and the old rush of fear and desire — fear of the strength of his own desire, maybe, or of its discovery — helped push him to his feet.

She detached herself from Gallagher and held out her hand. "Mr. Paz," she said quietly, the little touch of British inflection she'd come back with from a year at Oxford still in her voice. "I'm grateful."

He kept her hand a second too long, and she took it back. "You look . . . well," he said, unable to bring himself to call her señora to her face. Snappy opening, he thought.

She smiled a quick, noncommittal thank-you, then stepped aside for Gallagher, at whom she glanced the way she might have at somebody who'd tried to sell her chewing gum on the street. "You know Mr. Gallagher, I'm sure," she said. Gallagher, apparently less grateful, held Paz's hand not too long, just too hard.

"Paz," he said.

"Gallagher." Paz had never particularly liked Gallagher when he'd broken him in for this job or when they'd worked together before that — once on an illegal computer technology sale to the East Germans, once on cross-service "flying squad" detail when they'd bodyguarded a secretary of state through Argentina. But he respected him as an agent, the triteness of that distinction notwithstanding. He was half Cheyenne, erect and broad and Errol Flynn handsome, except for the absence of the thin mustache, and maybe six years younger than Paz. Add the fact he'd been tapped for Paz's job when Paz had given it up and there was plenty not to like him for. But he'd worked his way up the right way: to make his latest rank, he'd spent three weeks under cover on a leaky boat full of Dominican dopers and Mafia hit men to set up a bust. Alone, in the middle of an ocean. He'd paid his dues.

Gallagher engineered Maritza into a chair next to him and across the table from Paz, and ordered a rum-heavy *campechano* for himself, a Dubonnet for her. Dubonnet still, Paz thought. He took a hefty drink of his brandy and soda and held Gallagher's eyes. "You two work together fairly often these days?"

"Part of the job," Gallagher said. "Just like it was when you were here."

Maritza shot him a sharp look, then gave her head a quick shake. "No," she said. "Not quite the same." Then, as if to change the subject as fast as possible, she flicked open her eelskin briefcase. Down to business, Paz thought. No small talk, even. The Maritza of the telephone. That was another thing that had changed. There had always been a streak of the Latin aristocrat in her — take her or leave her, that was your problem — which had been part of her appeal to him. It brought him back to a piece of his pre-Bess background he'd walked away from, but whose style he could still appreciate. She did it well, but that nervous, impatient imperiousness she'd shown on the telephone when she knew she was being overheard seemed more insistent than he remembered. He wondered whether it was for Gallagher's benefit now, or for his. You could build a good grudge in five years.

The baguettes of her wedding ring caught a stray sliver of

light and flashed as she handed a photocopy of a government form across the table to him. "I thought you might want this," she said, her voice cool as the rainy night air that blew in from the open back door, but her hand less than perfectly steady.

"What is it?" he asked her, conscious of keeping his own voice's tight control.

"I should think everyone who knew of the codex's existence before it was missing is listed there. It's the permission form for the excavations."

Paz fumbled his glasses out of his pocket. He hadn't needed glasses the last time they'd been together. He made an unnecessary show of putting them on. "Everyone?" he said.

"I can't speak for what was told to close family, of course. But we had all agreed that no good purpose would be served by the news going outside ourselves until we were sure of what we had."

Paz looked up at Gallagher over his glasses. Gallagher said, "My name's not on there. I never even saw the form until that thing showed up missing."

Gallagher folds this hand, then, Paz thought. And Maritza wanted to get down to business, the painless country of business. All right. "Forgive me," Paz said to her. "I'm puzzled. If I remember, there was a time when nobody was taking anything the baron did very seriously. Why the change?"

Her smile was less formal this time, more genuine. "We didn't when he began this time, either. But his dig was privately financed. So . . ." She held up her palm in a "what did we have to lose" gesture.

"And that's why you let him keep the codex with him? Because the financing was his?"

"Not really. It was a . . . delicate situation. I was in the process of trying to get him to bring it here to us so we could mount a larger translation project. But what could I have done? Forced it away from him? No. I was trying to be patient."

And so, Paz thought, we know who's probably being blamed

for this mess — which would explain some of her urgency. "But you *are* sure of what you had?"

"Absolutely," Maritza said sharply, as if she were a little offended. "We had the paper tested — you know that." Paz nodded. "But even before that — well, I staked my reputation on it. The colors, the figures, just . . . *cómo le puedo explicar?* Have you ever seen a Maya codex, Mr. Paz?"

"Only Aztec ones, as originals."

She wagged her finger. "They're nothing like the Maya. For me the Aztec codices are like cartoons compared to this one. They don't have *writing*, you see, and that makes all the difference. And the figures on the Maya ones are so much richer, more . . . alive. They're more lovely, too, and I think more frightening in a less obvious way: they're part human, part god, part animal — like us, no? And the whole codex is such an intricate thing, with those sensible, square hieroglyphs all over it like the text for the illustrations, though of course they're much more than that. To me Maya codices have always looked at least as impressive as illuminated medieval manuscripts, except that they lacked the poetry and the stories — they had too much to do with astronomy and calendars. But *this* one, Mr. Paz, this was going to tell us the whole story of the beginnings of civilization here, and it was even more exciting because it might well have been the *first* one. I saw the Hebrew letters on it, and the ships, and the six-pointed star, and I knew that no matter what else I did in my life, if I could just see this project through, I would have done enough. And I *know* what to look for."

"I'm sure you do," Paz said, meaning no more than that but doubting she'd think so. Her voice had lost its distance now, and she leaned forward across the table toward him, as enthusiastic as she'd been in her grad-student days. Gallagher's eyes moved from her to Paz and back, reading, trying to decipher the two of them, Paz was sure. Just as he was doing himself. Cops, he thought. Knowing what to look for.

To hide, Paz lowered his eyes and scanned the form. Von Hummel was the "supplicant." Maritza de la Torre was listed as supervising authority, and Humboldt Méndez J. was archaeological liaison. Stanley's name was there, too, along with four others Paz didn't immediately recognize.

"Méndez was the one found dead?" Paz asked.

"Yes," Maritza said, a little huskily.

"How?"

Maritza looked to Gallagher, as if she were deferring to his superior knowledge of things violent.

"It was in his driveway in Polanco," Gallagher said flatly. "He'd opened the gate, so it might have been somebody he knew. They used a machete or maybe a big knife, the cops say, and it was at night in the rain, so nobody saw anything. There could have been one guy or half a dozen. Nothing missing from the house. His wife didn't even know anything had happened till Señora de la Torre showed up and found him."

Collosini, Paz thought. Collosini and the blood from a knife wound. Then he put that to the side for now, too. "*You* found him?"

"I had an appointment with him."

"What about?"

"I don't know."

"Excuse me?"

She'd pulled back from the table by now and had stiffened, imperious — or nervous — again. "He had called me earlier that day and said he needed to talk with me. I don't know. He wouldn't tell me what about."

"And that's all?"

"Should there be more, Mr. Paz?" she said and turned to stare beyond him at the square of darkness that was the open back doorway. Paz turned to check it. All he saw was darkness. She'd dismissed him, but even in dismissal he admired the style of it. Gallagher smiled.

Paz asked him, "What did his wife know?"

"She said he came in on the morning flight from Veracruz, didn't say boo to anybody, and closed himself up in his study with his books until he went outside to answer the bell at the gate. Just left the house for a short lunch. The cops searched his house — searched the houses of everybody on that list who's in country, in fact — twice. First time when the codex turned up missing, then again when Méndez went down. Nothing. And if somebody had come after him to rip off the codex, how come they showed up three days *after* everybody who knew it existed had already been told it was gone." He tapped a file folder he'd brought with him. "I got you all the background stuff we had on the principals in the files here and in the stateside computer, which is not much, plus the police reports — on everything. So far as I can tell, what there is for *you* to do you got to do in Veracruz. I'm glad it's your mess." He was still smiling.

Paz nodded, and dreaded the thick folder of Spanish bureaucratese. And no, he thought, not everybody had known the codex was missing, but if Collosini had been expecting to be able to broker it safely in any case, he wouldn't have risked such a visible murder for it. Collosini stayed shunted to the side for now.

"Will I find much recent on Baron von Hummel in there?"

Gallagher shook his head. "Foreign national. And we don't have the police reports on him from Veracruz yet."

Maritza finished her Dubonnet and looked away from them again toward the empty doorway, from which the smell of *la mota*, of pot smoke, rolled in on the damp breeze. She gave her head a rapid shake, as if she'd felt her hair brush a spider web. It was a familiar gesture, though Paz had to see it to realize he remembered it: she seemed to use it as a physical way of blurring, softening, the edges of any thought she didn't like. "All night," she said, "I called him in his house in Veracruz to tell him about Humboldt Méndez. Nobódy answered me. In the morning I called the police. They found his house torn up, things broken, but his clothes still there. It must have happened in the night, too, because the housekeeper served him dinner before she left." She was silent a moment, watching her darkness. "He was a very old man. The only thing 'recent' about him was that he was very happy that he was going to get the recognition he deserved before he died. Was."

Gallagher reached as if to touch her arm, then saw Paz watching him, stopped, and self-consciously made a little tent out of his fingers on the table. You didn't need to be a cop, Paz thought, to read that. There was an embarrassed gruffness in Gallagher's voice when he said to Paz, "The state judicial police are on it. The Federales, too. They've got his place sealed. See it for yourself when you get down there."

Paz shot him a look. "Lots of luck," he said.

"They're taking this one seriously. Too much pressure."

"Why the pressure? Why the hell am I here, by the way?"

Gallagher sighed. Paz, the sigh said, was miserably out of touch. "You don't know? We're about to hit them with another hot dog scheme to go after the drug honchos. And their national debt's up for renegotiation again. Everybody's cooperating their asses — " He looked at Maritza again. "— tails off."

"Always the last to know," Paz said. Even Harmon had guessed it right. He slipped his glasses off and rubbed his eyes heavily. The wrong way, Teri would have told him. He felt a shot of guilt, thinking of Teri.

Maritza had given her attention back to the table, where she slowly twirled her Dubonnet glass between her hands. "Drink?" Paz said.

"Thank you, no." She gave him a slight, sad smile and locked her eyes on his for a moment. "For me it's late," she said, and Paz imagined an implied "don't you remember?" left hanging.

"Yep," Gallagher said. "Bedtime." He stood and put a

proprietary hand on the back of Maritza's chair. Maritza looked at him as if he'd just tried to sell her chewing gum again.

Outside on narrow Dolores — faceless, urban Latin American, with its oilcloth restaurants and steel-shuttered shops and aimless crowds — misty rain still peppered the air. Maritza turned up the collar of her raincoat, and Gallagher said, "I've got you set up with your contact in Veracruz."

"Army? Police? Customs?" You went with whichever was most reliable, less on the take, Paz knew. In different parts of the country, in different countries, you looked for your coop-eration — sometimes protection — from whatever authority you could get the most from. And stay alive with the longest. You knew your man first, then worried about channels.

"You're lucky. Customs. Teodoro."

"Looking up. He still *comandante?*"

Gallagher flashed his toothy Errol Flynn grin, willing to charm, Paz supposed, now that the worst of his evening was over. "Like his daddy before him. And if he has any say, his son after him." He checked his watch. "I got you the first flight out. Nothing for you here."

And don't let the door hit me in the butt as I leave, Paz thought. "What time?"

"Six. There's not another one till five in the evening. Only run two a day."

"Christ, not six," Paz said. He considered for a moment, already imagining the dawn damp — a few hours from now — setting his stiffening muscles like concrete after another half-night's sleep. He *should* take the flight and not lose one of his twelve remaining days. But the trail was already cold, wasn't it? And he did need some time to chew his way through all that paper they'd dumped on him, didn't he? "Does the train still run?"

"Beats me."

Maritza pulled her coat tighter against the wet wind. "It

leaves at eight. You can be in Veracruz almost at the same time the five o'clock airplane would get you there. It's better, the train."

The train was right, then: it was appropriate that last journeys into things be taken on trains. "Tickets a problem?"

"Not first-class ones. What is your hotel, Mr. Paz?"

"The Fremont."

"I don't know it."

"It's walking distance."

"Not tonight. It's wet." She pointed to a white Mercedes parked half on the sidewalk. It managed to block a driveway, an alley, and a fire hydrant all at once. A shabby, tan-uniformed parking cop leaned against it, guarding it. "Please." Gallagher's smile froze.

"There's no need."

"Not everything's a matter of need, Mr. Paz. It's my pleasure. Please."

Paz caught Gallagher's eye. "In that case, thank you," Paz said. "It *is* wet."

Gallagher and his frozen smile followed them to the car. When he leaned into the window on Paz's side of the car to say good night, his face sobered. He spoke softly so that Maritza, who was paying off the cop, couldn't hear. "Quintus, this is my goddamn turf now. Don't forget it. So far as I'm concerned, if you have to be window dressing, that's what the hell you are. Report in before you even shit, you got me? You're a damn good Customs cop, but I don't like your being here right now, and if you fuck anything up I'll pull your tongue out."

He straightened up and smiled amiably at Maritza. As they drove away, he stood waving goodbye like a schoolboy. He must have done those three weeks on a leaky boat, Paz decided, like a boy scout on a camping trip.

"Whatever you're thinking, Quint," Maritza said as they stopped at the corner for a parade of cross traffic. "Don't. He's married. I've had my fill of that. And I don't make a habit of attachés, either."

"That's not what he would like."

"What he would like and what he will get are not the same thing. I want you to believe that."

Paz squinted through the headlights of the cross traffic to the block ahead. The no-name bar Maritza had introduced him to — the bar they'd gone to the last night he'd seen her — had been on that block, squeezed between two worn Chinese restaurants and above a no-name taco stand. There was nothing there now: restaurants, bar, all of it, had been replaced by an empty space, a blackness. "The bar's gone," he said.

Maritza followed his look. *"El terremoto,"* she said.

"Ah. Of course," he said. "The earthquake."

She stared ahead at the traffic. "I'll tell you why I used to like to go there with you, Quint. Did you ever guess why?"

"I don't think I ever tried."

"It was a place that made no sense, *entiendes?* Do you remember the old woman customer with the fat arms who used to come and stand up and sing all those ancient Piaf songs for everybody? And the little gray lawyer who wore those ties that were always so out of date and who played the piano for her? Do you remember the night he played his whole awful Cosmic Suite for us, and we had to listen to it all, then clap, too?"

"I remember," Paz said.

"We never knew where they came from or where they went when the bar closed at night. And I never asked them. I didn't *want* them to have sensible stories to their lives, because if they didn't, maybe you and I didn't have to, either. You know?"

There was a break in the traffic and Maritza floored the car through it. "I know," Paz said. A retreat to monosyllables, he thought, the safety of monosyllables.

"And then you did the sensible thing," she said. "And then I did. You're a very sensible man, Quintus Paz, no?"

"No," Paz said. As she slalomed the Mercedes between a couple of honking Fords, onto the access road for the bright river of the Reforma, he pointed to the right, past the white wedding cake Palace of Fine Arts. "That way."

She wheeled out into a traffic circle and headed to the left. "I live this way," she said. "You still like nightcaps, don't you?"

Paz let his eyes travel ahead to the golden angel on top of the soaring monument to the Heroes of the Revolution, in the center of the next traffic circle, the *glorieta*. At night the smog softened everything, added an aura to lights, made the world seem as it must have been when this Aztec city was hidden in a mist from its now vanished lake. Even gap-toothed as the boulevard was because of the earthquake, its hotels, its statues, its billion lights, made it the world's grandest midway. For this moment, he was in love with a city again, a love that had outlasted most others in his life.

"Won't that disturb your husband?" he said.

"This is our town house," she said. "My husband is in business in Monterrey. He comes here on weekends."

Don't, he thought. Then, "I still like nightcaps."

It was wrong from the moment they got out of the car on the little cul-de-sac that was just far enough away from the trendy cafés and bars of the Zona Rosa to be quiet and fashionable. It's the business suit, he decided as they stood inches apart in the tiny elevator and she loosened her tie. Or, as they stepped into the mammoth living-cum-dining-room of the top-floor apartment, maybe it's the presence of another man, a husband here.

Or, as she turned to him and smiled, coat off, shoes off, from the dark mahogany bar and asked him what he'd have to drink, he thought, maybe it's just a song I've heard too many times, in Bahia or Macao or Ankara, a song I'm tired of. He had planned to call Teri when he got back to the hotel, but it would be too late. The shot of guilt came back, but it was as much disappointment as guilt now. The very bones of his shoulders hurt where the *chino*'s knees had ground into them, and his gut ached where the tan-suited man had decked him. He'd have another drink to try to get the feeling back that he'd had riding down the Reforma with her, where he'd mixed up loves, but he'd wind up drunk and useless.

He moved around the room to try to stay alert. The walls were hung everywhere with grotesque wooden folk masks, and homemade harps depended from the ceiling. It was a cavern of a room, the kind his grandfather's house in Buenos Aires had had its share of: dark wood, alcoves, parquet floors, a long, narrow balcony. On every available surface, even on the grand piano, things hunched and watched him: stone skulls; clay dancers in the flayed skins of sacrifices; blank-faced priests with labyrinthine headdresses; the staring god Chac-mool, cupping his hands to hold twitching human hearts; lame or dying penitents praying to the Virgin in fading *retablo* paintings. A staircase curved up another level to what he assumed were bedrooms (with another man's suits beside hers in the closets) and a kitchen (where she made the other man breakfast). From the windows he could look across rooftops to a smog-blurred Chapultepec Castle on its lighted hill, and he wondered how often doomed Maximilian and mad Carlota had looked out from that castle over this chilly, high capital they'd come from Europe to rule, and loved and feared such civilized barbarity, too.

Maritza handed him his drink. In the car they'd done some cautious, safe catching up — his new job, her husband's business, neither of which interested the other much. Now he realized he didn't have a damn thing else to say to her. "The nightcap," he said.

"Are you hungry?" she said.

"Thanks, no," he said. "You don't smile much these days."

She smiled. "Being a woman in a position of power is very difficult in Mexico. Smiling can be disastrous."

"Even for a woman who went to Oxford?"

"One of its lesser colleges."

"Aha."

There was a silence.

"We have a ghost here," she said. "He shows up there, on the stair landing. Sometime during the forties he came home and found his wife with another man. He stood on the landing and shot them as they came to the head of the stairs. He comes back. At night I can hear him there sometimes."

"Does your husband hear him, too?"

"No. He doesn't believe in him."

"Aha."

There was another silence.

"Are you still married?" she said.

"Yes," he lied, and thought, in a way, it's not a lie. "So are you."

"Do you still carry a gun?"

"Yes. Do you love your husband?"

"Where is it — under your coat?"

"Yes. Shall we have our drinks and discuss my gun for the evening?"

She sighed, sat on a white couch, and took a cigarette from an onyx box. "I'm sorry, Quint. It's just that I've been terrified to walk in here alone every night since . . . all that happened. Thank you for coming."

He tried a smile. "I couldn't do the sensible thing twice."

She lit her cigarette and looked up at him evenly. "For a year after you left I think I wanted you dead. Or me dead. I had never felt so worthless, so . . . *discarded*. Then I met Francisco, my husband, and *ya*" — she gave a halfhearted little flip of her hand — "it was over. What was it you used to say about you and Bess? Nothing kills wanting like not being wanted?" She looked away, then down. She shook her head in that spider web gesture again. "I don't want to cry, Quint. Just help me. Please. I'm afraid. I'm afraid of everything since this last weekend."

He sat beside her, tried to think of something to say that wouldn't sound fatuous, and failed. Even her perfume was the same as it had been, he noticed. He didn't risk taking her hand. "The police give you a hard time?"

"They've questioned me. Endlessly."

"If nobody but the people whose names are on that form knew about the codex, one of you took it, you know."

"Yes, I do know. If I had taken it, would I have insisted that you come here even after the baron disappeared? And could I have been in two cities at once when Humboldt was killed? And why would I kill him? And *could* I have, with a machete or a big knife, since he was much stronger than I am? And if the codex was already missing, why would these things have happened to the baron and to Humboldt *after* the fact? You tell me that, because I haven't slept for two nights trying to figure it all out."

"I don't know. I don't know anything yet."

"Then please, please don't *you* try to interrogate me about those things. I can't stand to answer any more questions from anybody."

You come late to the party, Paz thought, you get the cold hors d'oeuvres and keep your mouth shut. "First, we don't interrogate these days — we interview." He tried another smile he didn't believe in, waited for a reaction, but got none. "Second, I can't do either one because the treaty says I can't. I couldn't arrest anybody, either. I'd have to get one of *your* people to do all that for me. Technically I'm harmless."

She looked more worried than comforted. "Then how do you expect to find the codex?"

He gave her an exaggerated wink. "Secret gringo ways. The treaty says I can't tell."

"No. Don't *humor* me, Quint! You can't tell me because my name is on that list. That's the reason."

He hesitated. "Yes."

"But you *will* try."

"That's why I'm here."

She relaxed. "What does the treaty say about your staying overnight here?"

Paz sloshed his drink a couple of times, then had a brief staring contest with a stone corn god on a bookshelf. "Where?"

"*Here*, I said."

"Where here? Here here or upstairs here?"

She leveled her eyes at him again. "Wherever you choose."

He met her look. "You never answered my question about your husband."

"The answer is yes, I love my husband."

"Why isn't he here?"

"I told him not to come. He has his business to run."

And so you'll take me instead, to keep him from knowing you're afraid, Paz thought. He should be insulted, he supposed. He wasn't. He was sad and, he realized, more than a little relieved.

"This couch make a bed?"

Too quickly, she said, "I'll get sheets."

As he lay on the lumpy pull-out mattress, he listened. He heard her walking around upstairs, getting undressed. Maybe it was the business suit after all, he thought. Or was it an attack of virtue? Or, he'd no doubt think tomorrow, of stupidity.

As he listened, he felt more and more disoriented. What he took at first to be wind was tires hissing on pavement. What seemed to be blowing rain, he saw when he got up to look out the window, was the sound of men who were working late to gut an earthquake-damaged building, shoveling debris down some sort of makeshift metal chute. The central heat that kept coming on in this building without heat was the aging elevator starting. From the street came other, even less placeable sounds — intermittent scraping, blowing, whistling sounds. Or *was* that what they were?

He'd been standing at the window a good five minutes trying

to get the sounds to make sense before he realized that the silent things were more important. It was the silent movement of an elbow hanging out of the window of a blue Dodge parked on the street below that caught his eye first. Then a hazy face through the windshield, tilting up toward Paz's window. Then fifty feet to the left, on top of a pile of rubble, a shoulder that moved into a shaft of streetlight as a body shifted to take a quick look at the blue Dodge around the edge of a wall. The building, apparently Maritza's apartment, was being watched — and the one who was watching the building was being watched.

Slowly he backed away from the window, grateful that the lights of the city made it darker inside the apartment than out. He listened again. The small sounds from the upstairs bedroom had stopped.

He dressed as quietly as possible, no coat, pistol in his belt, shoes in his hand. Under the blank, minatory stares of the demons on the shelves, he propped the door slightly open with a little stone fertility goddess and, still shoeless, climbed the uncarpeted stairs to the roof, where the *portero*, the super, lived. From the *portero*'s unpainted concrete bunker the sounds of sleep remained steady — a snore, the quick breaths of children — as he tiptoed by on the wet tarpaper.

At the edge of the roof he put his shoes on. From there it was only a few feet down to the next roof, then a fire escape dropped into the darkness of the alley. He breathed deeply to clear the last brandy fumes from his head and slipped over the parapet.

At the mouth of the cat-and-garbage-can-clogged alley, he pulled the .45 out of his belt and clicked the safety off. He concentrated for a few seconds and brought back some of the Israeli antiterrorist training he'd been sure he'd never need when he'd endured it a couple of months before. Stand at a distance from the corner, a short side step, immobility, then a quick sideways nod of your head to see around the corner before *you* could be seen. Then again, and again, until, like a figure in an old magic lantern show, you'd bobbed your way to a clear view around the corner.

From this angle, the pile of rubble on which he'd seen the shoulder move was a small, rugged hill. An abandoned hill now, he saw as he bobbed the whole thing into sight from the end of the alley. Once he was sure of that, he stayed low and scuttled along the street to the corner. Then, step-nod, step-nod, first the wall and then the Dodge came into view, obscure in the puddling streetlight, the car a long lump among other long lumps backed up to the curb into diagonal parking spaces.

He waited. When a solitary taxi rocked onto the street from Avenida Insurgentes, he tensed. Then, just as the taxi was between himself and the Dodge, its headlights glaring into the eyes of whoever was behind the Dodge's wheel, he darted. By the time the taxi was hissing around the next corner onto Calle Biarritz, he had drawn himself up on the far side of the street, next to one of the long lumps, fifty or so feet away from the Dodge.

Even as he crouched his way closer along the dark sidewalk, he couldn't see past the streetlight's glare on the windshield of the Dodge well enough to make out the face behind the wheel. He *could* see that there was nobody on the shotgun side and that the window was up. That meant he'd have to work his way behind the car, then up along the driver's side to the open window. He slipped his shoes off again. The sidewalk was damp and rough to his bare feet. He felt the shell of a snail crumble silently beneath his arch as he moved around the back bumper of the Dodge. He checked the plate as he did: DF — Distrito Federal — local, no help.

He was three feet away from the arm hanging from the window when it moved, casually slid another few inches out the window. The arm was in the sleeve of a sport jacket, which was woven in an odd check-and-herringbone pattern washed into gray-on-gray by the pale light. But gray-on-gray was enough: Paz didn't need to see the colors. Slowly he stood, and in one motion clicked the .45's safety back on and brought the butt down hard on the arm. The arm jerked wildly back into the car, and the man the arm belonged to grabbed for something on the seat beside him as the door flew open.

"Gallagher, what the *fuck* are you doing here?" Paz said, loud enough to freeze the bastard with his torso twisted halfway out the door and the revolver in mid-arc, on its way to firing position.

"Asshole stunt," Gallagher said across the car seat as Paz pulled the shotgun-side door closed behind him. "I might not have stopped in time." Gallagher laid the revolver on the seat between them and massaged his arm.

"You did," Paz said. His anger was cooling enough for him to know Gallagher was right. He didn't want to talk about it — or think about it. "I've got a question on the table." He leaned to tie a shoe. "You going to answer it?"

"Collosini's dead."

Paz tied the other shoe.

"Argentine accent, the cops said. Christ almighty, Paz, I *worked* with you in Argentina! And did you think *my* informants didn't know about Collosini, too? For God's sake, Paz."

"Gallagher, I'm tired, I'm very tired. I didn't sleep last night. I probably won't sleep much tonight. I don't particularly want to be here, and I'm a short-timer — twelve days. I want to go to bed."

"You going to stonewall me?"

"No. I'm just tired."

Gallagher studied him in the dim light. "I ought to send your ass home. Now."

"Then do."

Gallagher studied him some more. "Throw you in that briar patch? Uh-uh. You got some windows to dress for me. Here's my deal. You go to Veracruz, talk to Teodoro, work his informants — if he's willing — ask whatever questions you, and he, want. You come up with something reasonable, you run it by me. If it looks good, I follow up — *I* do — put it into the computer and get whoever stateside working on it we need to. By the numbers. You run everything by *me*, I give you whatever help I can, and you go out in glory. But I want to know if you heard me before: I'm juggling too many goddamn political balls right now for you to make me drop one. Collosini was one too many, and you haven't even fucking started yet. No more."

"You follow me here?"

"I didn't have to. I know where she lives."

"Aha."

"Forget it. I went to a cocktail party here once. With half the goddamned embassy. As for you, all I had to do was watch how fucking nervous she got Saturday when she came in to tell me the anthropological institute 'officially' wanted you to come down. Tonight was just confirmation."

"Glad I didn't disappoint you. Or did you maybe expect to find red strobe lights going in the bedroom?"

"No, just you. I knew you'd spot me."

Paz supposed that was as close to a compliment as he'd ever get from Gallagher. He rolled his window down; there was still no sign of the figure on the rubble pile. "Look," he said. "I'm on the couch. She's in the bedroom. If it matters to you."

Gallagher pursed his lips and gave a series of slow, ambiguous little nods like a mechanical doll winding down. Paz had seen him do the same thing to make a suspect sweat. "Pretty heavy with you and Maritza, was it?"

The quick, sharp return of Paz's anger surprised him. "It was a long time ago, Gallagher. It's over. You've got open season if you want it. Talk to her husband about it." He popped the door open.

"Close the damned door," Gallagher said. Paz eased it to, but didn't latch it. "Your brother-in-law's on that list of names. You all right about that?"

"When I'm not, I'll let you know."

"He's in with this expedition outfit big-money, maybe bigger than you think. A year ago he gave some financial guarantees to a couple of local lien holders for a show that Collosini did the sets for. Three months ago two of the other people on that list, both backers, bought a big hunk of your brother-in-law's new airline — all handled by Mexican banks. One of those two people is in the States, so there's no reason for him to have jacked around with Mexican banks, except that the transaction was in dollars that came from an offshore bank in the Grand Turks. *Both* buy-ins came that way, in fact. You still all right about everything?"

Gallagher was as stone-faced as one of Maritza's idols, but Paz knew he was enjoying himself. In all the time he'd been in Mexico, Paz had never been able to get to the Mexican banks. Gallagher knew that. "Congratulations," Paz said. Gallagher gave him a modestly regal nod. "How'd you work that?"

"Few drinks, a few favors. Mexican banking's not as cushy as it was before the banks were nationalized. Times are hard."

"Who are the backers?"

"One of them you may know, the guy in the States. He's this farm-team Hollywood actor named Peter Lovinger. He's supposedly doing some kind of documentary about the codex: *In Search of*, whatever. That's why he's hard to make on a currency violation. He's got access to money from backers in forty-three and a half different countries, so far as I can tell. You ever seen him?"

"Not in anything to speak of." Paz had a vague image of a short man, balding, thin, and ferret-faced, looking furtive in a dark confessional, but he could remember nothing else about the movie at all. Or the actor.

"Me neither. He lurks a lot, you know? Every time I've seen him he was fucking lurking. Actors that just *lurk* shouldn't have that kind of money, right? But who knows? Maybe he's better at making deals than he is movies." Gallagher leaned forward and peered absently up at Maritza's apartment. Paz would give odds he'd spent more than one night here, watching. "The other guy you'll meet in Veracruz. His name is Receta y Precio. One of those high-tone, double-named mothers, so walk easy — hell, he could be a relative of yours. The land the codex was found on used to be his before the government took it and gave it to the Indians — *his* Indians, you know? That kind. He makes cheap-shit movies down here and owns a string of movie theatres in California where he shows them, which is his connection with Lovinger. And he makes soap."

"Soap," Paz said.

"Herbal stuff. Squeezes junk out of plants in the jungle and ships it to a factory in the States. And he's got this expensive hobby — he's turning half the jungle into a bwana sahib wild animal preserve. I got checks running on his finances here and stateside. I'll let you know." He picked up his revolver from the seat between them and slipped it back inside his coat, a signal that he was ready to leave. "I'll also let you know what I find out about the connection with your brother-in-law."

"Don't go to any trouble," Paz said.

"No trouble. One last thing. You'll want to check in with the consul down there. He's the fiduciary for the whole turkey shoot. He's on your list, too. Straight-arrow State Department type — wears fucking button-down pajamas. He'll have a car for you."

For me a car, and for you a daily report on me, Paz figured. No deal. He pushed the door open again, got out, then leaned in through the window. "You didn't tell me what your bankers gave you on Maritza, *cuate*."

"Nothing to tell. Her old man fabricates re-bars in Monterrey. They've got a decent bank account, but nothing out of line, no strange transactions. Ditto with Humboldt Méndez. I've got a local in Monterrey looking at how Mr. Maritza's business is doing, but it's taking time. I'll be back to you." He dug a car key out of his pocket. "You got one more name on that list. He's probably never been inside a bank in his life, so I don't know jack shit about him, but I wouldn't sweat him. He was your baron's head boy, Indian name of Salomón Katun. Check him with Teodoro when you get to Veracruz. Anything else?"

"Just this. You were being watched. I'd go on home."

Gallagher started the car and smiled benignly. "You mean that little guy who was sitting on the rock pile over there? Nah, he's watching *you*. He was there when I got here. *You* figure him out."

In five hours it would be time to get up. Even Gallagher wouldn't be able to murder sleep tonight, Paz thought as he centered his .45 on the end table beside the couch. Trying to think now would be as useless as crying, which hadn't helped get him through the divorce, either. He had a mess on his hands; that was enough to decide tonight. He folded his pants over a chair.

One last time he went to the window to check for the figure on the rubble pile. Nothing. The little guy, Gallagher had said. Paz had thought the man at Collosini's, the hawk man, *el halcón*, was a child at first. Had he been tracked somehow, all through the maze of Mexico City? How about it, Ethelbert, was that possible?

Tomorrow. He could even wait until tomorrow to be afraid, if he was going to be. He slipped back beneath the faintly scented sheets Maritza had given him and pulled the covers up against the chill. The scent was Maritza's perfume again.

At the creaking from the landing, he whipped his head around on his pillow, fully ready to see the ghost of the wronged husband walking toward him. He didn't let himself be sure that it was Maritza in a nightgown until she quietly pulled the covers back and slid in beside him. He didn't move when she did, but waited. She stayed on her side of the bed, not touching him.

Softly she said, "If we close our eyes and just listen to each other breathe, we can pretend we're anybody."

"Is that why you came down?"

"Yes. Was it a good idea?"

"It was a good idea."

He closed his eyes and felt her warmth even across the cold landscape of sheets between them. He thought about asking her whether she knew somebody named Collosini, or a little man with no eyes, but he didn't want to know that right now. He didn't want to hear her tell the truth about it; he didn't want to hear her lie about it. It was no way to work an investigation.

He drifted. Without thinking, he slid his hand across the sheets and touched Maritza's arm with his fingertips, and after a while, as he kept drifting, she was Teri. Then Bess, that first trip here, when he had lain awake in wonder, listening to her breath grow slower and slower, moving toward sleep. Then she was nobody, and he was already on a train heading down out of the cold mountains, heading toward the white city of Veracruz and the sea.

FIVE

To reach Veracruz, which was to the southeast, the train left Mexico City heading north. Of course, Paz thought. Of course. All in keeping.

But as they crept away from the city, he realized direction no longer mattered here. What he saw through the dusty window of the Ferrocarriles Nacionales de México coach would have been the same in any direction. Where he remembered green fields broken occasionally by a ruined hacienda or an adobe farmstead, chickens and children now choked the mud streets of crazy-quilt shantytowns. Everywhere outdoor cooking fires sent smoke rising to meet the haze of the morning, and faces, a collage of faces that he thought might well stretch all the way to the ocean, turned to watch the train. He recalled the atavistic faces of the scavengers in the ruins, their lives a notch down from even this, and saw the invisible eyes and skull face of the little man from Collosini's workyard, *el halcón*, and tried to think of some real link between all those lives and his. He couldn't.

In the half light of dawn he'd slipped out of bed to go to the bathroom, and, gray against the gray rubble, as still as the broken concrete, *el halcón* had been waiting again. This time Paz had been sure it was him. They had stared at each other for a full minute through the window, like different species on either side of an aquarium glass in the murky light. Then the man had scuttled over the crest of the rubble hill and disappeared into a leftover pool of darkness. He hadn't come back.

Unaccountably, Paz had felt no active fear as they had watched each other, only a kind of wariness. It had been the feeling he'd had in the presence of animals he knew had the potential to be deadly, but only if you got too close to them, cornered them. In fact, seeing him from a safe distance, Paz had felt there was something almost protective about the little man's still presence. No way in hell could he have explained why he felt any of that, or have defended it. Was it what people had felt when they'd put those empty-eyed idols of Maritza's into niches in their mud walls?

Later, nervous in the morning light, Maritza had stuffed him with mango and papaya, eggs and bacon, spicy beans and sweet bread, hot buttered *bolillo* rolls and thick coffee — and had promised him she'd ask the *portero*'s wife and oldest son to take his place on the couch for the next few days. And he'd promised to keep her informed. Neither of them mentioned the night before. This awkward morning had been an even worse time to pump her about Collosini and the rest than the night had been. He'd had the sense that she kept his mouth full so they *couldn't* talk, in fact. He hadn't objected.

So now, sleepy and stuffed, as he tried to slog through the Mexican police reports in the sun-heated coach — reports pecked out on manual typewriters with moribund ribbons — his concentration fuzzed like a distant TV station.

He kept seeing instead Gallagher and Stanley, dour, secretive, boy scout Stanley, whom Gallagher was already dogging and would keep dogging until he found what there was to find. That was a mercy to which Paz knew for certain he couldn't abandon Stanley — love him or not — and Mary Margaret. Conflict of interest? *There* was a quick irrelevancy for you.

As long as he just worked the case here in Mexico, didn't approach Stanley directly, ran fast and kept low, he could buy a few days — which was all he had left anyway. A codex, a murder, a kidnapping, an airline, offshore banks, a dead fence, a man with a skull for a face, and his own family. What were the connections?

It was logical, he figured, for Stanley to accept investment money from an actor who might do PR for him and from a Mexican with the right contacts who might smooth things with the government for him — especially if Stanley had come to know them through their all having backed the dig for the codex. But what had Mary Margaret said? None of the backers knew who the others were. Inoperative statement, Paz thought.

And what was logical about Stanley's standing good for Collosini's debts? Damn Gallagher, he thought. Damn Stanley.

What was important now was to stay with the starting point, to keep it simple, and to realize what was in his control and what wasn't. If he didn't, he'd lose himself in string pulling: jerk this one, see what falls; jerk that one, watch what comes down. Gallagher wasn't in his control, might in fact have to be worked *against*; but the information Gallagher had access to had to be in Paz's control. He was partially OK there — if nothing else, Gallagher was a pro. He might make Paz sweat for it, but he'd never really hold back any information he needed.

Then, on top of that, whatever was happening in the States — including whatever was happening with Stanley — wasn't in his control. He could depend on Teri to let him know what was going on, but she couldn't *do* anything about it. What he had to work with directly, what it was truly in his control to deal with, was a stack of Mexican police reports, a consul and a customs *comandante* in Veracruz, a soap magnate, and the knowledge that somebody was worried enough about his being here to have him watched. Those would have to do.

The starting point was still the codex. It might not even be the reason he was here now, but it was the *key* to the reason. With so little else under his control, he thought, lose sight of that, and he risked losing the whole iceberg.

Breakfast and lack of sleep were winning. The words on the police reports ran together when he went back to them. He rested his head on the cool window and let the rhythm of the train and of the faces passing outside lull him. All those people, worrying about feeding their kids, what the hell did they care whether this codex was ever found or not? Then he thought, there's another quick irrelevancy. It wasn't those people's salvation but his own he was after, and always had been after. He closed his eyes and let the train's rhythm wipe away the faces, too.

When, groggy, he opened his eyes again, the train was stopped somewhere in the middle of an empty valley deep in late-morning woods. Sunlight mottled the pine straw that lay deeply drifted over the ground, and to his right he could see the white, high humps of the volcano Ixtaccíhuatl, just being grazed by the thunderheads building for the regular evening's rain. From the view and from the cold, he knew they were somewhere near the high pass through the sierra, a couple of miles up. But why stopped? There shouldn't be anything for miles but a woodcutter's shack or two. He straightened his shoulder holster and got up to follow the other passengers, most of whom were making their way off the train.

Outside, people were stretching, examining pine cones, taking kids off into the bushes to pee, picking clumps of wildflowers. Their voices and the throb of the idling engine were the only sounds Paz could make out besides the rising and falling whoosh of the wind in the tall pines. Still puzzled, he walked along the tracks to the engine, which was stopped at a small wooden bridge over a fast, clear creek.

In the creek, the engineer and fireman stood in their underwear, soaping themselves down. Paz nodded to them. With great dignity, they nodded back.

He felt a quiet burst of pure love. Then he turned away so they wouldn't see his smile and took a deep breath. No bitter yellow smell of smog. He bent to the creek and splashed icy water on his face. Somewhere behind him, where the first slopes of the volcano began, the shantytowns ended, and with them the murderous traffic, the earthquake rubble. He took another deep breath to make sure the bitter yellow odor was gone. He smelled only pines.

The crater of one kind of volcano, he realized, wasn't above him but behind him. He felt for a moment what he supposed must be the temporary relief of a refugee.

He turned back toward his coach. As he did, he caught only a glimpse of part of an old suit coat, the bony shape of the head of the man stepping up into a second-class car down the train. But that was enough. His relief had been even more temporary than he had expected.

Once out of the sierra and onto the plains of Puebla, the train clacked slowly past the eucalyptus groves of Huejotzingo, among the church-topped pyramids of Cholula, then through the stone dignity of grande dame Puebla herself. At each stop, Paz checked the passengers who got off. *El halcón* was never among them. Paz hadn't expected him to be.

Beyond Puebla, the train gathered speed through open farm-lands whose richness thinned as the air did, the higher they climbed on their final, gradual ascent before the sharp fall to the sea. When the last clump of houses had flashed by and disappeared into the distance, Paz got to his feet. There would be no stops for miles now, no chance for anybody to leave the train. And a man who jumped, he saw as he made his way between the two swaying first-class cars, would have his face torn off by the cinders and the hard, stoney ground before he stopped rolling. This time, the son of a bitch would *have* to talk to him.

He stood for a long time on the jolting platform between the first- and second-class cars, the wind whipping his coattails against his legs. In the car he'd just left, the formal, efficient conductor, like a last symbol of order, turned his back and sat down.

He felt a tingling begin in his chest and move out along his arms and legs. It was a familiar feeling. With the ground blurring past and the air full of the damp smell of the earth, this could be the train out of the echoing Retiro station in Buenos Aires, heading through the pampa toward his grandfather's estancia and a hunt with the old man's gauchos. The feeling was the same, the tingling, and with it something between excitement and dread.

As the train began to buck and lash its way into the rough track of the miles-long curve before the Orizaba Pass, he checked to see that a bullet was chambered in the .45. He'd cornered the man once before and had learned. To hell with Harmon's warnings, with treaties.

For a foothold he found a steel maintenance step on the end of the coach and, yesterday's sore muscles trembling from the effort, carefully heaved himself up. On top of the car he stayed flat and crawled. He didn't look up until his fingers found the lip of the overhang on the far end of the car, which he'd decided was easily six times the length of a reasonable passenger coach. He lay a moment, letting his heart-beat slow, watching the rushing sweep of fields. Two *campesinos* had stopped their plowing behind burros to stare at him like, he thought, the farmers in the painting of Icarus falling from the sun. He tightened his courage, then swung over the edge and down onto the platform.

Downwind now. *Behind* his man. He allowed himself a brief moment of gratitude that he wasn't five years older, wasn't in even worse shape.

Inside the coach, the heavy door clacked shut behind him and abruptly snapped off the sound of the wind. Faces, the same kinds of faces that had turned to watch the train's progress through the shantytowns, now turned briefly to watch him as he moved up the aisle, steadying himself on seat backs. The faces belonged to women in black rebozos, thick-handed men in tire-soled huaraches, listless children — all of whom seemed to clutch things: plastic bags, boxes, paper-wrapped bundles.

El halcón was almost hidden by his seat back; Paz was only two seats away from him, stepping aside for a bathroom-bound woman in a red dress who'd gotten up from her seat across the aisle from *el halcón*, before he made him. He sat in an aisle seat with his head slightly turned, so that Paz could see just enough of his profile to be certain it was him.

Paz made a quick check of what he had. In the window seat next to *el halcón* a thin, bored boy of maybe eight hung over the seat and tried to get the attention of the woman behind him. The boy was clearly from a family of *campesinos*, with his frayed but clean shirt and his soup bowl haircut, freshly trimmed for his train trip. The woman whose attention he was trying to get might have been his grandmother — Paz could see wisps of gray hair poking from beneath her rebozo. As long as the boy found her more interesting than what was going on next to him, it would go all right. Notice him, Paz silently begged the grandmother. Keep him busy.

He slipped into the seat the woman in the red dress had vacated. Casually, he leaned forward, unbuttoned his coat, let it hang open, and slid the .45 from its holster. An old man next to him, who reeked of home-brewed pulque, launched into a riff of snores. Paz turned partially toward *el halcón* and held the .45 so that the butt was visible but the rest remained hidden by his coat. It was a reminder, a negotiating point, and, he hoped to God, nothing more.

El halcón looked at Paz but gave no sign of recognition. Close up, his face seemed truly misshapen, though Paz couldn't identify any particular feature as deformed. It was its thinness, the predominance of bone over flesh, the deepness of the eye sockets that combined to give the effect, like a landscape whose proportions are simply wrong. There were eyes in the sockets, Paz saw now, small and deep brown, almost black. He was reminded again of the thing in the cage at Collosini's, and felt somehow that even across the aisle he'd come too close, that he'd entered a kind of charged space.

"You know who I am," Paz said, raising his voice just above the clacking of the wheels. "What do you want with me?"

The man stared, said nothing. He carried a bundle as the others did, except that his was wrapped in a bright woven scarf. With his eyes steadily on Paz, he began untying it.

"Look, damn it, you've got to *want* something."

Blankness, stone. Just as there had been at Collosini's. Paz tried again the question he'd asked then.

"*Habla español? Do* you speak Spanish?"

In the string of sounds *el halcón* answered him with, Paz made out one word, "*español.*" The man spat the word, as if he'd tasted something filthy. His voice was high, flutelike, and the sounds of the language he spoke were like the sounds Paz had heard birds make in the jungles he was heading toward. What would the language be? Otomi? Totonac? Mother of God, he thought, how do you talk to the bastard when you don't even know what language he speaks?

El halcón's bundle was untied now, and slowly, so as to attract nobody's attention but Paz's, he pulled a hunting knife from it. Paz tightened his grip on the .45, flicked off the safety. He'd have to wait till the man moved, fire upward at him to make sure he didn't hit the boy. He braced. But the man simply held the knife loosely in his lap, almost as if he were mocking Paz and the pistol. His eyes left Paz's and darted to the boy beside him, then found Paz's again. In one fluid motion he turned the tip of the knife toward the bench of the seat, drove it in, then drew the blade upward nearly a foot through the imitation leather.

For a long moment the two of them sat with their eyes locked, Paz hearing the low sound of voices, the clack-*clack*, clack-*clack* of the wheels, smelling the mustiness of the seats and the pungency of the manured fields that seeped into the coach in spite of the closed windows. *El halcón* motioned with his chin toward the front of the car, a signal for Paz to leave. Paz shook his head. *El halcón* flicked his eyes to the boy, drew the knife up through another three inches of seat, and motioned again.

This part, Paz realized, he hadn't missed. This part was a nightmare come back, like the dream Ethelbert had been afraid of. He remembered the look on the face of the fat, pleading businessman on the DC-10 at the Ankara airport as the Libyan had put the Uzi to the back of his head, then the way the Libyan, who was barely old enough to shave — Craig's age, maybe — had grunted when Paz's heavy .45 slug caught him in the back as he rolled the fat businessman's body out onto the tarmac, where it hit with a sound like an overstuffed duffel bag. And he remembered the way his own temple had burned all that night from the little trough the Libyan kid's bullet had made in it as the kid was going down.

He slid the .45 back into its holster and snapped the holster shut. There was no point to negotiate from now; even the blunt reminder of the .45 was useless.

And then the woman whose seat Paz had taken was standing between *el halcón* and himself, saying to excuse her, but he had her seat, would he mind moving? The ordinariness of her request almost overwhelmed him for a moment. He mumbled something and got up. By the time he and the woman had done their seat-changing shuffle in the aisle, the knife was gone, replaced in the bright scarf bundle, and *el halcón* was staring straight ahead, as if Paz had already ceased to exist.

At the door of the car Paz turned. *El halcón* was still staring at the seat back in front of him, his eyes invisible again at this distance. Beside him, the boy had given up on his grandmother and seemed to be asking him what he had in his bundle. *El halcón* ignored him.

As the train slowed in the high country around the base of the cloud-swaddled volcanic cone of Orizaba, whose snows the first Spaniards had spotted like a beacon fire from far out at sea, fog began to swallow the world.

It ate first at the mountains, then at the grim haciendas in the middle distance. The haciendas, brown as the brown soil and rock of the treeless plains around them, seemed still to rule here, as if even the revolution had forgotten these scanty corn fields and great plantings of huge, tequila-giving maguey cactus that pocked the bare ground like prehistoric lilies. By the time the train began its slow switchback plunge down thousands of feet to the jungle mountains of Veracruz, the haciendas, huts, ragged children, hard-faced peasants, bony dogs, burros, mules — all had become images only half glimpsed in old, glaucous mirrors of cloud and fog.

Paz was part of it all. He hadn't been able to bring himself to go back inside any of the coaches; the tingling he'd felt earlier had turned into a heaviness, as if his own weight were too much for him to carry. For over half an hour he'd stood between cars, flattening himself against the end wall of a coach and pulling his coat tighter around him as the cold and fog grew, trying to get his angry frustration to blow away in the wet wind and his breathing to settle into some kind of regular rhythm. There was nothing more he could do now, he told himself. Any commotion and he lost, even if he was able to get the boy away from *el halcón*. An explanation to the Mexican cops would eventually involve Collosini, and then Gallagher, unless he killed *el halcón*. He couldn't take either option. What he could do was wait, just wait.

By the time the first white, thatched huts and luminous green forests of Veracruz began to appear through the pale belly fur of the clouds, his breathing was even again and he had argued himself back into reasonableness, or something near it. Soon the train would stop at Córdoba. *El halcón* would be gone before then; he wouldn't give Paz the chance at him that a busy station would afford. Wait, just wait.

When the cars squealed out of the last series of switchbacks before the long valley the train would follow to the sea, Paz knew the engineer wouldn't bother to gather speed again before the railroad yard at Córdoba. Already coffee warehouses, thick patches of huts, a sprawling brewery were erasing the forest alongside the tracks. Paz used the heel of his hand to wipe a clear space in the grime that grayed the window in the door to the coach. *El halcón*'s seat was empty. The boy was in his grandmother's lap, asleep. Paz leaned back against the end of the car, slid down it until he was squatting, then lowered his head and let the heaviness drain.

(

$IX

THE WHITE, HOT CITY of Veracruz was a place of firsts. When Cortés had landed near here to found his first settlement of the New World — his city of the True Cross, his Vera Cruz — he made his first ally, the nameless Fat Lord of the Totonac city of Cempaola. Not much had changed, Paz thought gratefully, as Comandante Teodoro Alcalde, spit-shined, Fat Customs Lord of the Heroic Port of Veracruz and ally, roared his bright-red Suzuki 750 cc racing bike through the gate, across the parking lot, up the ramp, in the door of his customs yard office building — scattering lesser lords — and slid to a stop a foot from Paz's chair. With grave ceremony, he dismounted while the designated lesser lords exchanged his helmet for his hat and took his motorcycle away to stable it. Then he adjusted his chromed .45 — his *escuadra*, the macho gun of choice in Mexico — in his belt, faced Paz, and held out his arms; if feathered capes had still been on the market, Paz decided, maidens would have appeared and draped one over his shoulders. That he had to make do with his tailored tan and olive uniform seemed almost punishment.

"Quintus," he said magisterially. "You prick hair. Give me a hug."

Paz backslapped and was backslapped while Teodoro, a foot

shorter and floating in clouds of confiscated French shaving lotion, said, "You look ten years older. Where the hell have you been?"

"Getting old," Paz told him. "*Mira, viejo,* couldn't you find a *tank* to ride in here on?"

"That's next. As soon as your government tries to slip one through here to Nicaragua, I will have one." He pulled away, his eyes doing a quick study of Paz's face. That's all he ever needed, Paz knew, a quick study. French perfume and red motorcycles notwithstanding, he never needed a second look.

"They're easier to find than a Maya codex, Teodoro," Paz said and saw Teodoro stiffen. Mistake, he thought. Joke, but not about business, not in Teodoro's kingdom.

Teodoro glared at thc lesser lords, since he couldn't properly glare at Paz. Some of them smiled idiotically, some struck macho poses, all of them silently acknowledging that *el jefe,* the chief, was among them. "Why was this man, my *amigo,* kept waiting here?" Teodoro demanded. "Why didn't someone take him to my office and get him something to drink?" He scanned the room, with its long, scarred counter and file cabinets and ancient TV and its tall chalkboards where all the ships in port were listed, as if he'd just discovered it and found it loathsome. Without waiting for an answer, he took Paz's arm and said, "I apologize, Quintus. We'll talk in my office, no?"

"Feel better?" Paz asked him as they headed for the great marble stairway up to his office. The building was more like a British colonial palace than a customhouse: a stained glass dome with angels of commerce on it ruled over a grand foyer, from which the stairway swept up to a massive encircling balcony. Heavy wooden doors led from that to offices, hall-ways — dungeons, for all Paz knew. The plaque outside said the English had in fact built it, back during the Porfiriato (in Mexico, Victorian things weren't Victorian; they were Porfiriato, after the once and not-quite-forever dictator, Porfirio

Díaz). Bronze-grilled French windows, open to the constant sea wind, looked out over the docks, where huge cranes hovered over freighters like steel pterodactyls.

Teodoro worked the crowd — customs brokers, lottery sales-men, hangers-out — that made the whole place as confused and busy as the banks of the Ganges. He slapped backs, shook hands: *el jefe* knew everybody and everybody knew *el jefe*. "Do I feel better?" he said above the echoing babble. "Who can feel better when the people who work for him are morons? *Carajo*! I can't even get them to button their collars and shave!" He bought a sheet of lottery tickets from a smiling old woman, winked at her, tore a couple off and stuffed them in her skirt pocket, and waited for her to cross herself and bless the ones he'd kept.

Paz thought, this is not the federal building in Tucson, Ethelbert. You'd like it here.

In Teodoro's office — piled high with confiscated stereos, crates of whiskey, cigarettes, weapons — a sergeant appeared magically with coffee as soon as they sat down. Teodoro slapped at a loose paper that the ceiling fan stirred, then poured a shot of Cuban rum into both cups and handed Paz one. Some things had changed in the office — the seven kids in the photographs were older, the wife a little pudgier, Teodoro's father in his own customs uniform a little grayer — but the confusion was the same. Teodoro had done well: he knew the difference between a bribe and a gift, and had let the gifts carry him. Paz trusted him because he knew how far to trust him.

He listened silently and sadly to Paz's news of the divorce. His small nods and perfunctory attempts at sympathy were eloquent with the pity of a Mexican family man who under-stood how such decadence was commonplace up there across the border, but who wasn't about to forgive it yet was too courteous to say so. The sadness in his heavy face deepened even more when Paz told him he was leaving the service, the ultimate divorce, though it did ease some when Paz explained the new job with Stanley. Teodoro was already beginning, Paz was sure, to run through dates for his and the family's discount vacations to Disneyland. Life went on.

He sweetened his coffee with a little more rum when Paz was done. "Changes," he said. "Always changes, Quintus." *Keentoos*, he pronounced it. "Here, for example. When you were attaché, you needed an arrest, some protection, information, you came to me. What you did while you were here that I didn't know about, I didn't know about — unless it could get me in trouble." He sipped his coffee and looked at Paz with heavy-lidded nostalgia. "I still don't know how you got aboard that *maldito* Czech freighter to find out those crates were full of computer parts — and I don't want to. You don't want to tell me yet, do you?"

Paz smiled and shook his head. "Old trouble you don't need, Teodoro."

The nostalgia vanished. "No, and not new trouble, either, Quintus. *Mira*. Now you are no longer attaché. Now there are new politics. In the jungles the *drogistas* pay the peasants enough to make them take risks every day that ten years ago would have been something only crazy people did. You know they killed twenty state policemen at once, no? You heard about that — twenty *at once* with machine guns, like a war, Quintus. Everywhere everything is dangerous, for you and for me. I will help you when I can, but almost anything you do could get me in trouble. *Comprendes?* You have only a few days left on your job. I have more."

"Gallagher," Paz said. "It's Gallagher. *Verdad?*"

Teodoro shrugged, his face as sad as it had been when he was listening to Paz tell about his divorce. "It doesn't matter, Quintus. What matters is if we are going to understand each other. What you do when you return *allá*" — he gestured vaguely toward the north — "is your concern. Here, it is mine. I will help you get as much information as I reasonably can to take home with you, where you are welcome to use it as you wish. If you want to interview someone, I will invite him here to my office and we will do it together, according to the treaty. If you want to leave the city, I will be glad to furnish you a car and driver. If — " He caught himself, and his voice lost its 'official' edge, as if he had seen his Disneyland trips flapping away out to sea. "I'm sorry, my friend," he said more gently.

He and Teodoro were dancing, then: new rules, new steps. Lead when you should follow and you could trip, fall, and maybe not get up. Paz understood that, understood that he was as alone here as he had been in Mexico City — Gallagher had seen to that. *El halcón*, Collosini, anything that could get him sent home was off limits between Teodoro and himself now. By the numbers, Gallagher had told him, and by the numbers Gallagher had made sure it would be. First Harmon, now Gallagher, he thought. Rule followers, goddamned rule followers. He hugged slow anger tight to him, kept it from escaping into this cluttered room, where it would ricochet back at him.

"Von Hummel's apartment," he said. "I'll want to see that."

Teodoro rummaged beneath a stack of bills of lading, dug a key out, and lobbed it across the desk to Paz. "The police have been through it. There's not much there now, but I have arranged for you to visit the police archives tomorrow. He was a friend of yours, no?"

"Of my father's."

"I'm sorry. I only met him a few times when he came in to me to clear some equipment through. He seemed very nervous, I thought."

"He always was. Are we saying 'was' on purpose?"

Teodoro cocked his head and held his hands out in a "who knows" gesture. "There is a big, deep sea out there, Quintus, for things to disappear into. I see no reason why someone would only kidnap him, unless there was a request for ransom. And there has been none."

"Nothing from your informants?"

"Nothing. I'm told none of the regular *contrabandistas* admits to handling a codex. I had no idea Baron von Hummel was looking for something so valuable or I would have been better prepared beforehand. I was not informed. I apologize." He was clearly more affronted than apologetic.

Paz dug in the pocket of his suit bag and handed Teodoro the form with the list of names Maritza had given him. "Three of those names are of people I'll want to interview. Can you handle it?"

Teodoro shoved the paper to arm's length and glanced over it. "I think Carlos Receta y Precio has probably been expecting you. I will find out if he will be free to talk with us soon."

"If he'll be *free* to?"

Teodoro reached behind himself, tore open a carton of cigarettes at random, and pulled a pack out. He lit a cigarette silently, seriously. "Quintus, Carlos Receta y Precio's first cousin on his mother's side, Anselmo, is subsecretary of the Ministry of the Interior in Mexico City. His father was a member of the supreme court. Another cousin, Dagoberto, will be governor of Chiapas State after the next elections. If he will be free to see us, he will see us."

Mexico, Paz thought, and then remembered the time he was allowed to talk to a senator with crooked relatives only after a month of negotiating and even at that only with the Commissioner of Customs sitting in. "Where?" he said.

"Here or at his animal preserve in the mountains, near Papantla and the place where the excavations were. It will be at his convenience." He stubbed the cigarette out after the second draw. It had been only a prop. "Salomón Katun, the native assistant of Baron von Hummel, you will see here. It is safer. He has no police record, understand, except for some fights when he was a young man, that sort of thing. I don't know him, but the government considers that as *cacique* of his village he is . . . politically uncooperative."

"Meaning?"

"His village votes for the opposition — the opposition on the left. And Katun is an *indigenista*, one of those impossible Indians who wants to separate his people from Mexico. You will want to go there, go to the excavations, no?"

"I will."

"Then I would feel more comfortable if he remains with us until you come back."

Paz felt a small surprise. This cautious Teodoro, this politician, was new to him. "You're really worried, aren't you?" he said.

Teodoro went for another cigarette. "You are still my friend, Quintus," he said.

"Thank you. And . . . ?"

Teodoro stubbed out his unlit cigarette and rolled his chair back from his desk so that he could get at a bottom drawer. As he reached for it he said, "Quintus, would you close my door, please? And lock it."

Paz did, then stopped beside the paper-littered desk as Teodoro spread three mug shots in front of him on it. He arranged them carefully, the way a stamp collector might arrange a new issue series he'd just come by. Then he stood so Paz could move in and get a better look.

The faces in the photos were all men, all somewhere around thirty, all Mexican. Besides that, Paz could tell only that he didn't like them. But in a mug shot even a priest looked like an ax murderer. "Do I know them, Teodoro?"

"No. I don't think you want to. These photographs were passed on to me from the Federal Police in Mexico City. They are *pistoleros* who came into Mexico from Panama about a month ago. Two weeks ago they were picked up for starting a fight that ended in a shooting at the bar of the Camino Real Hotel in Mexico City. Besides the guns, they were all carrying too much cash — dollars — and one of them had a deposit slip from a bank for even more. The Federales began to investigate, but no more than began. I think there will be no more information going out, ever. Do you understand me, Quintus? I have seen investigations stop this way before. I am not responsible for what the Federales in Mexico City do when *la mordida*, the right money to the right person, is involved."

"Then why did the mug shots come to you?"

"*Mira*, all of these *pendejos* tried to leave the country before the investigation was stopped. After it *did* stop they left for Los Angeles, but I got these photographs before that. And all of them were leaving from Veracruz. Why did they do that, when it is so much easier to fly from Mexico City? Eh? I will tell you this, Quintus. I *know* at least one of these men visited your consulate here. I had him watched the whole time he was in Veracruz. Why would he go to your consulate? If he wanted a visa, say, why would he come here for it? Could that perhaps have something to do with the reason they *all* left from here? Could their visas have been especially arranged for by Señor Henningsen, your consul?"

Paz picked up one of the photographs and looked more closely at the half-shaven, walleyed face in it. No, this wasn't a man he liked to imagine being in Los Angeles — or on the planet. The face, and the thought of where it was and why, gave his slow anger a focus, and it quickened. "Who in my government knows about this, Teodoro? Gallagher? The State Department?"

"Nobody, Quintus. Nobody from your government but you. The investigation is stopped, *over*. I have no authority to report it to anyone."

"Then what are you going to do with these photographs?"

Teodoro held his palms up as if he were checking for rain. "What photographs, Quintus? I threw some photographs away last week as soon as I was told I shouldn't have received them." He pulled another photograph, one that looked as if it had been taken from a distance with a close-up lens, from his pocket and handed it to Paz. It showed a man — the man whose photo Paz was holding — coming out of the American consulate in Veracruz. "I threw everything connected with that case away, in fact. Could you mean *those* photographs?"

Paz picked up the rest of the photographs and slipped them into his coat pocket. "Those photographs," he said.

"*Bueno.*" Teodoro stooped to his bottom drawer again, grunting from the effort. Where the photographs had been on his desk he now smoothed a wrinkled captain's manifest from a freighter and a smudged bill of lading. "These are dated just at the beginning of Baron von Hummel's project. Most of the items are what you would expect a project such as his to need — tents, drills, and such things. Except for this." He pointed to a faint carbon-copied item on the bill of lading. Paz dug for his glasses. Teodoro motioned for him not to bother. "Two diamond-toothed chain saw blades, Quintus. Given the name of the person who signed for this shipment, who was Señor Henningsen, and the nature of the project, we did not examine the papers very carefully at the time. I wish we had."

Paz remembered ten years ago, when he was attaché: the diamond-toothed chain saw blades he'd traced on a hunch then had been going to the Yucatán. It hadn't been just Maya stelae that had been disappearing out of the country then, but whole carved façades of temples. With a diamond-toothed blade, you simply sliced them off like bread, left bare stone, got the façades to a fast boat, and in a week they were crated and waiting in a dealer's warehouse in Miami or New Orleans, on their way to people with too much money who'd gotten them looted-to-order. The blades had given customs on both sides of the border as sure a trail to the dealers and the slicers as footprints in snow. And the hunch had gotten Paz a letter of commendation from *el señor presidente* López Portillo himself. A letter he'd left in the drawer of a dresser in what was Bess's house now. He remembered that, too, then quickly erased it.

Henningsen was fiduciary of the baron's dig. Even though there was no legitimate use for blades like those on this dig, could he have just signed for the shipment, not knowing what he had?

He erased that thought, too. If something as big as what he figured — the slicing up of a whole city — was going on, a man who sold visas to Panamanian gunmen wouldn't be in it by accident. "Who sent them?"

"One of the backers. They were consigned at Galveston by the one named Lovinger." He put the papers down. "For at least five years Lovinger has been making films with Carlos Receta y Precio, Quintus. I know. He has made three of them here in Veracruz. And that is our business."

Paz scooped up the papers too quickly, too angrily. "You want these?"

Teodoro said only, "I have copies."

"You don't think it's all Henningsen. The codex, everything," Paz said, thinking, no, not all Henningsen, because Stanley's name and airline showed up on Collosini's desk. Because Stanley was a business partner of Peter Lovinger's *and* of Carlos Receta y Precio's. Because Baron von Hummel would have had to know what was going on out there in that vine-wrapped ancient city, too. Because a whole village of separationist Indians would have had to know that somebody was carting off their history and have kept quiet about it.

But what Gallagher and Teodoro and a cabal of bankers and politicians and bureaucrats had left him with was Henningsen. Keep it simple, he'd told himself on the train. He had no other choice.

Teodoro shook his head slowly. "No. It's because I know there has to be more than Henningsen I am afraid for you. I can help you only a little bit, and a little bit will not be enough this time."

"Henningsen has diplomatic immunity. No matter how corrupt he is, you can't even talk to him if he doesn't want you to."

"We both know that, Quintus."

"He has to talk to me."

"Quintus, I've told you, you may not — "

"He's the American consul, damn it, Teodoro. I'm an American citizen. And that's my business." The anger broke away, slashed out before Paz could pull it tight to him again.

Teodoro started to speak but stopped. Then he looked away and said stiffly, "Yes, it is."

Paz heard his own voice coming out as stiffly. "I'll be glad to talk to Receta y Precio and Salomón Katun whenever you can arrange it. I'll be grateful if you can do it soon. I only have eleven days left."

Teodoro shoved his bottom drawer closed with a spit-shined shoe and nodded. "Where are you staying? I'll see you get there."

"The Mocambo, I hope. I haven't got reservations."

"You will by the time you get there." He unlocked the door and called for his sergeant again. Then he turned back to the room and started stuffing liquor, coffee, perfume, and boxes of unidentifiable other things into a shopping bag he pulled from the confusion of his stacks of confiscated goods. It was a Care package. Teodoro had never yet let him leave his office without one. Paz felt as small as he knew he was.

A quiet, cloudless sunset was already shading into night over the jungles to the west when Paz got into his room. He took a chance and called the consulate anyway. He was surprised when the phone was answered on the first ring. The voice was a man's, with only a hint of a gringo accent in its Spanish.

Paz said, "William Henningsen, *por favor.*"

The voice switched to English. "Is this Mr. Paz?"

"Paz, yes."

"My God, man, I thought you'd never get here. I sent a driver to meet your train but he said he couldn't find you. So far as *I* could tell, the only place he looked for you was in the bar. But I do have a car for you, assuming your driver sobers up by the morning."

Gallagher was a man of his word, Paz thought. "You're working late, Mr. Henningsen."

"Waiting for *you*. They called me from Mexico City this morning to say you were coming. Where are you?"

"At the Mocambo."

"Way out there on the beach? God, just you and the monkeys and the last of the grand hotels. You're a romantic, aren't you?" He laughed — at what, Paz couldn't conceive. The laugh had a forced heartiness to it that Paz was sure they taught in some State Department training school. "Well, you've been with Comandante Alcalde, I suppose. His office just told me you'd dropped by. I was about to call around to the hotels."

"I managed fine, thanks. Comandante Alcalde and I are old friends."

"Well, then. Do you have dinner plans, too?"

"Yes, I do," Paz lied. "But I could probably be talked into a drink before dinner." He'd had drinks with as bad, maybe worse. But he wouldn't eat with them.

"I'm on my way. How will I know you?"

"I'll be on the verandah by the dining room. Ask the head waiter."

"Half an hour," Henningsen said cheerfully. "I'll be prompt."

Paz knew he had time to call Harmon, knew he ought to call Harmon, knew he wouldn't call Harmon. He called Teri instead. There was no answer. It was around six in Tucson. He was sure she should be home — no matter where she went in the evening, she always stopped to feed the cat and change first. He added a mild worry about her to the stack, tested some of Teodoro's single-malt Scotch, scraped some whiskers off, and tried some of Teodoro's shaving lotion that made him smell like a Turkish whore.

Teodoro was right, he knew: he was walking into a swamp. But what Teodoro didn't know about was Stanley, or the sense (Paz realized he never put it into words) that there was something he had to make up to Maritza, or that there was an old, old debt to Baron von Hummel for the memory of some clean days with his old man, or about bangs and whimpers.

Teodoro didn't know about all that foxfire pulling him on into the swamp.

He told himself he'd know when he was about to get too deep into the swamp, that he was OK still. He told himself that, repeated it to make sure he'd heard himself, and went to meet William Henningsen.

In a *guayabera* shirt whose loose tails hid the .45 in his belt, Paz was ready on the verandah with a rum, Coke, and soda water *campechano* by the time the man who was unmistakeably Henningsen showed up. He and Henningsen would be alone out here on this hot night. That meant Teodoro's guard dog couldn't risk getting any more conspicuously close than he already was, sitting by himself by the door to the lobby with his out-of-place mestizo cop face and his heavy cop shoes and his obvious lack of interest in the leftover morning edition of *Uno más uno* he was pretending to read.

Henningsen was hurried, dressed very untouristy in twills and topsiders and a button-down blue oxford shirt, and his blow-dried newscaster's hair was as neat as a toupee. Paz never had gotten over being a little amazed at how bottom feeders so often made such a success of looking like anything but bottom feeders. He put him at thirty-five or so, maybe a jogger and a racquetball player. State Department, new style.

He attacked Paz with a smarmy smile and a Rotarian's handshake. "Mr. Paz?" He was a couple of inches taller than Paz's five ten, as Scandinavian blond as Paz was Argentine-and-black-Irish dark.

"Mr. Henningsen."

Henningsen sat and carefully swiped at a swatch of sprayed-stiff hair the ceiling fan above their table blew down across his forehead. He ordered a G and T and said airily, "Well, at last, Mr. Paz. Your reputation precedes you, you know. As many people as have been waiting for you to get to Mexico, you're a dignitary for us." He laughed his forced laugh again.

It was dark now, and all through the gardens below the

verandah, around the pool, up into the fronds of the palms, lights had come on. The breeze had died and the ceiling fan did little besides force hot air down to make Paz's glass sweat and to turn his own sweat to stinging salt more quickly. From somewhere down among the home folks' cafés and bars along the beach, he could hear a *jarocho* band's harp and marimba and guitar take up. Suddenly he wanted to be there, with Teri, not up here drinking a drink he didn't want with this pompous son of a bitch. To try to make small talk with him was more than he could bear. With a kind of release that was almost pleasure, he let his anger go, opened his arms and let it leap away from him across the table toward the grinning lie from *Gentleman's Quarterly.*

"I'll want to see the books for the expedition," he said abruptly.

Henningsen looked uncertain a moment, then his smile melted. "I acted in a private capacity, Mr. Paz. Those are not U.S. government documents. I don't think you have the right to see them."

"You have a problem with my seeing them?"

"Yes, I do. It's a matter of principle. Fiduciary responsibility is a position of trust, isn't it? Personally, I have nothing to hide, so if you'd care to take it out of my hands by getting a subpoena from the Mexican attorney general's office, I'd be only too glad."

They both knew a subpoena could take months, years, with the right bribes slowing it down. There were quicker routes. "Were you the first one to go to Collosini, Henningsen? Or were you surprised to find out there had been somebody there before you?"

In the silence from Henningsen, the fan whirred. Behind them in the dining room someone dropped a glass. Through the palms, a nearly full moon was rising and painting a long triangle of light across the sea toward them. The distant *jarocho* band swung into "La Bamba."

"You're not more than a flunky in this," Paz went on. "You

don't even have the ante to draw a chair up to the table. But if you saw the chance to grab one easy, portable thing that you had a broker all set up to handle, why not?" The waiter brought Henningsen's drink. Henningsen didn't touch it. "If it's any comfort to you, Collosini never did get it, either. Which I think lets you off the hook. You wouldn't have risked holding on to the thing longer than it would have taken you to be on the next plane to Mexico City."

"You're insulting," Henningsen said.

Now Paz laughed, genuinely. "Insulting? Is that what I am?"

Henningsen got up and dropped a wad of pesos beside his drink. "Good evening, Mr. Paz."

"Henningsen?" Paz pulled Teodoro's photos from his shirt pocket, unwrapped them from the bill of lading and captain's manifest he'd put them in, and spread them on the table like a full house in a poker game. Then he dropped the manifest and bill of lading in front of them like a bet.

"What are those supposed to be," Henningsen said, his bravado making a last stand.

"If you're cooperative, you might, just *might* get away with losing your job. Your people just detest scandals, don't they? If you're not cooperative, I promise you I'll get a goddamned hammer on your head from Customs that will make it impossible for any federal attorney *not* to prosecute you. Do you understand me?"

"There are rights — "

"Rights, hell! We're in Mexico, you ass." He downed the *campechano*, rewrapped the photos, and got to his feet. "Let's walk." He checked to make sure Teodoro's guard dog stayed put, then led the way across the verandah and down a flight of stone stairs into the half light of the garden. Henningsen hesitated a moment, then followed. When they were out of sight of the tables on the verandah, Paz drew up and faced him. "I just got those photographs today. Right now only two people who count know about you, and the other one of us has already forgotten he ever knew. I can put the photos and a report on a plane to the embassy tomorrow morning, or I can wait and make a report that *also* mentions how cooperative you've been. It's all up to me."

Henningsen picked a leaf off a bush almost petulantly, and didn't meet Paz's eyes. "What do you want?"

"First of all, do you show me the expedition's books before or after you've put your rake-off back? I don't give a damn if you're ever prosecuted on that. But part of that money's my sister's and I want it back, *entiendes?*"

"Yes," Henningsen said, still sulky.

"Then I want to know who the other person who went to Collosini was. Did you have a partner who was screwing you? Is that why two of you showed up?"

Henningsen threw down the leaf, surrendering. "I had no idea anyone else had gone to him. I wouldn't have needed a partner, would I? I knew where the codex was, I knew where the letters authenticating it were, I had the contact. What more could a partner have given me?"

"How did you have the contact?"

Henningsen hesitated, then said curtly, "Previous dealings."

"Who else could have had it?"

"Everyone, really. We all conceivably could have had some contact with Collosini, either on the buying or selling end. Even your brother-in-law." At the mention of Stanley, Paz was certain he saw a small smirk on Henningsen's face.

The little patience he had left for the man evaporated. In a single quick, hard motion he hooked Henningsen's foot with his own, jerked it from under him, and drove both palms into Henningsen's shoulder with the full weight of his body behind him. Henningsen spun and went down face first in a soft flower bed beside the path, Paz on top of him, straddling him, pulling his arm up tight into a hammer lock until Henningsen cried out as sharply as if Paz had flung hot water at him. Paz's loosed anger had talons now, was on its own, beating its wings and clawing.

"What about my brother-in-law?" His mouth was just beside

Henningsen's ear and he felt his voice metallic, fast, almost slurred. "What about my brother-in-law and Collosini?"

Henningsen spat dirt. "I only meant — "

"Try this, *pendejo*. Try that the whole thing was you and Humboldt Méndez. Try that Collosini told one of you that the other had come to see him, too, and you decided to split the profits instead of risking the whole damn deal in a fight. Try that Méndez got the codex and screwed you over, you had him killed, then had the baron kidnapped to scatter the trail. Even if it's not true, how long can I arrange to get you kept in a Mexican jail until it's sorted out? How long?" He jerked upward on Henningsen's arm another half inch.

Henningsen bucked once, then lay rigid and still. His sentences came in broken, staccato bursts littered with sharp intakes of breath like small sobs. "Collosini has something he's . . . using on your brother-in-law. I don't know what. I've got it all second hand. For God's sake, ease . . . up on my arm."

"Second hand from who?"

"Peter Lovinger. He and Collosini . . . worked together once."

"On what?"

"God, ease up!"

Paz shoved the arm upward again. "On what?"

"Oh, dear *Jesus*. The same thing. Collosini was using stage sets to get things out of the country, and Lovinger was going to use . . . film sets. He had contacts in Los Angeles, he said, that Collosini didn't have. It didn't last long. Lovinger . . . shorted Collosini on something."

"Why did Lovinger tell you that?"

"Because he worked with me, too."

With his free hand, Paz scooped up a lump of loose, wet dirt. He worked it into Henningsen's sprayed blond hair, deep, down to the scalp. The heart of his anger beat a little more slowly as he did. The son of a gaucho had done that to *his* hair once in a fight behind his grandfather's stables. He knew now how good it must have felt. He eased up on the hammer lock. "Visas?"

"At first he just wanted actors, cameramen, who'd work cheap. The others just lately — and just the three Panamanians you know about. I swear that."

"What did he want with Panamanian hoods?"

"I don't know. He wouldn't talk about it to me. He paid me and I signed the visas. I don't know."

"Where's Baron von Hummel? Is he dead?"

"I don't know."

"Who has the codex?"

"I don't know."

Paz shoved again. "Who did you forward the saw blades to?"

"Salomón Katun. I sent . . . everything care of him. Please, oh *shit*."

"Why didn't Méndez catch on?"

"I don't know. Maritza de la Torre . . . kept him on a short leash, kept him in Mexico City and said there wasn't a . . . budget to explore the rest of the site. He complained about that every . . . time I saw him."

"Maritza? What about Maritza?"

"Nothing. I don't know anything about her. I just know what Méndez said."

"What's Lovinger's connection with Carlos Receta y Precio?"

"They make movies."

Paz picked up another handful of wet dirt and smeared it along the side of Henningsen's face. "What else, *cabrón?*"

"I don't know. Receta y Precio doesn't . . . need money, so I don't know. Listen, Paz, Lovinger will have me killed if he . . . knows I've said anything at all. It doesn't matter now if I tell you whatever else I know. I might as well. I've got no reason to lie. Please, ease up!"

"Killed by the same Indian who got to Méndez? And Collosini? The one he's had following me? Or have *you* had the man doing it?"

"My God! I sold some visas. I'm not a hit man. I went to
. . . Georgetown, Paz! I didn't even know Collosini was dead."

Paz gave him that one. He'd talked about Collosini in the
present tense. He eased up on the arm. "Once more, Henningsen. What about my brother-in-law and Lovinger and Receta
y Precio? Why are they buying into his airline? Why are he
and my sister backing the dig with them?"

Henningsen was squirming now that the hammer lock was
looser, squirming and trying frantically to turn his head away
from Paz's hand and the mud. *"I don't know.* It could be
legitimate — even if Lovinger knows what Collosini had on
your brother-in-law, it could all still be legitimate, couldn't
it? They've got to launder money somewhere, don't they? I
offered, but they . . . Look, go ask them. Friday night, just
bloody go up to Receta y Precio's and *ask* them. All three at
once. Just please, please let me sit up. Oh, Jesus, please."

Paz's anger was quiet now, almost asleep. He sat up straight
and looked at his muddy hand in the weak light. It was a thing
he nearly failed to recognize, a hand that might have been
somebody else's. He remembered looking at it that way before,
after hunts in Argentina when he would pull it out of the
innards of a deer he was gutting, seeing the blood on it,
wondering that it was *his* hand that had done that to the deer.
He had to remind himself who Henningsen was to keep from
feeling ashamed.

"What about Friday night?" he said quietly. He let go of
Henningsen's arm, levered himself off him, and watched
Henningsen roll over and work himself into a sitting position.
They sat facing each other in the dirt.

Henningsen dabbed at the mud on his face with a shirtsleeve,
then massaged his arm. "You enjoyed that," he said.

"Not entirely," Paz said.

"It wasn't necessary."

"Yes, yes it was. Friday night."

"I'm meeting your brother-in-law at the airport. Peter called me this afternoon and asked me to meet your sister and him and handle customs clearance, then fly up with them. He wants all the backers together for a conference."

"Why?"

"Receta y Precio got some kind of letter. From Humboldt Méndez."

"A letter? What about?"

"That's all I know — a letter. Peter just tells me bits and snatches of things when the mood hits him."

Paz thought a moment. "Are they bringing their own plane down?"

"Yes."

"What time."

"Five-thirty. We have to be at Receta y Precio's at six-thirty."

Paz stood and brushed the dirt off his pants. He held out his hand to Henningsen, who didn't take it as he got to his feet.

"My brother-in-law might be bringing his confidential secretary along. A male secretary," Paz said. "Tell Lovinger that. Don't be definite, but tell him my brother-in-law takes his confidential secretary on business trips."

Realization dawned bleak as February on Henningsen's streaked face. "Oh, dear God, Paz, you can't ask me to — "

"You'll meet the plane — I'll tell you where when the time comes; it won't be at the airport — and if necessary, in Papantla you'll introduce me to Lovinger and Receta y Precio as Stanley's confidential secretary, then you can go away. It's not hard."

"I can't. No, I can't."

"You don't have a choice. You try to walk and you're an exile the rest of your life. My word on that."

Henningsen took a step backward, as if he were getting ready to run. "You'll have to get me out of Mexico, Paz. Immediately afterward. You'll have to protect me. I won't live a week."

"I'll do my best," Paz said, and thought, for what that'll be worth after this.

Henningsen tried to smooth his mud-caked hair and brought

his hand away in horror. "Oh, God," he said, and turned away toward the sea. "Oh, dear, dear God."

Paz got to Mary Margaret on her direct line. Stanley wouldn't have liked that if he'd been home; he wanted everyone, even Paz, to go through his gatekeepers. He said surprises made him nervous. He would have been nervous tonight.

"Quint, I've been frantic," Mary Margaret said. "We've got to go to Mexico Friday. I didn't know what on *earth* to say when Stanley told me Peter Lovinger had called."

"Did he tell you what it was about?"

"Just that it had to do with the codex, so he wanted both of us to come. I thought that you probably knew about it."

"When's Stanley coming back?"

"Friday morning."

"Can I reach him?"

"No. He's off looking at some ranch property in New Mexico. Can I have him call *you* as soon as he gets back?"

"Friday's too late. Got a pencil?"

"Wait a — oh, why do they never write when you . . . Yes, I have one."

"Just south of Veracruz there's a town called Boca del Río. You remember it?"

"I remember it. I used to be bored witless when Daddy would take us there."

"It doesn't have much of an airstrip — it should handle the Conquest but not the Lear. I want you to clear customs in Mexico City and *not* in Veracruz, then put down in Boca del Río, maybe about five o'clock to be sure. I'll meet you at the airstrip. Then we'll all go to Papantla and everything else will be according to schedule. Am I going too fast?"

"No, but — "

"Lovinger might call back. If he does, tell your gatekeeper to confirm that you could be bringing Stanley's confidential secretary with you. Tell her the man's name is . . ." Who knew the name Quintero? Collosini, only Collosini. ". . . Quintero, if Lovinger wants to know, and that he's Argentine." As he had done with Henningsen, he left his cover open. But the question wasn't whether or not he was going; it was only *how* he'd want to go when the time came.

"Quintero like grandfather's gardener?"

"Like grandfather's gardener," he said, feeling a surprise rush of closeness with her. "And don't tell him anything else. Be perfectly pleasant. It's important, Meg. Act as if nothing at all is out of the ordinary. But tell Stanley: whatever he does, *be there.* Tell him I've got an OK from Customs for this. Do you understand? Customs knows what I'm doing."

"What is it, Quint? What's so important?"

"It's all right," he said. "It's just a diversion. Think of it as a game."

"Quint, I'm *not eight.*"

"Then ask Stanley," he said.

SEVEN

WHAT IF, Paz thought as he sat on the edge of his bed with his shoes off and tuned out the babble of a dubbed *Dallas* episode from the TV. What if you had set yourself up in the business of smuggling artifacts out of Mexico, and you came across a way to have an entire ancient city just for yourself to loot at will, with all the proper government forms stamped and approved by all the proper authorities? Suddenly a system such as Collosini's would seem much too slow and cumbersome for the scale you were working on.

Then what if somehow you saw a way to move in on an airline whose sole business was between Mexico and the United States? An airline for which you could pick your employees so that a few key people handled everything at each step and in each city — the *pistoleros?* — and the rest of your business operated perfectly legitimately, even profitably. (After all, no matter how big your windfall in artifacts was, your supply of them and your market for them would of necessity be limited. You'd want something left over.) You'd even have complete freedom to choose the flights you sent things on, a piece or two at a time, steadily, day after day. Eight, ten flights a day, every day, steadily.

And what if you had found some kind of leverage and could

arrange to hide behind a successful, respected American businessman? A businessman who might have had no idea what had been going on at first except that he'd been pressured into letting you buy into his airline (secretly, but for Gallagher's slipping a Mexican banker a few bucks), thinking that all you wanted from him was a piece of a business that was bound to make you a fat profit.

It was beautiful; it covered all the bases. The pieces of it he had almost fit, too — all except the *pistoleros*. If you were dealing with antiquities, as Lovinger was, would you want Panamanian hoods running your operation? Or were they only enforcers to use against your airline people? Why would you need to import enforcers for that?

But for now the pieces fit closely enough to make an arpeggio of dread run through him, like a chill. He thought of Customs confiscating Stanley's airline, of the tangle of offshore bank dealings that could make it impossible for Stanley to prove he *wasn't* behind the scheme. And no matter how much Paz might believe Stanley was clean, he recognized that even he couldn't know he was now. He pictured years of trials, suits and countersuits, property seizures, possible bankruptcies — all public, all ready made for the press. Who would Mary Margaret be at the end of that? Who would his mother be? Who would he be?

What in God's name might Stanley have gotten himself — gotten all of them — into?

Paz had been sent to find a Maya codex a century or so ago. It was almost, he felt, as if he'd begun to slice a bad spot out of an apple, but the more he cut away the more rot he found. Or even as if he'd been meant to find the rot.

Frustrated, he got up, slapped the Off button on the TV, and opened the sliding door that led to the tiny private patio outside his room. Even above the rumble of his air conditioner he could hear the *jarocho* band working the bars along the beach. He half expected to see *el halcón*'s still figure in the dimness between the circles of light from the streetlamps along the beach road. He thought he might almost welcome him as something fixed, material, to deal with.

He switched off the air conditioner and left the door open to the steady breeze that had come up off the water, a breeze that brought the faint sea scent of ripeness and decay in with it.

He knew he had to keep cutting at the rot, faster now, more deeply: it was spreading, metastasizing, to consume his own family, just as it had already somehow consumed Baron von Hummel. It was flatly impossible for him to believe that it was chance that caused all of these people — Stanley and Mary Margaret, Peter Lovinger, Carlos Receta y Precio, Baron von Hummel, Henningsen — to converge at one precise point: the codex. Especially now. Some kind of long, hidden fuse had been lit when the codex disappeared, a fuse that had been burning toward this emergency meeting called about a letter from a man who was dead because of that disappearance. Something had changed, something that was apparently going to drastically affect everyone involved in this business. So for their own salvation (and Paz's), Stanley and Mary Margaret *had* to keep their appointment Friday, and he had to be with them.

A gust of sea wind blew the curtains out and curled through the room around him. He understood that when he stepped on Stanley's plane Friday he would totally cut himself off from anyone he could turn to for help: Teodoro, Gallagher, Harmon, Customs itself. He would be as alone as he had been in that great, cold, echoing house of his grandfather's in Buenos Aires, those endless weeks when he'd been dumped there and left to imagine the time when the decision to go or stay, to abandon or preserve a family, would be his.

Even though the wind was warm, he crossed his arms over his chest and buried his hands beneath them.

.　　　.　　　.

After dinner, he thought the hotel operator had gotten him the wrong number when a man's voice answered Teri's phone.

"I'm sorry," Paz said. "I'm trying to reach Teresa Sánchez."

"She's out," the voice said. It was surly and more than a little slurred.

Paz listened to the line hiss a moment. "When do you expect her?"

"Hell, I don't know. Half an hour, maybe. Who's this?"

"Quintus Paz. Who am I talking to?"

"Buddy. You're talking to Buddy."

"I don't know you."

"Naw, probably not. You the guy she works for?"

"With, not for."

"Yeah. Look, she went to take her cat somewhere, she said. Why don't you call her at work tomorrow? She's not working now, right?"

"No, she's not working now. But —"

"Check."

Paz heard the sound of the receiver clattering hard in its cradle before the dial tone took over again. He clicked the disconnect button a half-dozen quick times to get the hotel operator back.

"Señor Paz?" the operator said. "You have had a call while you were talking. I have a message for you."

"I want the number I was just talking to back," Paz said, telling himself not to panic, that he didn't know enough to panic yet.

"Si, señor. Un momentito, before I forget, please. This message is from a Señorita Teri. She says to tell you that everything is all right and that she will call you back, but that you please will not call her at her house. Have you understood that, señor?"

"That was all?" Paz said.

"Si, señor. I'm trying your number again now. Please hang up and I will call you back."

"No," Paz said. "Let it go."

He stared at the gray phone as if he were waiting for it to give him the rest of the message. You didn't go out to a pay phone, he thought, and leave a message for your boyfriend not to call you at home if you were in any kind of danger. Nor did you tell him that if you'd picked up some man and brought him home. At least Teri didn't, nor would she pick up some man in the first place. His incipient panic eased. But who the hell was Buddy? He ran through the names of people she knew at work, of family — or as many of the scores of nieces and nephews and cousins as he could remember. No Buddy.

He reached for the phone again, then let his hand fall. She was a grown woman who said she would call *him* back. She had a pistol and she was trained to use it. If she said she was all right, she was all right. Let it go, he told himself, let it go and learn to wait. Buddy was an old friend from high school, a cousin he'd never heard of. You've been a cop too long; you've learned too well to mistrust *everything*.

Except one thing. He picked up the receiver and asked the operator for Craig's number.

Bess answered.

When she found out it was him, her voice turned wintery. Quickly, before she could hand the phone over to Craig, he said, "I'm at the Mocambo." Trying to maintain any kind of security procedure was ridiculous at this point. Everybody who mattered in this thing already knew he was in Veracruz.

There was a pause. "How is it?" she asked at length.

"Not changed much. A new wing, but basically the same."

"Is the head waiter — Alfonso — still there?"

"Haven't seen him." The man had been Bess's favorite, he remembered. Always knew her name, always sat them at a table facing the sea, which she liked.

"Well," she said. "It's changed, then. People always did matter less to you than places, didn't they?"

"Don't, Bess," he said.

"I'll get Craig."

"Bess? You remember that huipil you bought in Mexico City? When was it — seventy, seventy-one?"

Her voice softened. "It was a long time ago, Quint."

"For the most part, Mexico was pretty good, wasn't it? In those days."

"Quint," she said. "I wanted to tell you this before you left. Maybe it's easier when you're so far away now . . . God, I don't know. Quint?"

"I'm still here."

"Quint, I think I'm getting married."

The pause was his now. He could hear the surf picking up outside, and still the harp of the *jarocho* band rising and falling on the wind. "Somebody I know?"

"I don't think so. His name is David. He owns a plumbing supply business and he's got a son about Craig's age. They seem to get along."

He took a deep breath. "Congratulations." The static on the line made the distance between them seem immense, he thought, aware of the sad irony of that. "Plumbers stay put."

"I waited a long time, Quint."

"Yes," he said. "Yes, you did."

"I'll get Craig," she said again.

"All right." He felt his eyes sting and thought, Christ, I didn't even do this when my father died.

Gratefully, he listened to Craig ramble about soccer practice, about a car he wanted now that he was about to get his license, about needing more money since he was going to be driving. Then he tried to picture Craig at a dinner table — the cherry-wood table they'd bought in San Diego — with Bess and a man named David, and with another boy sitting across from him, a boy without a face, who Craig would introduce to people as his stepbrother. He couldn't make it work. What worked here was the past, not the future.

"Do you remember the Mocambo at all?" he asked finally.

"You know what I remember about that place, Dad?" Craig said, his voice cheerful and oblivious. "It had the biggest swimming pool I think I ever saw. Is it still there?"

"I haven't had a chance to check," Paz said. "Not much swimming time this trip."

"That's a shame. Live it up a little, hey?"

"Do my best, old kid."

When he hung up, he wiped the sting away from his eyes with a corner of the bedspread. What the hell had he expected? Here he was, fifteen hundred miles from home again, lonely in a hotel room, and he was expecting everybody else to be waiting around to make *him* feel better? He ought to be used to this. Hadn't it always been the same — even when he and Mary Margaret were embassy hopping with the old man — popping in and out of lives and places and feeling always like some distant relative, some foreign cousin?

Almost as an afterthought he dug out his notebook, picked up the phone again, and dialed Maritza's number. He'd promised to keep her posted, hadn't he? But the *portero's* wife answered. Señora de la Torre was out, and wouldn't be back until late. Paz left the message that there was no news on the codex yet, and that he was at the Mocambo if Señora de la Torre needed him.

He undressed, then found his swimming trunks in his suit bag. OK, old kid, he thought. Live it up. He made a last check of the beach road from the patio door. Still no *halcón*, though the shape of a man, much too large for *el halcón*, moved aimlessly among the palms. Another one of Teodoro's guard dogs? No, Teodoro did the best with what he had to work with: the man wouldn't be so obvious if he were Teodoro's. Somebody from the hotel, Paz decided, working his own loneliness out. No professional would just loiter like that. He locked the door, wedged his fake ID's behind the toilet tank, and wrapped his .45 and his room key in a towel to take with him.

Outside, he was almost alone with the hotel. The patient guard dog he'd seen before dinner had moved out onto the verandah, where he had a view of the breezeway that ran by Paz's room. Besides him, only a solitary couple, silhouetted in the lights from the verandah, walked slowly along the great circular promenade that hung over the gardens like a balcony from an Escher drawing. The woman's easy gait reminded him of Teri's.

He headed through the gardens toward the pool. The guard dog heaved to his feet to watch. Of all the hotels Paz had slept in since he'd first come to this one forty years ago, when he dreamed of hotels he dreamed of the Mocambo. It was precisely the wrong place to be tonight: he needed something hard and modern, a place with a noisy band and flashing lights. When he and Mary Margaret had been brought here for vacations as kids, this place had been a gigantic, landlocked Moorish ship for them, not quite real even then, its arches disappearing behind arches and its great verandah and promenade like a prow reaching out from this green hillside toward the sea, trying to find its way back.

A ghost ship tonight, he thought. He wished he'd talked to Teri.

To confuse his guard dog, he ducked into the garden entrance to the ballroom, whose tiled dance floor was broken by two perfect ovals of swimming pool. He had a vague memory of Mary Margaret trying to drown him in one of those shallow pools when she couldn't have been more than five. He had a clearer memory of Bess laughing on their first trip to Veracruz, saying she was sure she'd seen Humphrey Bogart slip behind one of the pink, lily-shaped columns around the pools, and Bacall disappear through a mysterious door in the back. He'd told her it was OK because no doubt Sidney Greenstreet would be waiting for her there with steamship tickets to someplace safe, then she'd hummed "As Time Goes By" from the wrong movie, and they'd danced, all by themselves, around the empty pools.

There it came again, he thought. The past, bushwhacking you. He stepped out into the garden again and got a look at the verandah. No guard dog.

He took one of the tiled walks down the hill to the big pool Craig had remembered. As he passed the old part of the hotel he picked out certain rooms, certain doors. See that room? the booze-tinted voice told him. His old man was looming over him as they walked — tall, stooped, his face already elephant-skinned from chain smoking those unfiltered Delicados. That's the room where García Lorca stayed. Same one they give that poet Neruda when he's here. And that room? Watch for the old-timer who comes out of it. He's Léon Felipe, best damn poet of them all. He lives here. And then another night: Hear that cello music from the ballroom? Remember it when you grow up, *chamaco*. The man who's playing it is named Pablo Casals.

Ghosts, all ghosts now. Every one of them.

He was close enough to see that the pool, three times the size of any Olympic pool, was deserted when he heard the sounds from the hedges that surrounded it — something large, man-sized, moving slowly through them, getting in position to watch. Teodoro's guard dog had gone out the front and around the side of the hotel, then, to cut him off.

Paz veered down the hill toward the beach road. A deserted pool and a heavy-shoed cop with nothing to do but watch you do belly flops, he thought. No thanks.

At the edge of the beach, he stopped for a beer at one of the open-sided, thatched bars where the *jarocho* band was setting up its marimba, then remembered he hadn't brought any money. He stayed to listen a minute anyway, to break his mood. The musicians were dressed in the loose white smocks, embroidered bandannas, white pantaloons, and short-brimmed straw hats of mountain Indians. They looked toward Paz hopefully, figuring him for a bigger tip than they'd get from the half-dozen local drunks who still lingered around the bar's rusting metal tables decorated with Carta Blanca beer logos. Paz avoided their eyes.

He fled again, this time along the deserted beach itself. Not even a dog on it, he saw, all the way from the breakwater on his left to the arm of jungly land that ended his view a couple of miles to his right. End of the line here, the sea, no farther back you could go than the sea.

He checked again to make sure nobody was watching, then wedged the towel-wrapped pistol and key into a crevice between two hunks of concrete at the head of the breakwater. From there he walked a hundred yards or so farther down the beach to a point where the only sounds were the surf and the wind, which blew a fine powder of sand against his legs, and the only light the fully risen moon. He scanned the beach a last time, waded into the surf, and dove.

He was already beyond the breakers, far enough from shore so that his feet touched only the colder water of an undertow if he lowered them, when he looked back to the beach and saw that no, no, it wasn't deserted after all. There was a man on it. A man who, when he stood up from Paz's towel with Paz's .45 in his hand, he could make out clearly in the moonlight. Even in this wind, Henningsen's newscaster hair was in place.

And he'd told the bastard not to walk! Why should he walk? Of course the man Paz had seen across the beach road from his patio and had heard crashing around like a water buffalo in the bushes by the pool hadn't been a professional. Henningsen was an amateur everything, but Paz had been even more of one: rusty, yes, and worse. He'd blown his concentration, wandered, let himself become as self-absorbed as a fifteen-year-old — and had handed his head to the man. The rawest agent in Customs knew better than that. He treaded water and fought to think. All Henningsen had to do was keep him away from the shore long enough, and no one would ever know about the visas, the visit to Collosini, the money skimmed from the baron's expedition. Paz had drowned, had gotten too far from shore, that's all. No wounds on the body, nothing. He'd even left the son of a bitch his room key, so he could stop off for the photographs on his way out!

The concrete breakwater was on Paz's right now as he faced the beach. He could make the couple of hundred feet to it easily — but not as easily as Henningsen could. Forget the spit of land to his left. More than a mile in open surf? He hadn't been that strong a swimmer when he was twenty.

Something brushed his foot in the colder water of the undertow. He recoiled from it, lost his balance, and was buried in a swell. He gagged at the taste of the salt water, imagining what it would be like if that taste was the last one you ever knew, then sputtered back to his breath and shouted, "Henningsen!" Don't panic, he told himself, making the words form themselves consciously in his mind. Concentrate, and for God's sake, don't panic. He won't shoot you because he won't want a police investigation; he won't want to have a bullet hole in the body if he can help it.

"Henningsen!" There was a chance the wind would carry his words to the beach even over the surf. "Henningsen, they'll catch those visas anyway, damn it. They'll come for you. They'll figure this out!"

If Henningsen heard, he gave no sign. He dropped to one knee and braced the pistol, target shooter's position. How good was he? The range was long for a pistol, and Paz hadn't brought an extra clip. If Henningsen was wild, what were the chances that he could be drawn, that he'd empty the clip? Paz damned the bright moon to hell, and let the waves carry him slowly closer to shore, stretching his toes to search for something solid each time he slid into the trough of a swell. He felt nothing.

Henningsen's first shot splatted into the water a yard to the left of Paz's head. The second shot hit roughly the same distance to the right. Henningsen lowered the pistol and gave Paz a thumbs-up sign. His message was clear. He could shoot.

Paz kicked into a backstroke and moved farther out to sea.

He was surprised at what slow progress he made against the swells, at how weak his kicks were, and how short his breath came already. He had to relax, to save what energy he had left. Of all deaths, drowning had always been the last he'd have chosen; he somehow had always thought of it as getting lost in his grandfather's endless, cold house and never finding his way out. He imagined the sensation of letting go, sinking, losing the sense of up or down, of light or dark — it would be like dying twice, a death before death in such a miserably *alien* place. For a moment, in his fear he felt immensely sorry for himself, and then he thought, no, by God, no, whatever else, I won't drown. He looked up at the moon, which didn't give a damn that he was afraid of drowning, and saw that a solitary cloud, a scout for a thunderstorm building over the gulf, was stalking it. He felt a cramp in the arch of his sole turn his foot into a painful claw, and he relaxed and kept himself afloat as best he could with his arms alone while the cramp eased, and he let the moon help him make his decision.

When the cloud found the moon, he let himself go under. He had one advantage: that *he* knew what he was going to do but Henningsen didn't.

He surfaced first five or so yards to his left, toward the distant spit of land. Enough light spilled from behind the cloud to make seeing harder but not impossible, and he made sure he stayed above water until Henningsen saw him and moved to follow him along the beach. With luck, Henningsen would try to pace him, stay ahead of him. That would put even more distance between them.

When he went under this time, he twisted and swam to his right, swam hard. Screw using his strength up — he wouldn't need it again if this didn't work.

When he broke water for air, his chest in a panic even if he wasn't, he didn't risk staying above water long enough to clear his eyes and check Henningsen. He had to keep Henningsen from getting a make on him as long as he could. It wouldn't take Henningsen long to figure out he'd been suckered, anyway.

But if Paz was going to make the jetty and get a decent running start from there, ten yards, ten seconds, could make all the difference. He saw the shadowy shape of the jetty rising from the water in front of him, and dove again.

Two more lungfuls of air, and he saw the first blurred outline of the jetty ahead of him through the dark water. The thing was made of great broken hunks of concrete, and the gray, angular shapes he saw could have been buildings, skyscrapers, thrown into the sea by some cataclysm. He knew he had to chance looking for Henningsen now, before he exposed himself, a perfect target, on top of that concrete wasteland.

He clung to the first shape, bracing himself against the breaking surf. No matter that it was covered with a coat of slime and barnacles — it was solid, was everything water wasn't. He wiped his eyes clear and checked what he could see of the rest of the breakwater from where he was, which wasn't much. Everywhere the jumbled shapes blocked his view, so that he could see only short stretches along the top of the thing. Henningsen wasn't on any of those.

Nor was he on the beach. They were both on the jetty, then, both hidden: Henningsen on top, where he could run, Paz below, where he could only crawl. But assuming the moon stayed out of the way, Paz's enemy, the water, was his friend now. If he worked himself back to the beach, keeping his body beneath it, and praying that the jutting pieces of the breakwater would hide the rest of him, he might, just might make the beach. From there, a broken-field sprint and he was in among the cabañas, then the trees . . .

He looked up to check the moon just as the cloud slid past it, then, with the breakers beside him shining viciously in the clear light, he moved, feeling like some shelled sea thing scuttling for the next slimy dark place. But when Henningsen stood up from behind a jagged concrete rampart a dozen feet away, he knew that the light didn't matter. Henningsen had made him long before, had been waiting for him.

"Let it go, man, for God's sake," Paz shouted up at him with what breath he had left. "Too many people know about those pictures."

"You told me only two knew, Paz." There was no heartiness in Henningsen's voice now; it was as cold as the moonlight. "I'm here, and someone else is at the second place. You were, I believe, only with Comandante Alcalde today, weren't you?"

"Henningsen, Christ, anybody touches him and they'll cut your heart out and dance in your skin — you *know* that." Gaucho! Paz thought. Teodoro had given him those pictures thinking he was giving them to a man who had good sense, had trusted him. But in truth he'd given them to a man who was so busy with the past that he let the present eat both of them up. Well, here it was, here was the present, standing over him in blow-dried hair with a .45 pointing at him. What was he going to do with it? He eased himself out of the water, a couple of feet closer to Henningsen. Henningsen didn't react.

Paz made sure he had a purchase on the slippery concrete and slowly stood. He wasn't certain what he was doing, or why — bluffing, bravado, fear, stupidity, maybe all of them. All he knew, dimly, was that he'd had a decision to make — now, in this present that might be forever — and he'd made it. He wouldn't go back into the water, he wouldn't let it happen that way.

"*You'll* have to do it, Henningsen," he said. "I won't drown."

"Yes, Paz, you will."

As Paz took a step up, Henningsen took two down, so that they were almost close enough to touch fingertips. Paz knew that with no firm foothold, tired as he was and ten years older than Henningsen, it would be stupid to lunge for him. Almost by instinct he held out his hand. "Let it go, man. Help me up."

For a moment, as Henningsen's left hand rose, Paz thought it had worked, that Henningsen was going to make that easy gesture and it would be done. That was why he didn't even try to duck when Henningsen flung his handful of sand and why he stood astonished and blind while Henningsen gave him a quick shove back into the surf. "I brought your mud back, Paz," he heard Henningsen say as he fell into the darkness.

He felt little besides his astonishment at first, only the power of the waves tumbling him under the water and then the cold as he sank deeper. A memory flashed: an agent he'd known on an assignment in Turkey once, whom the undertow in the Black Sea had taken. It had kept the man swirling for hours like a rag in a clothes dryer, down to the bottom of the sea, then up top, then down again, until, when the fishing boat had pulled him out at last, parts of him had been scraped away to the bone. Paz fought to keep his eyes open so the water could do its cleansing work, and pushed upward against the cold with strength he'd been sure he didn't have.

He felt the concrete before he broke the surface and clung to it as he rose the last few feet. The sand was gone from his eyes, but it and the salt water had left the world around him as indistinct as if he were seeing it through a thick bottle. He saw a figure on the jetty above him who he knew had to be Henningsen. "For the love of God, Henningsen!" he shouted, and the figure started down the concrete maze toward him. Then there was another shape behind Henningsen's, a much smaller shape, and Paz could make out only that this one was dressed in the smock and pantaloons and straw hat of a *jarocho*. Was the man *with* Henningsen, or did Henningsen even know he was there?

The answer came when the shape raised something long and straight that hung briefly against the sky, then fell on Henningsen just where his shoulder met his neck — and Paz knew who the man was. Henningsen stiffened, seemed to start to turn, but his shoulder and head were suddenly at a strange angle to each other, and his motion turned into a vague half twist, as if he were in a diving competition. Then he launched awkwardly out over the jutting concrete and disappeared.

The other man stood a moment, perhaps waiting for Paz to

make some sort of move himself. Paz could do no more than keep his hold on the slippery jetty with one hand and try to squeeze clearer vision back into his eyes with the thumb and forefinger of the other. If he moved, he would have strength only to let go and slide back into the water. He wouldn't do that.

As Paz's vision blinked more and more clear, the man scrambled down the concrete toward him. Paz waited, expecting — what, he didn't know. Then as the man squatted and held out his hand, the shape of a face beneath the straw hat formed. And even though Paz still couldn't see the features well, he recognized the dark holes where the man's eyes were hidden, the face so thin that it was almost a skull.

"*Gracias, muchísimas gracias,*" he managed to mumble as *el halcón*, with a grip whose strength would have impressed Paz in a man twice his size, hauled him onto a reasonably flat, dry slab of concrete.

And then he was gone. Just as easily as he'd disappeared from the passenger coach earlier, he was gone.

When Paz worked up enough breath to get to his knees, the beach, too, was empty. His attempt to call out backfired. He retched, sent dinner's langostino and all the sea water he'd swallowed back where it came from, and found some relief.

He looked at Henningsen as little as possible as he dragged him higher up on the breakwater, where he would stay put as the tide rose. Henningsen's shoulder was severed down to his rib cage, and that was enough to want to see. Luckily, the .45 had landed on the jetty, wedged between two hunks of concrete, glinting in the moonlight. Paz hugged it tightly to him as he wove back along the breakwater, cursing his weakness and slowness. Henningsen had said other people were on their way to the "second place," to Teodoro.

Back in the hotel, in his wet bathing suit still, he called Teodoro's house first, then his office. No answer in either place. He knew there was no way around calling the cops about Henningsen. The body was here, he was here, the two of them had had a drink together earlier tonight: even the Mexican cops would make that connection. But could he risk telling them to find Teodoro, to warn him? Teodoro had given him those pictures against orders. Would Teodoro be better off facing Henningsen's friends or his own "colleagues"?

At least, he decided, there'd be no surprises for Teodoro with the cops. He'd stand some chance. He asked the operator to connect him with the office of the Federales; Gallagher would ream him for not getting in touch with the embassy first, but let him. Time mattered too much now.

The phone rang once on the other end before the door to his room splintered open. He threw the phone at the bed lamp and snatched the .45 off the table beside it. In another motion he was behind the bed, drawing down on the darkness where the door had been; whoever was there had known enough to unscrew the lightbulbs from the breezeway outside, too. The blind facing the blind, and Paz prayed that the next light didn't come from the muzzle of a pistol.

A voice came from the direction of the door. "Keentoos?"

"Holy Mary, Mother of God," Paz breathed. "I'm here, Teodoro. I'm all right."

Until Friday now. There were no longer eleven days left; at the most what he could hope for was somehow to stay here and stay alive through Friday. It was Thursday morning. He'd had two hours of sleep after the Federales and the state judicial police and the Mexican customs cops had had at him.

The three hoods who had gone after Teodoro — Paz figured he himself must have been considered easier pickings, since Henningsen alone had come for him — were just as dead as Henningsen. Not as dramatically dead, but as effectively: they hadn't made it through the first rank of lesser lords surrounding *el jefe.* Teodoro had protected Paz as well as he could from the Federales, had kept them at bay until morning, when

Gallagher could get involved on the Mexico City end. As Paz read it so far, he wasn't going to have to take the fall for Henningsen. The cops seemed to accept his story that he hadn't seen who had taken Henningsen down: given his state — under water and blinded — he had made his explanation stick. Teodoro had the photos back, so Paz lied and said he'd gotten on to Henningsen through a tip from the LAPD, who'd picked up one of the distributors Henningsen had sent north. It wasn't a very good lie for the long run, but he didn't have a long run.

Teodoro wouldn't need a good lie to explain the three dead hoods who'd come for him. Any explanation the *comandante* chose to give was a good one. If the three had shot one another over a three-card monte game, they had shot one another over a three-card monte game.

It was Thursday morning, he was waiting for a call from Gallagher to be put through, and Teri was coming down. That's all he knew: she'd left word with the hotel operator while he was in town at the headquarters of the Federales, about five in the morning. "Arriving on Mexicana flight at five," the message read. "Have some things for you." Only that. Nobody answered at her house, not even Buddy, and Paz wasn't about to call Harmon. She'd had to have left on the morning milk-run flight to make the connection to Veracruz; she was already in the air. Reluctantly, he stacked that mystery to the side with all the others for the moment and answered Gallagher's call.

Gallagher's voice was angry, but it was also a little bemused. "You even," he said, "got a U.S. consul killed. That's fucking amazing. Nobody in Customs has ever done that before, I don't think." It was the first time they'd been able to talk with any privacy since the Federales had gotten Gallagher out of bed at two in the morning.

"I'll spot you one," Paz said.

"You'll do nothing for me, Paz, but get your ass out of my territory. I want you out, State wants you out, the deputy commissioner wants you out. When the Mexican government can get it together enough to want you out, they'll want you out. *Damn* it, but didn't I warn you? Do you realize the heat I'm taking to get you out of the country without a stink?"

"When?"

"You're being escorted out. I'm escorting you personally. The Mexican authorities are handing you over to me at the Veracruz airport. Understood?"

"When?"

"Five o'clock flight. Today. I don't look forward to the company."

"I'm not done here yet, Gallagher."

"The hell you're not. I wouldn't trust you to go to the can without a federal officer beside you. State and the DEA and I will debrief you here. Internal Affairs wants you as soon as you get home."

Paz laughed. "What are they going to do, retire me?"

"That's enough, Paz, that's e-fucking-nough. You're to confine yourself to the city of Veracruz, take *no* further action on this case, and cooperate with the Mexican authorities to the fullest extent until I come to take charge of you. That's not a request."

"I didn't take it as one."

When he hung up, he showered and went back to bed. His eyes were on fire from the sand and salt water and lack of sleep, and his fingertips were raw from the concrete of the breakwater. His mind was Jell-O. He justified going to bed by telling himself that it was the last luxury he would allow himself, that he was forty-five years old and had to admit it. He was no good to anybody in this shape.

He slept hard until one. When he woke up he showered again, fished his *salvoconducto* and fake ID's from behind the toilet tank, dressed, folded a clean shirt and pair of underwear and flattened them as inconspicuously as possible beneath the shirt he had on. In spite of the heat, he wore a coat over his shoulder holster; he would need to be dressed well. He slipped a toothbrush, razor, and tie into a pocket of the coat and dropped the room key behind the dresser. He wouldn't need it.

At the door, he stopped to check the room a last time. It was much more than a hotel room he was leaving, he told himself very deliberately, very consciously. He knew that it wasn't as if he were making a choice: his choice had been made even before Gallagher had ordered him off the case. He had made some of it when Harmon first mentioned Baron von Hummel, some of it when he saw Stanley's name on the paper at Collosini's, some of it in Maritza's apartment, and the rest after he spoke to Mary Margaret on the phone last night. What was tough was realizing how irrevocably that choice would be made when he walked out of this room.

He flicked out the light, stepped through the door, and closed it softly behind him.

Outside, he nodded at his guard dogs (there were three now: one from Mexican customs and two Federales) and crossed from the breezeway up to the verandah and into the lobby. One of the Federales and Teodoro's man detached themselves and followed.

At the long circular drive that led to the hotel, he took his time negotiating the fare into Veracruz with the taxi driver, so that his two guard dogs had time to make it to their big Monte Carlo cruiser. Then, as his cab pulled into the smoking, roaring traffic, he thought: in a little over three hours, not only will I have no place to go for help, but my friends will be my enemies.

EIGHT

THE TAXI SWUNG onto Avila Camacho, the broad *malecón* drive that followed the bay into town. The concrete benches along it were emptying as the afternoon heat came on; in spite of the breeze from the sea, the moisture the sun was boiling out of the ground from the summer's rains was enough to prostrate even veteran Veracruz bench sitters. Paz savored the wind from the taxi's open window, knowing he'd miss it when he got out.

He told the driver to go slowly, so that the Monte Carlo could keep them in sight easily. Until five o'clock he was legal, and he wanted to keep it that way.

He was certain of few things at this point — in some ways fewer than yesterday — but one of those was that Henningsen hadn't given him away to Peter Lovinger. Henningsen had been terrified of Lovinger: the last thing he would have done was go to him with news of his conversation with Paz. Nor would a man like Lovinger — assuming he had as much at stake as Paz was betting he did — have condoned such a clumsy, obvious stunt as Henningsen had tried. Henningsen had panicked.

Yet if it hadn't been for *el halcón*, it wouldn't have mattered to Paz ever again what anybody's motive for anything was. *El halcón*'s hawkish face had hovered over him at the beginning and at the end of the two fitful hours of sleep he'd managed before he talked to Gallagher this morning. The man who had tried to kill him in Mexico City had saved his life last night. It made no sense at all, none. He knew that if for no other reason than to make sense of *el halcón* he would have to go up into those jungle mountains tomorrow.

The *malecón* petered out among the narrower streets of the old part of the city. "*Ya dónde?*" the cabby said. "Where now?" Paz gave him an address he'd memorized from Maritza's list of names, and the cabby cut off a honking bus to swerve onto a side street to the left.

Another thing Henningsen's death had done was to get him in trouble sooner than he'd expected. He'd hoped to be back from Receta y Precio's meeting with something to show before he got sat on. So far it was only internal Customs Service trouble: he'd stepped on State's toes but he'd broken no laws.

There could be more trouble coming — there *would* be more coming. And he'd been shaken badly by Henningsen last night. Sometime during those two nightmare-ridden hours of sleep he'd had, he'd accepted that he might not be alive Saturday morning. Maybe that was why he'd slept so hard when he went back to bed: the forgotten nightmares had dealt with something, the risk had been calculated on some gut level, balanced against what was at stake, and accepted.

He didn't *want* to die, he knew that; he didn't want to be in trouble. But out of the deep anger that he'd felt yesterday (and he knew that he hadn't been angry just at Gallagher, at Harmon, at Teodoro and Henningsen and the dead ends on this case, but at *all* of the rules that had held his life down like guy ropes on a balloon for so many years), out of that anger had come an incredible sense of freedom, too. He'd known some of that sense on the train as he was working himself up to go after *el halcón*, when the odd tingling he'd felt as a boy on his way to a hunt had come back to him.

There had been no rules on the pampa but the rules the hunt itself imposed, rules that he'd been sure then he and the animal had understood without words, as he and *el halcón* had.

He could become a junkie of that freedom. Maybe that's what Harmon had meant when he'd said that without Customs he would be a gaucho, a barbarian. Was his hand in the innards of a deer, his hand grinding mud into Henningsen's hair, a result of that freedom, too?

And now he was barely more than a week away from being without Customs. What, he wondered, was he beginning to feel on the wind? He knew there was something to fear in it.

The baron's apartment was in the heart of the old quarter of the city, just off the *zocalo*, the central plaza, on the wrong end of a one-way street. Rather than swelter in the traffic-stalled cab, Paz decided to walk the long block to it. He told the cabby to pull over. The Monte Carlo eased into a bus stop behind them. While he was paying the fare, Paz kept his eye on the rear view mirror. He gave the Federál plenty of time to get out and slip into a doorway. The Monte Carlo's driver reached for his radio.

As Paz walked (slowly, so his shadow would have an easy time of it), he realized that he was in a world utterly lost — in one generation — to *his* world. It was a world before air conditioning. Above him people hung over balcony railings, immobile, hoping for breezes, watching the moving show of the street. Women in thin dresses still waited out the heat of the day in darkened rooms behind the iron-grilled windows he passed, white curtains still billowed against those grills in the breeze, music and voices still carried into the street through them. This was the definition of city that had existed since cities had. But it was a world that now, for a good hunk of the people on the planet (including himself), was being replaced by a great cool dead hum. He breathed the unfiltered street smells, afraid he was already remembering this the way the last of a species might.

And then he thought, no more of that. The present is what you stay alive in. Remember last night.

The baron's landlady, a heap in a rocking chair beside a window, her television set roaring a soap opera and her electric fan whizzing, waved him toward the door across the hall from hers. She'd apparently had enough of cops lately not to be impressed even by a gringo one. And between the noises in her room and the ones from the street, Paz could well believe she wouldn't have heard if someone had made off with half the Mexican navy from next door.

The baron's apartment was the baron. Wicker and rattan with worn cushions, heavy, carved antique Spanish tables, hand-woven Indian rugs, a careless and battered kitchen, a collection of pre-Columbian and colonial artifacts that made Maritza's look paltry. And books. Books in German, in English, in Spanish, in French, in Russian — leather-bound treatises to paperback novels, everywhere, on everything. The cops or the landlady had apparently put the rooms more or less back together after the police search, but the books had been too much for them. They rose in uneven stacks like Votan's towers of Babel all over the floor and tables; if he was hoping to turn up something the cops had missed, he'd need a week just to dig through those alone. One final dead end.

It was the pictures that drew him at last. There were maybe fifty of them scattered over the walls, mounted photographs that must have covered a period of at least as many years. In the living room he stopped with a shock before one of the baron, dark hair slicked back à la Robert Taylor, standing beside Paz's mother and father — and, skinny and bored, himself at twelve or so and Mary Margaret in tacky little twin pony tails at maybe six. Even his family was among the baron's artifacts.

And then he spotted the triptych, the three side-by-side Polaroids of the dig for the codex. They had to be of that dig, because Henningsen was in one, Maritza in another, each sweaty and limp, posing with pasted-on smiles in front of a low, partially cleared temple mound with the baron and six or eight other people Paz didn't recognize. But in all three, standing just slightly apart from the others, staring blankly toward the camera, was *el halcón.*

He stared back at *el halcón* a long moment, and, his excitement quickening, he reached for the photographs. As he did he heard the front door to the apartment click open in the foyer. He dropped his hand from the photograph to his shoulder holster and flattened himself against the wall. Then, from the foyer, "Keentoos?" He relaxed and stepped out in view of the door.

Teodoro was alone, much too tailored and spit-shined for a man who'd been up nearly as much of the night as Paz had. He came into the living room, majesty in the midst of disorder. "My man just told me on the radio you were here," he said. "You slept first?"

"I slept. You?"

Teodoro waved sleep away as unimportant. "But you talked to Gallagher."

"He called," Paz said.

"You know you have no right to be in this apartment now. He told you what your . . . status is."

"Yes. Can you do anything?"

Teodoro wagged his finger. "I don't want to, Quintus. You were very dangerous to yourself last night — and to me. I think you will be dangerous again if you stay. Do you understand, my friend? You are off the team. You can't keep playing if you are off the team, can you? I want to see that you meet Gallagher at the airport today, and I want to see that you are on the eight-in-the-morning flight with him. You will be, Quintus. *Entiendes?* A man who is off the team cannot expect to stay on the field without the other players doing what they must do to get him off the field, no matter if they are his friends. You understand this, I know."

"I'm in Mexico for a reason, Teodoro," Paz said.

Teodoro shrugged. "You can begin a great deal from the

States, Quintus, in the time you have left. You know about the saw blades now, and Peter Lovinger. And I have returned these to you." From somewhere beneath his tight uniform coat he maneuvered an envelope and handed it to Paz. Inside it Paz found the mug shots Teodoro had taken back from him last night, the bill of lading, and the captain's manifest. He tucked them in his own coat pocket, knowing he ought to thank Teodoro but not able to. Teodoro was trusting him again, and he felt guilty for letting him. "Someone else can finish for you. Let it go. You have a good life waiting."

"*Damn* it, Teodoro. That's not enough."

"It will have to be, my friend." Teodoro's face sank into sadness again. "For my part I will continue to do what I can from here. I will keep watch."

"And we both know that won't — " Paz caught himself.

Teodoro hesitated. "We both know, yes." To cover the awkwardness of the moment, he pointed past Paz to the photograph of the baron with Paz's family. "That's you," he said. "*Verdad?* You haven't changed that much, you know. And that's your father beside you?"

"That's him."

"You look like him." He stepped past Paz to the triptych. "And most of these you know, too, I imagine. Baron von Hummel, Señor Henningsen, Señora de la Torre, but maybe not this one." He pointed to a hulking, mustached, beefy man with a pleasant smile who would have fit well in a Kiwanis group portrait. "Humboldt Méndez." He crossed himself. "I think he was unlucky."

"Just that?" Paz said.

Teodoro shrugged again. "I don't see Peter Lovinger in any of these," he said, squinting as if he were trying to find something beyond the photographs themselves. "Perhaps Baron von Hummel didn't want to include him?" He took out a notepad and jotted something on it. "Or didn't want to have to look at him every day."

He pointed again. His finger paused at *el halcón*, then moved on. Paz's breath quickened. *Tell* me, Teodoro, he thought. Let me be sure. But Teodoro's finger moved on and stopped at a short man in American army combat fatigues who wore a pistol strapped around his waist. Everything about the man seemed square — head, shoulders, body — as if he were made of bricks or blocks of stone. In his fatigues he might have seemed a little ridiculous, like a little boy playing soldier, except for his eyes. They were expressionless, a gambler's eyes that faced straight into the camera, daring it to find out anything about him. An ocelot on a leash lay curled at his feet.

"Señor Receta y Precio," Teodoro said. Paz registered with a shock the connection of his imagined Frank Buck with this ice-eyed, aging little soldier in the photograph. "He supplied your army with soap during the Vietnam War. He told me once a general gave him a fatigue uniform like that in Saigon. I think he must have liked it." He started to turn away.

Paz stepped toward the pictures — too quickly, he was afraid, but Teodoro didn't seem to notice. "Who's this one?" He tapped the glass that covered *el halcón*'s face.

Teodoro scanned the triptych and made his "who knows" gesture with his hands. "He's in all of them," he said. "I would guess he's the native assistant, no? What's his name . . . ?"

Say it, Paz thought, *say it*. "Salomón Katun."

"Ah, *sí*. Salomón Katun." He checked his Rolex. "I will come to your hotel at four-thirty, Quintus. In a little over an hour. We will go to the airport together, no?"

He walked Teodoro as far as the *zocalo*, which was only two blocks short of the customhouse. The shadow stayed behind them. He was there, Paz knew, as a reminder.

The streets were filling with bored shopgirls and worried businessmen on their way back from the long afternoon's siesta. Tables at outdoor restaurants were starting to fill, and the noise of marimbas and TV soccer games from the bars was cranking up in volume. Paz found a table at a sidewalk café and wolfed a greasy ham and cheese torta, his first real meal since the dinner he'd lost on the breakwater last night. His guard dog sat at a table in front of the adjoining café, sipping a *café americano.*

It was less hunger than the hope that food would give him some sort of clarity, would stop his nerves and his mind from leaping, that made him eat. Since he'd left Mexico City, he'd spun further and further from what he *thought* he'd come here for, in spite of his resolution to stay close to the starting point: Baron von Hummel and the codex. Being in the baron's apartment, seeing his pictures, feeling his presence, reminded him that he'd been so caught up by the whirlwind he'd been spinning in that the baron had almost ceased to exist for him as a human being. He realized that he had been almost taking it for granted that the baron was dead, almost willing him to be dead because it was simpler to believe that he was. One part of the story, at least, would seem more sensible if he was. Now he'd been jerked back to the starting point, where he should be: who wanted him here, and why; who didn't want him here, and why.

He took the last piece of bread from his torta and broke it into two pieces. Here's Stanley, Mary Margaret, Carlos Receta y Precio, Henningsen, and Peter Lovinger, he said to himself, and dropped a piece of bread on one side of his plate. Here's Baron von Hummel and Salomón Katun, he said, and dropped the other piece on the opposite side of the plate. He slid the two pieces together, apart, together. Each time, they almost fit into a whole piece again, but not quite.

There had to be a *link.* What, damn it, what was the link?

He checked his watch: a few minutes after four. Teri's plane — which was also Gallagher's — was due in less than an hour. He squeezed the two pieces of bread on his plate together in a tight ball, then hurled it into the gutter. He got up, left a tip, and went inside the café to the cashier. Through the wavy glass of the window pane, he saw his guard dog anchor some pesos beneath his empty cup but keep his seat, waiting. Paz asked for the bathroom, which he found was at the end of a hallway that passed within three feet of the swinging doors into the kitchen. When he came out of the bathroom, he stopped at the entrance to the hallway and fumbled with his belt. His guard dog was lighting a cigarette and glancing around for an ashtray. Paz stepped through the swinging doors.

At the end of the alley behind the restaurant, he didn't risk waiting to flag a cab. He shoved his way onto an aged, rattling bus heading for a barrio he'd never heard of. He didn't care. They'd be looking for a man in a cab in any case, so he was better off staying on, then transferring. He swayed among the sweaty, packed bodies, remembering the way he'd stupidly thought in Mexico City how he'd enjoyed going under cover, becoming for a while one of the ones he hunted.

In front of the low, white airport terminal, built on marshland off the highway between Veracruz and the Mocambo, he surprised the cabby at the back end of the line of taxis when he ducked into the cab. The man started to protest that fares had to take the first taxi in line, up by the main entrance. Paz handed a five-thousand-peso note over the seat.

"Just stay in the line," Paz said. "Don't be in a hurry to move up." The man checked to see that the dispatcher wasn't watching (no neat yellow Volkswagens at this airport, only a sour-faced dispatcher with a sweaty cap and a crooked tin badge), mumbled something agreeable, and settled.

It had taken Paz three transfers to get here, and his sweaty hair was as plastered to his forehead as if he had been in a rain storm. The Mexicana 727 was already on the field, with stairs being shoved up against its door. When he'd gotten off the bus, staying low behind the crowd, he'd spotted the gently flashing light bar of the Federales' patrol car directly in front of the main entrance, and just behind that the big Ford of Mexican customs with ADUANA painted in green across the trunk. He slumped in the seat and waited. It was better that they'd gotten here before him, were inside already.

When the passengers started to come out, he saw first the two green hats of the Federales, clearing a way through the crowd. Then Teodoro's tan hat, then Gallagher, standing a whole head taller than anybody else around him. Then, looking uncomfortable and self-conscious, seeming to try to lose herself in the crowd, Maritza de la Torre. Paz sat up in the seat, caught himself, and slid low again.

She was still elegant, less severe now but nonetheless formal in a dark skirt and beige blouse. Gallagher and Teodoro were arguing. She stepped away from them as if she were going to ask the dispatcher for a cab, but Gallagher saw her and swept an arm out for her to stay close to him. She looked around her as if she were hoping for some kind of rescue, then seemed to give up and allowed one of the Federales to take her bag and put it in the customs cruiser.

Why hadn't she told Paz she was coming? Unless she herself hadn't known until the minute before she got on the plane, she'd had plenty of time to call him at the Mocambo. Even if this was nothing more than a routine business trip, why the hell hadn't she told him? She wasn't with Gallagher, not trying to edge away from him to get her own cab, as she'd done. Why was she here?

Paz's own cab moved up a car length as the line did. Teodoro held the customs cruiser's door open for Maritza. Then Teri stepped through the doors of the terminal.

In contrast to Maritza, she looked cool, loose, in a low-cut white sundress that made her dark hair seem even darker. Paz fought an impulse to lean out of the window and call to her, see her start walking to him, see her smile and be glad to see him. She stepped to the curb, set her bag down, and scanned the sandy scrubland around the terminal, seeming to be trying to get her bearings, or to make someone — Paz — appear from the waves of heat.

The Federales slammed the doors of their car almost simultaneously, as if they'd rehearsed it. Gallagher shook his head, glowered at Teodoro, and got in the back of the customs cruiser beside Maritza. Teodoro walked with stately dignity — *faster, walk faster, damn you,* Paz thought — around the front of the car and eased himself into the shotgun seat. Paz ducked as he gave one last professional glance around the loading area. The Federales switched their light bar off and, with a jerk as the transmission was dropped into gear, moved away from the curb. The customs cruiser followed, both cars moving toward the long drive that led to the highway.

"The woman in the white dress getting in the next cab," Paz said to his cabby. "Pull out of line and stop beside her. And stay in gear."

Teri looked surprised, but just for a moment, when he stepped out of his cab and grabbed her bag. With no questions, no hesitation, she followed him and slipped into the seat behind the bag he heaved in.

In the cab, he covered her hand with his and said to the cabby, "Stay behind the police cars. Once we see which direction they take on the highway, there's no need to stay close. I'll know where they're going."

Teri leaned over and smoothed back his wet hair. "Glad you could make it," she said.

His mouth went dry, coppery, when he looked at her. Not trusting himself to let go of any emotion yet, he said, "Want to tell me why you're here?"

She raised his hand, looked at the raw fingertips the concrete of the breakwater had left him with, and kissed them. Her own hand was unsteady. "You look like hell," she said.

"Does Harmon know you're here?"

"No."

"Then — "

She was working hard at not meeting his eyes. "Quint, I need to know what's going on right now, don't I? You go first. Please."

He thought of the slurred voice on the phone last night, realized he might not want to know why she'd come, and began.

He ran through for her what had happened since Monday — including what he'd just seen between Gallagher and Maritza — rushing, trying to keep it all as straight and as flat as if he were doing a debriefing. Even at that, it took him most of the drive into Veracruz to get it all out. And she'd listened the way she might have to a debriefing, calmly, asking a question now and again, then letting him go on. She'd learned her lessons at the academy in Glynco well, he thought, and for the hundredth time was impressed by her.

"Then Gallagher was the tall one with the mustache, and the woman is Maritza de la Torre?" Teri said. "I saw her get on the plane. You could have knocked her over with a feather when she saw him. No idea at all why she's here?"

"Nothing I'd go to court with," he said. "But if you want to get to Receta y Precio's in a hurry, this is the airport you'd come in to." He felt a queasy anger begin, then pushed it down, hard. He didn't need anger at something that could only be one more conjecture so far. When he'd run through everything for Teri, he'd left out himself and Maritza. Even that could come later, at a better time and place; now he needed a friend and a clear head.

They were coming into the old quarter along the *malecón*, past a trendy-looking restaurant called Señor Garlic's, and the sun was being eaten away by the tops of the hazy mountains to the west. Long shadows made the concrete benches tolerable again, so they were filling up. As soon as Paz had seen the two cruisers turn toward downtown, he'd known what the plan was. They weren't going to bother with the Mocambo but were going straight to Teodoro's office, where Gallagher could place the phone calls that would make Paz truly a fugitive. First, Gallagher would get his *salvoconducto* pulled, so that he could be busted on a gun charge. Then he'd get Paz's TDY orders revoked and his visa canceled, so Paz would officially be no better than a foreign civilian with an illegal gun. Unofficially, he'd be whatever the Mexican cops wanted him to be. What Gallagher would get under way with Washington Paz didn't know, or want to know. It would depend on how pissed he really was. Optimistically, Paz guessed he'd wait a day or so to make sure of his ground.

From Teodoro's office Paz figured they'd go to the Hotel Emporio. It was more Gallagher's style than the Mocambo: high-rise, on the waterfront, flashy disco, close to the bars and restaurants on the *zocalo*. And Maritza would want to stay clear of the beach hotels if she didn't want Paz to know she was in town — for whatever reason.

He told the cabby to drop them at the promenade along the *malecón*, beside the harbor, where the nightly carnival of Veracruz was warming up, and left Teri's bag at a tourist stand that seemed to specialize in banjos made from armadillo shells. Invisibility was harder to come by here than it had been in Mexico City, but because of the crowds he was still counting on its being possible. Hawkers jostled them in the crowd, selling soap and shells and shark's teeth, ships in bottles and straw shoes and hammocks, boxed Rice Krispies and hot-spiced boiled corn kernel "squites," fresh fruit ices and towers of cotton candy. Shore patrolmen, their long billy sticks swaying, threaded among cadets from the naval academy, whose white-gloved hands rested nonchalantly on the golden hilts of swords as they went *paseando* with their girlfriends. Beyond, in the harbor, ships with names like Campeche, Puebla, Odessa, Alexandria wore rigging lights like tiaras.

They joined an old man who sat oblivious on a bench with a book while the crowds swirled around him as if he were a rock in a stream. Paz satisfied himself that you could be five feet away and, unless you were looking hard, not get a make on Teri and himself. But from here they had a reasonable view across the boulevard, where, next to a statue of pot-bellied President Carranza, the Emporio rose.

Her eyes lost in the movement and colors, Teri said quietly, "Told you I'd get here someday."

"That you did."

He watched her focus narrow to the broad steps that led to the hotel, and as it did, her face grew more serious. It was a face whose changes he could watch for years, he thought, and still not understand much of what was behind them. His sense that there was something wholly unplaceable about her depended in part on that.

"Listen, Quint," she said. "If Stanley's airline deal falls apart because of this mess, it's not too late to stay in the service. Not yet. We can still find Gallagher and make an excuse."

"Is that why you came down?" he said.

She thought a moment before she answered. "Put it off as long as I can, huh?"

"Yep."

She kept her eyes on the hotel. "Maybe I put it off because I don't really know for sure myself why I did."

"Try me."

"OK," she said hesitantly. "OK. What happened was Harmon got me out of bed last night at three o'clock, ranting. He wanted to know if I'd heard from you, and I eventually got it out of him what was going on. When I hung up, I thought about the whole thing and decided, well, that I knew you wouldn't come home. I guess there were a lot of things going on in my head — your sister, Stanley, the baron, this being your last case — and I knew that no matter what Harmon and Gallagher told you, you just . . . wouldn't. So I thought about it some more and decided that I needed to be here. I don't know *really* why, just that you shouldn't be here by yourself, and that I was afraid for you because you were. Then, since Harmon kept me up half the night, he didn't think anything when I called in sick, and I got on a plane. I'm clear — through the weekend if I want. And you owe me three hundred and fourteen dollars, round trip." She turned her face toward the sky as if she were checking for rain. "You glad I came?"

"Except for the three hundred and fourteen dollars." Buddy hadn't told her he'd called, then.

"Well, there was something else, too." She leveled her eyes at the hotel again. "Don came by. I hadn't seen him in three years."

"Don?"

"My ex-husband, Don. What other Don?"

"Not Buddy."

"Oh, his family always called him Buddy, but I never could bring . . . " She faced him. "How did you know that?"

"I called."

"You *called*. The bastard didn't tell me. *You* didn't tell me."

"I would have gotten to it," he said.

"Damn. You mean you let me go on . . . "

She swung her head back forward. They stared at the hotel together for a long time. "What did he have to say?" Paz said finally.

"I'll tell you something, Quint. I married Don when I was nineteen and he was a back-up guitarist in a rock band, which I thought was absolutely exotic. You think things like that about men when you're nineteen. Then after I left him I thought, well, that's it. I'm done. That's what being in love and living with somebody adds up to — a guy coming in at four in the morning with his breath smelling like rotten weeds and either waking me up and wanting to make love, which he wasn't capable of by then, or waking me up by puking in the toilet. A toilet at that hour's an echo chamber, you know that? And then he's in bed until noon with a hangover while I'm off to work at seven, and by the time I get home at night he's got a beer in his hand again. That's glamour, right? That's exotic.

"So he shows up last night, late, and says he doesn't have a place to stay. Says he's been playing clubs back east, in Birmingham. He was high as a kite on something, and I put him on the couch — on the *couch*, damn it, Quint, and don't look at me that way. He kept saying that he was sorry for everything, and that he loved me and wanted me to come back to him. I couldn't kick him out. I just — couldn't.

"But I decided that *I* was getting out if he wanted to stay the next night, too. I took Herschel to the kennel and thought I'd probably just go to a motel after work. Then after Harmon called I started thinking, listening to Don snore the way he always does when he's high. *You* don't snore, Quint. It doesn't have to be the way it was with Don and me. It wasn't being in love and living with somebody that was the problem, it was being in love with *him*. Does that make any sense?"

"Yes," he said, and thought, the safety of monosyllables.

"Anyway, I was thinking about that, and I was thinking about Harmon's call and you down here, and I wanted to tell you all that before anything happened that might make it . . . too late to say it. I just, I just *needed* to be here, OK? Look, I don't just think I love you. I know I do. And there's no way on God's earth I'm getting on a plane north again until you get on it with me. So don't even bring it up."

Paz watched a kid hawk harbor tours, then watched a family of apprehensive, barefoot Indians in pantaloons and rebozos make their way through the crowds and down a dark back street.

"What are you thinking?" Teri asked him after a time.

"That the past is a Papago tracker," he said.

By the time the customs cruiser pulled up in front of the Emporio and Gallagher and Maritza got out, he'd told her about himself and Maritza. Then he was going to tell her about how he'd felt when he heard Bess was getting married, but suddenly that had to wait: Peter Lovinger was coming out of the downstairs disco in the Emporio.

Lovinger saw Maritza and was about to approach her, but drew up sharply when he spotted the ADUANA on the back of the cruiser, then Gallagher hulking out of the seat behind her. He stood for a moment, confused — long enough for Maritza to see him, too, and turn her back on him — and walked away rapidly toward the *zocalo.*

Teri spotted him first. Paz probably wouldn't have recognized the man in a different time or place. Ever since he'd talked to Gallagher about him, he'd been trying to bring his face back from half-remembered films. Gallagher was right: the man lurked. Walking away from Maritza, he seemed to head immediately for the nearest patch of shadow. He wasn't a big man, and Paz had to wait for him to cross the boulevard and come closer before he could make him out completely. He was thin-faced, thin-lipped, thin-nosed. As he moved in the crowds he twisted his body so that he walked almost sideways, slicing through them as if he were afraid of being touched. In his films he affected a kind of Montgomery Clift moroseness. The difference was that Clift had been merely treacly, whereas Lovinger had an edge of malice to him that Paz decided had to come from somewhere in the man's off-camera self. Paz thought of Stanley, the three *pistoleros,* the diamond-toothed saw blades, and was conscious of detesting the man without ever having spoken a word to him.

"You're sure it's him?" he asked Teri.

"Absolutely."

Paz got up. "Then let's stay with him."

"No, you go," Teri said. "One of us ought to stay here. Gallagher and Maritza won't recognize me."

Paz hesitated. Lovinger plunged ahead through the crowds; in seconds he'd be lost. Paz squeezed Teri's hand. "If they go anywhere, stick with them if you can — but not too far. I'll meet you back here in an hour, hour and a half. Let them go if you have to."

Teri squeezed back and nodded.

Paz didn't have far to follow. At the *zocalo,* Lovinger took an outside table at a brass-eagled restaurant called the Bar Imperial, asked for a menu, and ordered. The sun had dropped behind the tall U shape of the once-grand Hotel Diligencias;

the smell of the sea and the deep-green cool that seemed to radiate from the broad-leaved almond trees, the magnolias, the pines and palms and banana trees of the stone-paved *zocalo*, soothed the hot plaza like some biblical balm. The streets leading to it were filling again, but with slow strollers this time — families, couples holding hands, chaperoned girls, and prides of gangling boys. From the balcony of the white-frosted gingerbread loaf that was the Municipal Palace, a white-uniformed naval band was playing a concert to the changing colors of the fountains below them while the wandering marimba and guitar bands tuned up and waited their turn.

Paz was able to stay to the shadows behind an abutment of the Municipal Palace, to the side of Lovinger's table but close enough to read his face. The man was clearly anxious: his eyes were never still, pecking at people, dogs, anything that moved. He shooed away beggars and street vendors, and kept his eyes moving constantly over the *zocalo* even as he began to eat.

He had just finished his oyster cocktail when Maritza and Gallagher crossed the *zocalo*. Paz was relieved: Teri would be close by. He spotted her pulling up to a low wall behind a pillar at the front of the Municipal Palace, thirty feet away. She scanned the *zocalo*, saw him, and nodded. He settled in to watch the scene among Gallagher, Maritza, and Lovinger as if it were a dumb show, too far away to hear the words but not always needing to.

Gallagher was looking very pleased with himself; Maritza wasn't. They stopped to watch a street vendor demonstrate a plastic dancing chicken. He offered to buy it for her, she refused, looking trapped. They scanned the tables of the sidewalk cafés and bars, listened to a harpist for a while, approached the Bar Imperial, Gallagher apparently conscious of their making a good couple, of being seen. She turned when Lovinger called her name, surprised; Gallagher frowned. Lovinger embraced her, old friends, what a treat to find *you* here. Gallagher hung back, cop-suspicious, a married man with another woman. She nervously did the introductions, Lovinger all smiles, Gallagher recognizing the man and managing at best a green persimmon smile.

Lovinger was determined to talk to her, Paz thought. They'd planned to meet at the hotel, but Gallagher had blown that. (Had Lovinger come to pick her up to take her to Receta y Precio's tomorrow, and the airport had been too obvious a place to hook up?) Now Lovinger had a chance to make a meeting look accidental, and he was taking advantage of it and to hell with the risk. Paz felt the queasy anger he'd begun to feel at the airport come back, grow.

Lovinger asked them to join him, holding her chair; Gallagher, unhappy, reluctant, excused himself to go to the bathroom to shorten the time. Maritza and Lovinger watched until he was out of sight. Lovinger's face turned serious, annoyed; he motioned with his head toward Gallagher, said something, then waited for an answer. She picked up a straw, began to tie it into a knot, shook her head and answered him. He took the straw from her and flipped it away, making her meet his eyes. She shook her head again and said something emphatic.

Gallagher, Paz thought. He's asking her what the hell Gallagher is doing here.

Lovinger nodded, apparently satisfied. She leaned over the table, talking quickly and earnestly. Once she pointed in the direction of the beaches. Lovinger's face went from serious to distressed to stricken.

Henningsen. She's talked to Gallagher and she's telling him about Henningsen now, Paz thought. He realizes that I've talked to Henningsen, that Henningsen blew it, so that maybe his whole deal is blown, too. Which means he hasn't been in touch with Katun — if he ever has been — at least since last night. At the thought of Katun, he glanced at Teri. She was absorbed in the show, no one near her.

Now it was Lovinger's turn to talk fast and earnestly, gripping

Maritza's hand on the table, drilling her with his eyes. She heard him out, then gave her little shudder as if she'd just brushed a spider web, asked a question, got an answer, shook her head no, pulled her hand away. He talked fast again, she looked down at the table, hesitated, nodded yes, seeming to be close to tears. He handed her a napkin. Gallagher came back.

The meeting at Receta y Precio's and the letter, Paz thought. But why would she be here if she didn't already know about the meeting and the letter? Something else was going on, too, something Paz didn't know about. And whatever it was, it was bad news, very bad news for Maritza.

Gallagher kept standing, signaling they really ought to go. Lovinger's smile was weak, forced this time. He made no attempt to keep them, Maritza no attempt to stay. Gallagher and Maritza moved away down the line of restaurants. He indicated an open table at one, she shook her head no. She touched her cheek as if feeling for a fever. He bent to her solicitously, took her arm, and they arced across the *zocalo*, back toward the hotel, she walking stiffly. When they were out of sight, Lovinger called for his check, impatiently waving away the waiter's puzzled protest: *el señor's* dinner hadn't come yet.

Paz tried to find a word for the way he felt, so he could get a hold on it, defend himself against it. The closest he could come was *stunned*, in a physical, real sense, the way he'd felt once when a gun runner he'd trusted as an informant had caught him off guard with a rifle butt, out of Brownsville. Christ, Maritza was the one who'd called him down here to begin with!

Then he thought, of course she had been.

The rest hit him even harder, so literally hard that he leaned against the wall of the Municipal Palace to steady himself.

Maritza — the link.

When he'd first come upon Katun it was by accident. Katun

hadn't known who he was, and had tried to kill him. No one had known where Paz was then. In fact, no one in Mexico had even expected him to arrive until the evening flight, so Katun *couldn't* have been waiting for him at Collosini's. He had come to Collosini's for Collosini, had come to kill *him*. It wasn't that Katun had tried to kill Paz one minute and then protect him the next. If he'd tried to kill Paz at Collosini's, it was only because he had no idea who Paz was yet; Paz had been only some stranger who would be able to tie him to Collosini's murder.

But who in Mexico had known when Paz was expected to arrive? Only two people: Gallagher and Maritza.

Then Katun had shown up outside Maritza's apartment. Not to kill this time, only to watch, maybe to protect.

Who had known or suspected he was going to Maritza's apartment? Only two people: Gallagher and Maritza.

Then the train. Then the Mocambo.

Only two people.

Of those two people, who had known Salomón Katun?

Only one.

His anger washed over him as blindingly as the sea water had last night. For some reason he was being protected, yes — but no matter what the reason, he'd been lied to and manipulated. He felt betrayed, but more than betrayed. He felt used. All along, from the time Maritza had called him in Tucson to the night in her apartment, he'd been goddamn *used*. And he had no idea even what he'd been used for.

He made sure that Teri was still in place, then pushed away from the wall and went to the back of the Municipal Palace, so he could watch Maritza and Gallagher make their slow way down the street that would take them back to the Emporio, where Maritza's fever would get worse, Paz was sure, and she would have to go to bed early. He knew as he watched Maritza fade into the crowd that, whether he had a right to or not, he was feeling a far deeper kind of betrayal than he'd felt the night on the border out of Brownsville.

When he got back up to the front of the Municipal Palace, Lovinger's table was empty, and Lovinger was already at the far corner of the *zocalo*, waiting to cross the street in front of the Café Parroquia. He waved to a Land Rover that sat a few spaces from the corner on a side street, and an arm waved back at him from the driver's side, then pointed at something in the *zocalo*. Fifteen paces behind Lovinger, in the direction the driver of the Land Rover had pointed, Teri tried to fend off a hammock salesman, who blocked her view of Lovinger with the curtain of hammocks he held up for her. She hadn't seen the signals between Lovinger and the driver, but Paz knew that whoever was in the Land Rover could have seen her from the moment she stepped out to follow Lovinger.

She broke away from the hammock salesman and glanced back toward Paz. He motioned for her to wait. She shook her head and waved him on to catch up with her, then turned to follow Lovinger across the street.

She must have looked for Paz when Lovinger got up, Paz thought as he stepped into the *zocalo* after her, and assumed he was going around the palace to cut Lovinger off. Had he made himself clear enough about Lovinger? The bastard was behind at least two killings so far. If he thought somebody was following him . . .

Paz sped up. He was halfway across the *zocalo*, dodging the hammock salesman, when Lovinger reached the Land Rover. Lovinger kept walking, leading Teri, until she was a couple of paces beyond the Land Rover, too, then stopped. As he did, the driver of the Land Rover got out and circled the cab, to put himself behind her.

Teri caught the setup almost immediately, but even that was too late. She was a base runner caught in a run-down, blocked on one side by the Land Rover and on the other by the wall of the Parroquia. Paz broke into a run himself, just as the hammock salesman opened his arms and spread his hammocks like the wings of some huge, rainbow-colored bird. Paz sidestepped, but not in time. The salesman went down in a loose heap of hammocks with Paz on top of him, both of them tangled like netted fish.

If Teri had stopped and let Lovinger confront her, had tried to talk her way out of it, Paz might have had time to disentangle himself and make it to her. But she turned and threw a quick jab to the driver's stomach, then tried to run past him, which gave Lovinger the seconds he needed to grab her arms from the rear. Now they had no choice: a dozen people were watching, and a couple of sailors had already started toward them. It was either take her with them or let her go. The driver jerked open the door of the Land Rover, and Lovinger shoved Teri inside.

By the time Paz had fought loose from the hammocks and then through the traffic in front of the Parroquia, the Land Rover had turned the corner and disappeared north, onto the overpass that led to the Papantla highway. Frantically Paz tried to hail a taxi, realizing only when he saw the cop running toward him from the *zocalo* that he had his .45 in the hand he was waving at the taxis. He stopped to scoop Teri's purse away from a pair of street urchins, then ran, heading for the old part of the city and its dark labyrinth of alleys.

The Land Rover had gone north, toward Papantla, but Paz's only option had been to head south, to Boca del Río, where Stanley and Mary Margaret would put down tomorrow afternoon. He had no place else to go. No one would be looking for him here in this little backwater town, maybe not even Salomón Katun, who Paz supposed had headed back to his village when the wall of cops had formed around Paz last night.

And he had nobody to turn to, just as he'd told himself he wouldn't when he'd walked out of his hotel room this afternoon. Even if he called Teodoro, even if Teodoro agreed to help now, a customs *comandante* would be forced to yield the Federales and the army their territory. If Paz was right, if the fact the Land Rover had taken the Papantla highway backed his logic that Lovinger had taken Teri to the safety of the jungles and Receta y Precio's preserve, the heavy-handed presence of the army or Federales there could mean she'd simply disappear forever.

But no matter where she was, he had no place besides Receta y Precio's to begin to pick up a trail from. And he'd never make it onto Receta y Precio's property except through a side door. The cops would be expecting him to head north toward Papantla, first of all; he wouldn't have any kind of chance on the highway. Then this was Mexico: the property of men like Receta y Precio would be guarded better than a federal prison. The only reasonable way he had of coming in through a side door now was to land at Receta y Precio's airstrip tomorrow. Until then, he had to stay put and wait.

He sat on the edge of a twin bed, only the dim light of the bed lamp glowing, in a sky-blue, concrete-block hotel, two storeys, asphalt tile floors, beds with iron frames that had been painted and chipped and painted again. The shower drained into a hole in the middle of the bathroom floor. It was Boca del Río's best.

Once more the ante had been upped, this time in an increment so enormous he knew thinking about it could paralyze him. Yet how could he *not* think about it? What was the trick? How did you shut your mind down for twenty hours or so, as if it were a computer or a refrigerator? He remembered that the night before he'd left Tucson, Teri hadn't wanted to let go of him while they were making love, holding on as if she were afraid she would float away if he wasn't there to anchor her. Tonight he had let go of *her*.

He got up, conscious of moving very slowly, very deliberately, reminding himself that he was in control of his body, at least. Teri's purse lay on the cigarette-scorched Formica dresser top, and beside it sat the bottle of José Cuervo he'd bought from the bar downstairs. He opened the bottle, poured a tumbler two-thirds full, and drank it. Then he stared at Teri's purse, started to reach for it, but instead picked up the bottle and poured the tumbler full this time.

Where was she right now? What was happening to her? She'd come down because she was afraid for *him*, she'd said. He knew he could watch Lovinger and anybody connected with him, even Maritza, bleed to death in a ditch and not lift a finger to help, the way his grandfather claimed he had done to a Chilean cattle thief once. He could put them in the ditch.

He took the .45 out of its holster, checked the clip in it and switched the safety off before he laid it on the bedside table, then went to the window. He put his face close to the cool pane and scanned the scrubby clearing around the hotel. Just at the edge of the jungle, he thought he saw something move and flash palely in the moonlight, though he wasn't sure. It could have been no more than an iguana stirring the underbrush.

He stayed at the window a long time, watching.

NINE

BOCA DEL RÍO was a home-folks spa a few miles south of Veracruz. On Sundays when Paz's father hadn't been too bad, it had been good for lazy side trips from the Mocambo: fruit trees and seafood restaurants and a little bandstand and beaches where the Atoyac River spilled into the Mandinga estuary. Weekdays, like today, the small blue concrete-block hotel dozed empty in the sun while bored shopkeepers sat on its porch and watched families of monkeys in mango trees pick ticks off one another.

During the morning Paz tried to sleep, as if he were looking for sleep to send him answers; but each time he started to drift off, his thoughts circled and wheeled like birds. Two nights ago seemed ten years ago. What he had to do had looked so simple then: he would fly up under a reasonable cover to Receta y Precio's with Stanley, find out about a letter, listen to what they wanted from Stanley, get what else he could, in and out, take the heat when he got back. But two nights ago Peter Lovinger hadn't had Teri, and two nights ago Paz hadn't been pretty sure Maritza would be waiting at Receta y Precio's. Either of those circumstances would make trying to use a cover impossible. Hiding on the plane couldn't work now, either: since Maritza had surely told Lovinger that no one any longer knew where Paz was, Lovinger would surely be cautious enough to have the plane searched.

Worse, Paz didn't have twelve days. He had one.

The computer printouts he'd found folded into a side pocket of Teri's purse eased his mind on one point, at least. They contained the information he'd asked for on Collosini and Stanley. As best he could make out from the computerese, what Teri had found about Collosini was not much: nothing had come into the States from his company since the codex had disappeared. She'd sent a memo to Harmon suggesting that he request a hold on Collosini's company's next shipment, if there was one, but that was no help now.

It was the IRS information that told him most. Stanley had apparently paid a series of consultant's fees over the past couple of years, totaling over nine hundred thousand dollars, to an outfit called Afrimex, S.A., whose registered business agent in the United States was Peter Lovinger. So far as Paz could tell, Afrimex had done nothing but funnel that money through a Panamanian bank to various post-office-box banks in the Cayman and Grand Turk Islands. A telex from Gallagher that Teri had included noted that money from one of those banks had been used to buy into Stanley's airline. Before the payments to Afrimex, there were three consultant's fees that totaled about forty thousand dollars to Producciones Collosini, S.A. *Those* stopped about the time the fees to Afrimex had begun.

Whatever Stanley had with Collosini, he went bigger with Lovinger, Paz thought. If it was artifacts — and it had to be — that was what Lovinger had on Stanley. But Paz was convinced Stanley wasn't acting as any kind of dealer for them: his IRS papers showed he was worth just over forty-two million at last count. He wouldn't jeopardize that for a chance to pick up a few quick bucks on nine hundred thousand worth of artifacts. At least to that extent, Stanley was clean.

Paz flipped through the printouts again. This Afrimex used a Panamanian bank. The three hoods Henningsen had sent north were Panamanian. One more track, one more piece of sign, Ethelbert. But leading where? He still didn't know why those *pistoleros* were in Los Angeles. Or what they had to do with a missing Maya codex.

In the margins he found a couple of penciled notes in Teri's handwriting. One said, "Bank in Panama checked by Customs rep last year in arms transaction. No firm case. Bank itself checks out legitimate." The other read, "Info copy of telex from IRS to Gallagher in D.F. re Carlos Receta y Precio & Peter Lovinger (?who are these?) indicates money trouble — esp. Lovinger — heavy losses in overseas et al. investments."

Panama again, Paz thought. But arms? Was that a coincidence, or one more thing he had to try to shove into place — and how? The money trouble made more sense, and could explain Lovinger's hurry to get Stanley down here, especially if the letter from Humboldt Méndez was as full of bad news as Maritza's reaction had told him it was.

But it still gave him no clue at all to what the damned letter was *about*.

One day left, he thought. And he had to find a way to protect Teri, first of all, but there was so much else he couldn't let go of, either: Stanley and Mary Margaret, Baron von Hummel, the codex, a whole city of irreplaceable artifacts. A simple way — he didn't have time for anything else. It was as if he had hold of an equation that stretched all the way across Father Carnes's long blackboard at the Jesuit school in Buenos Aires, an equation whose solution had to equal one.

God, how he had hated that blackboard, those impossible equations. He remembered the feeling he'd had when he walked into that cold schoolroom: it was as if he'd gotten a piece of raw wool stuck somewhere in his throat, something blocking it that was expanding, choking him.

He looked at Teri's handwriting again, the familiar neat loops and even letters, then cleared his throat to try to drive away the cloying wool.

The twin-prop Conquest sent shimmers of late afternoon heat up from its aluminum body as it waited on the otherwise empty runway. Paz had told Mary Margaret the truth: the airstrip wasn't much, a windsock and a long, flat, sandy runway a couple of hundred yards beyond where the town's main street dribbled away into a trail through the thin jungle. It hadn't deteriorated much in the five years since Paz had seen it. He hadn't expected it to. As close to Veracruz as it was, it was too convenient to smugglers for their friends in the government to let it go entirely.

They talked beneath the dense shade of a banyan tree, Paz and Stanley and Mary Margaret, while the red-haired pilot roasted in the Conquest. The plane had come in early, as Paz had wanted, so they had an enforced time to talk. Even now Stanley wore his dark three-piece suit. Here, surrounded by the forest, he looked more like a hulking raven than ever. And Mary Margaret's jewels were as out of place among the bugs and sun and elephant grass as snow. They were dressed for Carlos Receta y Precio's country *finca*, or what they thought it would be.

Paz told them about Teri, believed their shock, and asked enough questions to get Stanley moving in the right direction. Then it was time to listen, to let what Stanley said become a room you combed, looking for the one overlooked thing, the one piece of evidence that would make the others snap into place, to see if he could hear the one number that would solve the equation.

Stanley was grave, embarrassed, formal, worried. As he spoke, he fiddled with his glasses and paced in a little invisible square. He talked more than Paz thought he'd ever heard him talk in the dozen years combined he'd been married to Mary Margaret, as if he'd been accumulating unspent words all those years like money. Mary Margaret stood close to him, looking off occasionally toward the airstrip. Stanley said he had told her on the plane down most of what he was now telling Paz.

Nonetheless, they were both clearly in pain, and Paz watched Mary Margaret, sharing that pain, as Stanley talked.

"Nine hundred thousand," he said to Stanley. "How did you get nine hundred thousand into the thing and still not understand what was going on?"

"I didn't *know* in the beginning that the pieces I was buying were illegal, Quint. They were small things at first — a potshard with a speech glyph on it, a little broken clay head of an idol — that I'd buy from a child at one of the ruins Mary took us to. And then I let myself go. I don't let myself go often; you know that. But I became obsessed with the whole idea of having part of a civilization that had utterly vanished. I was like so damned many other people who have private collections, I suppose — I didn't *want* to know what was illegal. I told myself that the pieces I was buying were better off with me than sitting in the basement of a Mexican museum, or buried in the grave of someone who had been dead six hundred years. I'm sorry," he said, not to Paz but to Mary Margaret. She looked away. Paz knew that even though she'd heard this already today, the second time was pounding it in, making it more real, like a death you have to get used to. He moved closer to her.

The pain deepened in Stanley's face but he went on. "I think I began to admit to myself that they probably were illegal — though I never did permit myself to research the law and know for sure — when I first dealt with Collosini directly. I'd heard my gallery owner mention his name on the telephone one day and had some of my people in Mexico City locate him, you see."

"Lovinger got to you through Collosini? It was Lovinger, wasn't it?"

"Lovinger. He came to me supposedly to talk about my investing in a film, which I would never have done — not in one of that man's, in any case. He mentioned Collosini, one thing led to another, and he asked me if I would be interested in buying some pieces from his own collection." He stopped his pacing abruptly and faced Paz. "Do you remember the museum robbery in Mexico City four years ago, Quint?"

"I do." The Museum of Anthropology. Paz remembered that the Customs bulletin on the robbery said that most archaeologists called it the loss of some of the finest pieces of pre-Columbian art ever discovered. Christ Jesus.

"The pieces he brought me — a Zapotec ball player, a woman in labor — were small ones. I had no reason to suspect they were from the museum. But that didn't matter, did it? Lovinger would have sworn that I knew all about it. I had even signed a receipt! That's how little I wanted to admit to myself what I might be involved in."

"Why didn't you talk to me, Stanley?"

Stanley took his glasses off, carefully wiped them, glanced at Mary Margaret, and put them back on. "I hired you for the airline because I hoped you would stop whatever they had in mind, Quint. *I* didn't know, but I hoped desperately that you would find out and stop it without my having to know. I'm sorry for that, too. It was cowardly."

Mary Margaret walked a few steps away toward the airstrip and turned back to face Stanley, as if she needed some kind of physical distance from him. She was near tears, Paz could see, and her face was drawn tight with fury. "For the love of *God*, Stanley! There are people *dead* in this. There are people missing, people Quint and I love — and who you might, too, if you'd ever taken the time." She turned away, took a step, turned back. "I have to know something, Stanley. Did the codex and that poor old man ever matter? Did any of us? In all this collecting and buying and selling you were doing, did any of you ever stop to remember what finding that codex *meant?*"

"Yes! What else can I do now that I'm not doing, Mary? All along I've thought of looking for that codex as a kind of, oh, reparation for what I'd done. I didn't know who the other backers were any more than you did. I didn't know until

Lovinger told me he and Receta y Precio wanted to buy into
the airline — and I didn't find out the reason he wanted for
them to do that till just this week. Then it was too late."

"Then you know what's been going on up there — the
looting, all of it?" Paz said.

"What looting?"

"Of the city the baron found the codex in, about Lovinger's
carting the whole damn thing off. Isn't that what you meant?"

"Oh, dear God," Mary Margaret said.

"No. I meant the drugs. I had no idea . . . I meant the drugs,
Quint. I thought surely your people would — well, it's your
business to know those things, isn't it? I meant the drugs
they're setting themselves up to smuggle on my airline."

Like tumblers in some huge lock, the pieces slammed into
place. The *pistoleros*, the overseas investments mentioned in
Teri's note, the laundering by Afrimex, the post-office-box
banks, the urgency to get Stanley down here if something was
going wrong with the artifacts scam, the airline itself. Paz had
looked at the surface and seen what there was, had seen how
those things could fit into the artifacts business, but he hadn't
seen what *might* be done with it all! Eight, ten flights a day,
steadily, he'd thought about Stanley's airline — so why limit
it to artifacts? If you had that kind of ironclad operation, why
just use it to make millions when you could almost as easily
make *tens* of millions, and, over a period of time, hundreds.
Take the money you make on artifacts and build on it, use it,
increase it fifty or a hundred times. It was classic, prudent
capitalism.

Paz took a breath, held it, then said, "Slowly, Stanley. Tell
me."

"Well, I got a telephone call two days ago. The man had
some kind of accent. He said we shouldn't fight each other —
talked about 'product' and said I shouldn't try to oppose him
by setting up my own distribution system. Suggested some
sort of partnership, in fact. I had no idea what he was talking

about until he mentioned the airline and some Panamanians, then I remembered the bank I'd sent Lovinger's money to. I tried to tell the man I had nothing to do with any of that, but he insisted I did. Then, the more I thought about it, the more I realized that yes, yes I did have something to do with it. And that I couldn't ignore it any longer."

"What did you tell him?"

"That I'd deliver his message. In person."

No wonder Lovinger had looked so desperate when Maritza had told him about Henningsen — as Paz was more sure than ever she'd done. He knew that if Paz got word out about his three Panamanians, his whole setup would be blown. He wasn't going just for wholesaling his drugs; he was going for control of the street action, too. The Panamanians were *tenientes*, lieutenants.

And Paz assumed he must have people standing in line to supply him. He could have started with Receta y Precio and the *mota* that could be grown on Receta y Precio's land — and maybe Katun's — to build a stock. Then, when Fiesta Airlines was in business, he could use those jungles on Receta y Precio's land to hide a whole transshipment operation, a "trampoline" for Colombian and Peruvian coke, Jamaican grass — it was unlimited. Instead of risking losing profits by sending the stuff north by airline mules or face having it interdicted by Customs planes and boats, growers would fight each other to plug into Lovinger's network.

No wonder there had been "money troubles" and overseas investments. If this was what Lovinger was setting up for, he'd have to have gone on the line with everything he had. And he'd have to be operating on a schedule with no slack at all. If something went wrong *any*where, he'd have suppliers, lenders, investors, buyers on him in a minute. And Paz knew those people, had faced them in courtrooms, bought information on their competitors from them in Bogotá hotel rooms, been shot at by them. If they suspected Lovinger wasn't about to deliver as promised, he'd be a dead man.

"And that's what you plan to do. Deliver his message in person," Paz said.

"Yes, Quint," Mary Margaret said firmly. "We do."

"But I'm even worse off than I was," Stanley said. "If Peter Lovinger can connect me with the artifacts, and now with this looting business, it strikes me that he's got a perfect case built against me — even without the drugs. Wouldn't you say, Quint?"

"So far."

"Then what about this letter? You think it might have something to do with the looting? You think it might affect what he's doing up there?"

"That's a strong possibility."

Stanley raised his arms a foot or so, then let them drop. "Nothing to be done. I got us into this affair, and I have to see what these people want from me now. They're clearly not going to go away."

"No."

"The important thing is Teri now, of course. If this business of theirs has gone foul, I've got some room to negotiate — go for what I can get and hope it's enough."

He looked at Paz and Mary Margaret, seeming to wait for them to dispute him, then brought his watch up and held his glasses steady. "Look here, Quint, we've barely got an hour. My pilot's melted out there."

Paz suddenly felt light, felt as if air had somehow replaced the thick mud that had seemed to fill his veins since last night. He watched the missing factor form in the equation and the answer write itself on that long blackboard in Father Carnes's classroom: one, the simplest number. Yes, he thought, by God, yes! He closed the two paces between himself and Stanley and hugged him. "Stanley, you're absolutely brilliant," he said. Stanley looked at him as if he might be dangerous.

Stanley had said "negotiate," and Paz had understood what Stanley had that tipped the scales completely. He had the simplest power of all, the one thing Lovinger didn't. He had money. If Lovinger had gotten bad news about his artifact business and was worried that Paz might be about to throw his drug distribution network off, too, he *had* to be thinking about money. *Stanley* had the control, could make terms — Stanley had understood that immediately. Habit again, Paz thought, a habit he has and I don't.

How Stanley could use that control, that power, Paz didn't know yet. But he had it to use — *they* had it to use. That was enough for now. He didn't have to go into Receta y Precio's under cover, and he didn't have to hide to get in. He could *walk* in: Lovinger needed Stanley, and more, he needed Paz. He felt as if he'd just come up for air from waters far deeper than he'd been in two nights ago.

Stanley, still puzzled, backed away from him, then grunted. "How's that hotel in town?" he asked.

"First rate," Paz said.

Stanley considered. "Lovinger insisted that Mary come along. I suppose I'd become unaccustomed to questioning him." He paced one of his squares off. "This whole thing has gotten to be more serious than I'd anticipated. Do you think Mary would be better off staying here?"

"Ask her."

"Stanley," Mary Margaret said. "You're on very thin ice."

"That's precisely why I have to keep on with this," Stanley said.

"Yes, you do. But that's not what I mean. I'm still your wife, am I not?"

"Of course."

"Then please stop being a jackass and let's get in the airplane." She raised her chin so that the diamonds of her necklace caught the sun and flashed, then turned sharply and strode toward the Conquest.

Stanley looked bewildered a moment, then said, "Well, Quintus," pushed his glasses nervously up on his nose, and followed.

Paz watched them go and, one last time, glanced behind him at the path back toward Boca del Río, where he imagined the weekend crowd beginning to fill up the little hotel, the shopkeepers waking up, a band taking its place on the white bandstand. It's going to be over soon, he thought. One way or another, it's going to be over. God help us. He eased the weight of his pistol against his side and walked the short path to the plane.

The Conquest shook cones off the sea pines it skimmed as it lumbered into the air from the dirt strip. Veracruz fell away behind it; the wind-slanted sea pines and prickly pear cactus of the sandy coast gave way to flat pastures and stands of elephant grass that could slice a walking man's legs as surely as could the machetes of the cane cutters in the shrinking patchwork of fields below. The pilot stayed low and followed the highway, which itself never risked getting lost by wandering too far from the coastline.

Stanley worked at the desk built into the front of the plane; Mary Margaret sat in the back and stared steadily out the window, lost in herself. Paz sat across from Stanley and watched him make notes in the margins of memos, scribble things on a yellow pad, punch a calculator. Paz saw the papers tremble in his hand, and noticed the way he had to read the same memo two or three times to make it stick. But still he envied him even that partial escape.

To negotiate, he thought. *Everything* had to be negotiated, and all at once. Teri first, and Teri alone if need be. He didn't think Lovinger would have hurt her yet, because he'd have no idea who she was. All her ID had been in her purse, so she could have come up with a safe cover — for the time being. But when it became clear that she was connected with Paz and his family, they'd know she was a negotiating piece. Her life might depend on the negotiations' not going wrong.

Baron von Hummel also had to be part of the bargaining.

Paz knew clearly what he had to do: that if it came to a choice of Teri or the baron, he had no choice. But if the power existed to negotiate for Teri, it existed to negotiate for the baron, too. If Lovinger didn't actually have the baron, he would know where he was. Lovinger's involvement in everything that had happened was too deep for him to claim a blank spot about him.

Then there was still Stanley to keep out of prison if possible, the family to protect. And for Customs, the codex to find and a smuggling operation to stop.

But how, damn it, how to negotiate? What to put on the table so that Lovinger would let them walk away with what they wanted — or walk away at all. The answer seemed close enough to touch, but Paz couldn't feel the *shape* of it yet.

He knew that part of the reason he wasn't thinking well was that this one mattered so much. He had gotten into this whole mess because of the past. But it was the future he was fighting for now — Teri's, Mary Margaret's, Stanley's, his own, and, indirectly, Craig's. Is it fun again, Paz? he asked himself. Is this what drove Bess away from you, this same damned obsessiveness that wouldn't allow you to back away from this case when you had the chance? At least he'd kept Bess, unlike Teri, a safe distance from it in the old days.

"How do you plan to play it?" he asked Stanley suddenly and probably too sharply.

"See what they want first," Stanley said. "You can't negotiate until you establish a floor." He went back to his work, hiding.

Paz pulled him back out of it. "This is a business transaction, then? Just that?"

Stanley paused a moment. "Essentially. If it weren't so scummy, I'd say this taking over of my airline was a brilliant business move. Lovinger's got a complete conveyor belt now — raw material all the way to consumer. Under other circumstances I'd admire him."

The more Paz thought about that, the more wrong it sounded. "You're not making sense, Stanley," he said.

"It *is* a good business move."

"No. About Lovinger. What's his track record in business?"

"So far as I know, he doesn't have much of one."

"No, he doesn't. He's just a B-movie actor. If he could put something like this together, why didn't he do it a long time ago?" What had Paz thought about this operation when Stanley had first told him about it? Classic, prudent capitalism. With a string of nothing but failing films behind him, what did Peter Lovinger know about any kind of capitalism? Paz's excitement began to build again. "Is Lovinger the only one you've met with?"

"Well, generally. I only met with him once when someone else was along. I mentioned it — the time that Lovinger brought Carlos Receta y Precio along to work out their buying into my airline. It was the first time I'd met Carlos at all, in fact. So far as I had been concerned before that, he was a kind of silent partner, maybe even an unwilling one, as I was."

But when there was some real business to conduct, Paz thought, he was there. Real business, not just blackmail, which was a simple enough transaction that anybody, even an actor, could handle it. "How did they work together?"

Stanley considered. "Carlos didn't say much. He let Lovinger do most of the talking, but I noticed that Lovinger kept glancing at him as he talked. It struck me at the time that he was looking for Carlos's approval, though I dismissed that because Carlos never bothered to give it. He seemed more than anything else to *tolerate* Lovinger. It was, oh, a kind of chemistry at work, I think, nothing I could pin down. Like watching two animals and recognizing almost right away which one is the dominant one. You should understand that, Quint. In your work you should. *I* understand it; I'd even say that of the two of them, I felt much more comfortable with Carlos. He's a businessman, after all." He went nervously back to his calculator and began to punch at it, apparently at random, as if it were a substitute for worry beads.

Paz breathed deeply and sank back in the seat. Again, *again* he'd looked at what was instead of what might be. Everywhere he'd looked, he'd seen Lovinger and had assumed Lovinger was all there was to see. It was as if he'd been following the tracks of a dog so closely that he hadn't seen the footprints of the man beside it. Maybe it was true, maybe he was too damned old, too rusty to be let loose at this anymore.

It should have been so clear all along. Carlos Receta y Precio. The key, the final link Paz had been groping for. Peter Lovinger wasn't behind this thing! He had the kinds of international connections Receta y Precio didn't have, and Receta y Precio was only too glad to use those. But it was Receta y Precio's show. It *had* to be. Receta y Precio was the one who had known about the artifacts; Christ, he had even once owned the whole city full of them. He had the jungle lands to grow the *mota* on and to use for the drug trampoline, he knew Salomón Katun, knew the baron, had the business sense. All he needed was someone to front for him. And he'd found his man.

In the end, then, Receta y Precio was a businessman and this was a business proposition. It was as simple as that for Stanley, and it would be for Receta y Precio, too. He and Stanley would understand each other, had common interests, a common sense of the way the world works, just as the man who had called Stanley to negotiate a partnership for dope distribution had assumed a commonality.

Paz had his answer.

"Stanley."

Stanley looked up from his calculator.

"Stanley, you know what you've just told me, don't you?"

"Yes. Yes, I think I do — now."

"Then I want you to tell Receta y Precio what you just said to me about admiring his business. Leave out the part about its being scummy, and tell him that."

"Why?"

"I want you to negotiate yourself into a full partnership with Receta y Precio."

"Pardon me?" Stanley took his glasses off.

"Agree to tide him over until he can put their operation back together, but you admire Receta y Precio's business sense so much you want a partnership in exchange. It won't come cheap, but I want you to keep him going. You negotiate deals that way every day, so it should be possible for you."

"That's absurd," Stanley said quietly.

"Is it? There's a very fine line, Stanley, between what you were doing when you bought those artifacts and a rip-off. You think they'll doubt your sincerity?"

Stanley hesitated. "I meant, why should I keep him in business?" he said, still quietly.

"Because Receta y Precio is a businessman. You're offering him the only thing he'll go for — the best business proposition he can get. You're offering him you and me together. Listen to me, Stanley. What does Receta y Precio know about me so far? He knows that I've disobeyed orders and have gone underground. Maritza's told him that. He knows that I've gotten an American consul killed and am in trouble for it — how serious, they don't know. They know that I'm a short-timer — just over a week to go in Customs, not retiring but flat quitting — and that I'm working with you. If he thinks I've turned, I've rolled over, I'm a gold mine to him.

"And so are you. Who'd he rather work with? Lovinger? Or you, with me in tow? Given your connections and mine, who's more valuable to him? You're wanting something from him, but you're offering him something in return that works to his benefit, too. How can he turn it down?"

Stanley's face stayed blank, gave nothing away. "And you expect them to give up Teri, too?"

"Why not? They'll have no way of knowing anything about her except that she's working with me. Does she look like a Customs cop to you?"

"That's all you want?"

"No. I want a case built and I want them to feel secure enough to keep coming to the States, where we can get at them. That's for Customs, Stanley, for the crown. For Mary Margaret, I want a husband who's not doing time in a federal prison. Ask your lawyers. Ask them how quick they'd jump at a chance to have you cooperate in a federal investigation right now."

"I see."

"No, you don't, not completely. If you're going to be a partner, I want you to insist on knowing everything. I want you to demand to know whatever they know about the codex, about Baron von Hummel, about Maritza de la Torre, about a man named Salomón Katun, and about why they made such a big deal of specifically getting *me* TDYed down here. You won't *get* everything they know about those things, of course, but if you're a negotiator, negotiate. Get what you can."

Stanley slowly put his glasses back on. "You have a high opinion of my abilities, Quint. Higher than I have."

"You can do it," Paz said.

Stanley turned his head and looked vaguely out the window. "I honestly don't know," he said.

"You've got to," Paz said. "It's all there is."

As they droned up the coast, towering, flat-bottomed clouds moved toward the land like overloaded barges. The pilot stayed with the highway, which was a careful line drawn between luminous green jungle mountains on one side and buff sand dunes on the other. From memory and imagination, Paz added details, the way he might have added them to one of Craig's model railroad landscapes. The blue coves would have white herons in them; rain water ponds would be covered in green, yellow, and purple hyacinth. His memory brought back clusters of mangos, bananas, coconuts, bright reddish cashew fruit; brought back thatched roofs, huts of clay, logs, cane, huts on stilts; a dozen dismal restaurants named Del Mar; villages where sausages and goats hung fly-heavy in the sun; orchids.

It was the country in which he had told Teri you could find Eden. Had she gotten here before him?

The clouds took over just as they banked inland toward Papantla, hurrying the dusk. Stanley stuck his head into the cockpit to check the coordinates for Receta y Precio's landing strip with his pilot. Then as the pilot began a banking descent, he backed out of the cockpit and pointed out a window on the right side of the plane. "Papantla," he said.

Paz leaned to the window, concentrating, remembering, making a mental map. From above, the Totonac town of Papantla was a postcard: narrow streets curving up and down the sides of low green mountains, red tiled roofs giving way to thatch as the streets turned into trails, a spired cathedral dominating it all. But Paz had been here before, a time when a squad of soldiers had been wiped out as they tried to raid a pot plantation. There was that, too, about these mountains where a thousand dirt tracks and paths led off into the covering jungles. If Receta y Precio was truly going into the business, he had been born in the right place.

The pilot circled. A couple or three miles from town at the end of a dirt road, an airstrip ran along the flat crest of a hill. Below it in the valley lay a long lake, and between the two a white housing compound took up a good five or six acres of the gently sloping hillside. Paz made out a large flat building he took to be the main house, a handful of outbuildings, and what appeared to be kennels or cages scattered haphazardly over the rest of the property, some partly hidden by trees at the edge of the lawns.

Then, a mile or two from the compound — past the lake and over the next hill — he saw a long, uneven double row of thatched huts lining what appeared to be no more than a widening of one of the trails that led from Papantla. At the end of the trail was a larger wooden building — a store? — and a hut roughly twice the size of the others.

The *cacique*'s hut, Paz thought. Salomón Katun's hut. He had a momentary sensation that was both dread and excitement, a sensation again that he remembered from his hunts as a boy. He and his grandfather's head gaucho had tracked a puma in the foothills of the Andes all day once, to a cave high on the face of a cliff. The old gaucho in his blousy *bombacho* pants and beret had sat to brew himself a gourd of maté tea, pointed to the cave and said nonchalantly, "There it is, boy. It's yours," and Paz had set off up the cliff alone. The sensation was the same now, like looking up at the cave just before he started up the cliff.

A hundred yards past the big wooden building was a small hillock with mounds of fresh dirt around it, and running in a long rectangle into the jungle from it were maybe a dozen smaller hillocks, discernible only as bumps in the thick vegetation. Temple mounds, Paz thought, the heart of the old city. The thatched huts along the trail seemed a vague reflection of it in a distorted, dim mirror. As the plane banked for a landing, Paz picked out a narrow path that led through the jungle from those huts to Receta y Precio's housing compound. He wouldn't want to try it after dark.

Mary Margaret turned from the window at last as the Conquest bumped down onto the grassy landing strip, and made a short *oh* sound. She fixed her eyes on the cabin of the plane as if it represented some final touch with civilization for her.

The pilot turned the tail of the plane and taxied back to the head of a well-maintained dirt road that led away down the hill toward the housing compound. A Land Rover waited on the road; in the fading light Paz could make out the form of a driver behind the windshield, but no more. When the pilot cut the engines a gust of wind from the approaching thunderstorm rocked the plane, and then the silence seemed utter. Mary Margaret, in some kind of instinctive reversion, crossed herself.

As the pilot lowered the door and steps, the Land Rover's engine started and it moved slowly toward the plane. The pilot helped Mary Margaret out first. Then Paz, making sure his coat was hanging free so he could reach the .45, made his way down the steep steps behind Stanley.

He'd just reached the bottom when the Land Rover jerked to a stop and the driver, a sawed-off shotgun in his hand, stepped dramatically down to meet them. Paz's detestation rose like the aftertaste of bad meat when he recognized him.

Peter Lovinger, in a bush jacket and faded jeans, smiling, shook Mary Margaret's and Stanley's hands, mumbling half phrases about how glad he was, but his eyes — and the shotgun — stayed on Paz. Paz spread his legs slightly, let his arms hang loose and ready, and waited for his turn. Lovinger's smile unbent as he approached Paz.

"Peter Lovinger," he said, and instead of offering his hand, gripped and steadied the shotgun with it. "And your name?"

"Quintus Paz." With a great effort Paz held himself absolutely still as Lovinger's shotgun rose upward and pointed toward his face.

TEN

LOVINGER HAD FRISKED THEM. Now, with Paz's .45 in his belt, he stayed maybe five yards behind them as they walked in a loose pack down the road ahead of him, his sawed-off shotgun trained steadily on them as if he were a guard on a prison gang. The road led from the airstrip downhill through a swatch of new-growth forest for a distance of four or five city blocks. Already the faded gray light was robbing the forest of green, was making the trees and underbrush lose their outlines and seem to close in on the road, as if they were only waiting for night to fall so they could take their own back.

"You're supposed to be a businessman," Lovinger said as they walked. His voice was vaguely familiar to Paz now, too — a little raspy, a little too carefully modulated, the kind of voice you could imagine oozing easily over Hollywood telephone wires by the hundreds making deals that never would happen. There was both a promise and a coldness in it. "We had a business appointment, Stanley."

"This is business," Stanley said over his shoulder.

"Bad business, Stanley. You're going to try to tell me this guy's on our side now, right? That's the way it's playing? Come on, Stanley."

"That's the way it's playing," Stanley said calmly, giving away nothing. Paz thought, you're impressive so far, Stanley.

"Try it on Carlos. Carlos likes freaky things. Hey, Paz."

"Yeah," Paz said.

"I thought this might happen. Do you believe that?"

"I don't know. Should I?"

"The Chicana. She's got a Spanish that's so full of border slang that even I could pick it up. Who else could she be connected with? You know what she tried? She wanted my autograph. Maybe without that *pocho* Spanish, but you know, I don't think she even knew it wasn't right. You people need a dialect coach."

"Is she here?"

"Ho," Lovinger said. "'Is she here?' See, I told you I knew this might happen. And goddamn it, we just don't need it right now. Nobody's got *time* for complications right now."

"Then don't complicate anything. Is she here?"

"She's fine, wherever she is," Lovinger said. "As long as *you're* fine, she's fine. Stay fine."

Not quite halfway down the road they passed the first of the cages Paz had seen from the air, partially hidden among carefully clipped hedges in a clearing. Mary Margaret started visibly when the deep, almost pained rumbling of a male lion came from the cage nearest the road, answering a peal of thunder. The lion, tongue lolling, watched them pass as if they were of no more interest to him than the pair of jet-black squirrels who bounded along the road ahead of them. The female lion, jaguars, and smaller cats, all of whom seemed to be up and pacing (The coming rain? Paz wondered. Feeding time?) watched them with the same deceptive marginal interest. Without the cages, would it be so marginal?

At the end of the road the land opened out into a small paradise. The acres of tree-dotted lawn surrounded a long, low modern house, all arches and white stucco, the size of a resort hotel. The house had a chapel attached to it, mission style, and everything swept gently down toward the deep blue lake and, beyond that, the green mountains rising toward the twilight clouds. An ostrich loped away from them as they left the road for the lawn, and a peacock warned them off with his psychedelic tail. With the garage, a couple of guest houses and the outbuildings, Teri could be any of a dozen places. Paz would need keys, time.

On the lawn in front of the house a man watched them approach, as still in that landscape as if he were posing for a Watteau painting. Only Receta y Precio wouldn't have worn his combat fatigues for Watteau. Nor would he have had an ocelot pacing on a leash beside him. He didn't move as they approached except to fling ice from an empty cocktail glass onto the perfect lawn.

Lovinger shouted a couple of names, and two men in boots and *guayabera* shirts trotted from the porch of the house, pistols drawn and looking serious and puzzled. As they did, Lovinger stepped up beside Paz and jerked him roughly out ahead of the others, then halted them all a few yards in front of Receta y Precio.

"Carlos," he said and shoved Paz another yard forward with the barrel of his shotgun, showing off Paz like a hunting trophy. The ocelot stopped its pacing and eyed him warily, its tail slowly swishing. "They came bearing gifts. Quintus Paz. Recognize the name?"

Receta y Precio nodded once, curtly and mechanically.

Lovinger said, "I told you it was stupid, Carlos. Didn't I? He shouldn't be within a thousand miles of here. Maybe you'll listen to *me* next time."

Receta y Precio ignored him; his eyes rested on Paz for a moment, then moved to each of the others' faces in turn, as if he were memorizing them, or judging them. His eyes showed no surprise, no anger; they were just as they'd been in the photograph on the baron's wall, the unreadable eyes of a gambler. "You were not invited here," he said to Paz. His voice was as high and thin as a girl's, Paz heard with a shock, but like his eyes it, too, was flat, emotionless, as cold and opaque as the water at the bottom of a well.

"In a roundabout way, I think I may have been," Paz said. This little man, he thought. I didn't know he existed a week ago. Now he controls nearly everything that matters about my life. Receta y Precio was almost grotesque, almost a dwarf, yet no one — ever — had controlled as much of Paz so directly. Paz felt a quick surge of hate for the man, felt something much stronger than the mere detestation he'd felt for Lovinger.

"The animal invites its tracker? Is that what you're telling me, Mr. Paz? Well, here I am. What will you do with me now?" He swept his arm around at Lovinger, his *pistoleros*, the jungles. "I am at home. You must be very sure of yourself."

"I am," Paz said, lying.

"So am I, Mr. Paz." He motioned to one of the *pistoleros*, the bigger of the two, a man who wore a pair of turquoise and gold earrings. "Bring them inside," he said.

He about-faced and, jerking the ocelot behind him, led the way to the house, all right angles as he walked. At the porch a houseboy scurried to meet him and hold the door, and Paz and the others followed him into a living room as big as a dance hall, which was all beamed ceilings and stuffed heads and had a stone fireplace that could have been the entrance to a mine shaft. Lovinger went straight for the sideboard bar. Receta y Precio gave the ocelot's leash to the houseboy and stopped at a high-backed easy chair in front of the empty fireplace. A woman's hand was resting on the arm of the chair, but nothing else of her was visible.

Receta y Precio leaned over the chair and the woman's hand rose to touch his sleeve. He said something to the woman, too low for Paz to hear, and she leaned around the back of the chair. Receta y Precio's focus never left her face. When she saw Paz she closed her eyes and let her hand slowly trail from Receta y Precio's sleeve to the chair arm, then she sank behind the chair back once more. She was Maritza.

Receta y Precio paced, as the cats in his cages had. But his steps were short and mechanical, as if some terrible tension were turning his muscles to rock. Lovinger sat on the arm of the companion chair to Maritza's and nervously stroked his own pant leg the way he might a dog while Maritza stared into the empty fireplace. Paz remembered what she had told him in Mexico City about wanting him dead, about feeling discarded when he'd left. She'd told him then that she'd gotten over it, had met her husband and gotten over it. And he'd believed her. Now, seeing her with Receta y Precio, he understood with a sense of almost physical loathing how totally he'd been used. Yet still, still he didn't know what he'd been used *for*.

No one else moved. The pilot had been led away by the houseboy, and Paz and Mary Margaret shared a white silk couch. Stanley leaned against the mantelpiece. A *pistolero* slouched beside each door to the room, and a maid with a round Indian face circulated noiselessly with a plate of *bocadillo* snacks.

"Mr. Paz's presence here changes things," Receta y Precio said to Stanley. "I had assumed that our representatives in Los Angeles would be in jeopardy if Mr. Paz had talked with Henningsen. Now you're telling me that's not the case? He doesn't intend to report that conversation? Am I correct?"

"You are," Stanley said.

Paz took the photos Teodoro had given him from his coat pocket and flipped them onto the coffee table in front of his couch. "Earnest money," he said.

"Not very," Lovinger said. "Who else has those?"

"Nobody," Paz said.

"Then how did you get them?"

"It's what I'm good at," Paz said. "It's why you need me."

Lovinger started to answer but Receta y Precio cut him off. "I would like some other kind of earnest money, some stronger kind, Stanley."

Stanley shrugged noncommittally. Paz had once seen him use that same gesture negotiating to buy a shopping center. "I want to do business with you," Stanley said. "I told you that."

"I had wanted to make absolutely certain our airline would begin operations on time when I first called you down here this week," Receta y Precio said. "Something had come up that made that essential."

"The schedule is printed and the tickets are sold, Carlos. Six weeks from tomorrow. What more can I tell you?"

"My congratulations." Receta y Precio stopped his pacing to play with a strand of Maritza's hair a moment. "Then there's one more thing. We suddenly find ourselves with a cash flow problem."

"Because of this letter you got?"

Receta y Precio nodded.

"Are we talking about a partnership now, Carlos?"

Lovinger broke in. "Don't complicate it, Carlos."

Receta y Precio said to him sharply, "If I want your opinion, I'll ask for it, Peter."

"I only think — "

"Terms, Stanley. What do you want? You want the woman Peter brought here, I imagine. I should say stupidly brought here. Who is she?"

Paz said, "She's my fiancée."

"What an old-fashioned word, Mr. Paz. She's just that?"

"Yes."

"You might have done much better to have tracked Peter with a good dog." He glanced at Maritza. She kept staring into the empty fireplace, not reacting. "Then what else, Stanley?"

Stanley rattled off percentages, asked for figures, suggested a division of duties. Receta y Precio listened without comment when he could and offered as little information as possible when Stanley asked him a direct question. All the time on the plane that Paz had thought Stanley was hiding in his papers, something else had apparently been going on in his mind, too, something that had worked as quick as his calculator. He sounded as if he'd been thinking his proposition out for weeks. His voice was strained and he kept clearing his throat from the effort of sounding convincing, confident. Paz was again impressed.

Finally Stanley went for broke. "Then there's my personal interest," he said. "Mine and my wife's."

"And that is . . . ?" Receta y Precio said.

"The codex. Baron von Hummel. Why my brother-in-law was involved in all this. I'll have a right to that information."

"You would, I suppose," Receta y Precio said. "Tell me, Stanley. For all that, how *much* could you help with the cash flow?"

"Within what kind of time frame?"

"Say, by Monday."

Stanley looked surprised. "I couldn't liquidate a great deal by then. We're talking about securities and bank accounts for the most part."

"We both understand that."

"Then . . . two million at the outside."

"Oh, Jesus, Stanley," Lovinger said. "Just that?"

Stanley flared. "If I knew more about the problem, I might be able to deal with it better, Peter. Why doesn't someone just tell me what we're talking about here and have done with it."

"Maritza," Receta y Precio said. "Hand Stanley the letter, please."

Without answering, Maritza stood and took an envelope with a handwritten address from the mantelpiece. It would have been too high, Paz saw with irony, for Receta y Precio to reach without her. She handed it to Stanley and, as she returned to her chair, caught Paz's eye for a moment. He tried to read the look. If he saw anything in it, he saw an appeal. But for what?

Stanley slipped a typed letter from the envelope and began to read. As he read, hunched over to catch the light from a floor lamp beside Maritza's chair, he seemed to sink deeper and deeper into himself until his dark suit was all there was of him. When he was done, he handed the letter to Receta y Precio. "I see," he said.

Mary Margaret was on her feet now. "You see what?"

"You may share it if you want," Receta y Precio said to Stanley.

Stanley said, "It was from Humboldt Méndez. It was a copy of a letter to several newspapers — *Excelsior, Uno más uno, El diario* — I don't remember them all. He says the codex we saw was fake. He says he has proof."

"No, it wasn't," Mary Margaret said without hesitation. "The baron had *tests* made. I don't know why this Méndez —"

"Méndez says he had tests made, too, Mary. The baron himself told him the codex was fake weeks ago, and gave him part of the codex to have tested for himself," Stanley said gently. "He claims only the first two pages of the thing were real, and those were the ones Baron von Hummel sent for testing. Read it yourself if you want — he's got the case made."

"No!" Mary Margaret said. "I don't care what he claims the baron said. Méndez is lying. Baron von Hummel spent his whole life looking for that codex."

Maritza spoke for the first time. Her voice was muffled, slow. As she began, she shook herself, and Paz was ambushed by the realization that the gesture was heartbreaking for him. "Humboldt was right. Baron von Hummel had found those two pages years before. He made the rest of the codex himself, working all those months of the dig. He was from Dresden, you remember. He knew what the Dresden Codex looked like as well as anyone alive."

"Why did he do it?" Paz said. "Why would he fake it?" All of this — Teri, the deaths — all of it because of a fake? Yet there had to be some sense to it — even those people at the no-name bar in Mexico City whose lives Maritza had *wanted* to make no sense did make sense to somebody.

Maritza turned to look at Paz and said, as if she hadn't heard him, "It was wonderful work, Quint. I truly believed it was real. So did Humboldt, until he had his own tests made. I wanted it to be real."

"Then where is he?" Paz said rapidly, making sure she knew he was speaking just to her. "Where is the baron?"

Receta y Precio crumpled the letter and flung it into the fireplace. "Baron von Hummel is no longer the point, not so far as our needs are concerned. The point is, Stanley, when that letter is published — which, given even the slowness of our mails, could be by tomorrow, since it was postmarked Monday — there will never be any more excavations."

"Then that's your cash flow problem, and the reason you want to get the airline in operation as soon as possible," Stanley said.

"Wanted, Stanley. Wanted. The airline is no longer an option either."

"What the hell does that mean, Carlos?" Lovinger said.

"A phone call from Los Angeles about an hour ago, Peter. You'd already gone up the hill to meet Stanley. We have no more *tenientes* in the United States. They were picked up sometime this morning."

"Paz," Lovinger said. "Paz, you bastard." He got to his feet and raised the shotgun.

"Put it down!" Receta y Precio ordered. "It doesn't matter how it happened. We're out of business — in both our businesses. Face that."

Gallagher again, Paz thought. He'd given Gallagher that cock-and-bull story about getting a tip on Henningsen from the LAPD, a for-the-time-being story. But Gallagher had checked it out before the time being was over. Paz had figured him for next week at least before he could get anything going. Damn computers, he thought. Damn Gallagher's efficiency.

Stanley kept trying. "A network like yours can still be put back together, Carlos. My offer stands."

"On two million dollars? No, Stanley. Once the word goes

out that we've fallen apart, even if by some miracle none of our *tenientes* talked to the police, we'll have suppliers, lenders, investors to deal with. Do you have any idea how much they would want to call in, Stanley? They won't wait the weeks, maybe months it would take to put a new operation together. And with no back-up from the artifacts . . . no. It's over. Everything is over."

"Then why did you let me go on about the partnership?"

"Would you have told me how much cash you were prepared to invest if there had been nothing to invest in? I'll be needing cash, you understand."

And now there was nothing to negotiate, Paz thought. Stanley's power had evaporated like a rain puddle, and something more basic than money had taken its place: the need to survive. Now it wasn't just Lovinger who was dead, it was Receta y Precio and Maritza, too, unless they ran quickly and hid utterly. They'd need Stanley for that — but only for a little while. The first to be gotten rid of would surely be Teri, and then himself.

Lovinger angrily crossed the room to the sideboard by the fireplace to make a drink. Paz heard the decanter chattering against the glass as he did. "Then let Mr. Paz tell us what the fuck we're going to do." He whirled on Paz, scattering whiskey. "How the goddamn hell about it, Paz? You got fifteen, sixteen million in change on you?" He hurled the glass in Paz's general direction: it hit a couch, bounced and smashed. As it did, Receta y Precio's startled ocelot screamed and jerked away from the houseboy. The maid with the *bocadillos* was crossing the room with a fresh tray, and tried to leap out of its way as it bounded for the door; it saw her movement and, disoriented, swerved and made a running pounce onto her. She shrieked and went down in a clatter of tray and plates with the ocelot, as big as a Doberman, on top of her.

The *pistolero* with the turquoise earrings, who'd been guarding the front door, ran for her, just as Receta y Precio snatched up the poker from beside the fireplace. The *pistolero* swatted at the ocelot with his .45 and the ocelot turned on him. The *pistolero* backed away and raised the .45.

"Leave it alone!" Receta y Precio shouted and charged the *pistolero* with the poker. The *pistolero* ducked as Receta y Precio brought the poker down on him.

Paz took his chance. In the confusion, he shoved himself up from the couch and made for the door the *pistolero* had been guarding, which was only a few running steps away. He reached the door and ducked through it just in time to hear the heavy explosion of Lovinger's shotgun from the room behind him, then the last, long scream of the ocelot.

A few drops of rain had already begun to blow onto the covered porch from the clouds that seemed to sit just above treetop level, and only a charcoal light was left beyond the range of the floodlights that surrounded the house. From the porch he had his choice of heading across an open patio, which seemed to act as a hub for the various wings of the house, or trying to circle the house from the outside. He could be trapped in the patio, he thought, or lost in one of the labyrinthine wings before he'd even begun to look for Teri. He broke into a run around the perimeter of the house, stopping only long enough to bang on the barred windows he passed and hope that she would hear and answer him.

He'd gone nearly halfway around when he found her. She was in what seemed to be a bedroom, and had apparently heard him coming. As he reached the room she swung a heavy onyx ashtray and the window covered him with a shower of glass. "Get something to smash the door, Quint. Hurry!" she shouted at him. "It's locked but I don't think there's a guard outside."

Paz turned to make a quick check of what was nearest and most useful. The garage seemed the best hope, maybe fifty yards away, beyond the end of the wing. "Stay away from the window," he shouted to Teri as he turned back to her. But she didn't hear him. She was screaming and covering her head as

Peter Lovinger, the door to the room open behind him, brought the barrel of the shotgun down hard across her arm. Paz lunged for the broken window. He never knew whether he made it. Out of the corner of his eye, just before he felt the flash of light that blocked out all light, he saw the earringed *pistolero* swinging the poker toward him.

The room he woke up in was a study with a single barred window. Somebody had dumped him in a recliner chair, and had left a bright architect's lamp shining in his face. His head hurt at the base of the right side of his skull, but when he touched the spot he felt only some rawness. No blood. He was a little groggy but still able to function. His watch told him he'd been there nearly an hour when he straggled to his feet.

The room was maybe nine by twelve, roughly the size of a jail cell. On the walls around him hung a gallery of photographs, and in all of them Receta y Precio glared at the camera. In some he was holding a dead animal, in others dead fish. In one of them Salomón Katun helped him hold up a dead buck. Interspersed among the photographs were framed maps and drawings, all of them labeled "Afrimex." In one drawing, faceless tourists lounged aboard houseboats on the lake and were being served by what looked like Zulus, who'd apparently brought them drinks on speedboats. Other drawings had the same blank tourists riding in small buses with bars for walls, like cages, while lions roamed free around them. The maps apparently were of Receta y Precio's property, and showed a web of trails through the jungle. Outlines of a couple of restaurants and a hotel behind fenced enclosures were sketched in near the entrance to the property.

This was Afrimex, then, Receta y Precio's dream: the people in cages and the animals roaming free — plus a good profit. It was what he was willing to loot a city for, to flood the gringos with drugs for. It would have disgusted a man like Baron von Hummel.

A door in one wall of the room seemed to lead to an adjoining room. Paz tried it and, as he'd expected, found it locked. He looked for a telephone, located an empty plug, and made a quick search of the desk drawers, then of the bookshelves. The nearest thing to a weapon he came across was a monogrammed letter opener. He had no idea where he was in the house, where Teri was, where Stanley and Mary Margaret were. It was like being in the fishbowl on a drug bust, he thought, being the guy set up to make the buy. You turned yourself into one big sensor nerve, held on, stayed alive, felt as little as you could. To keep his growing claustrophobia at bay, he began to pop the photographs one by one from their frames with the letter opener and rip them into small pieces, which he piled neatly on top of Receta y Precio's big carved mahogany desk.

There could be only one reason for the baron's revealing the codex was a fraud, Paz decided, no matter what the reasons for his faking it to begin with and no matter why he took so long to reveal that he had. He wanted to stop Receta y Precio. And he had. But because he wanted to stop him, Humboldt Méndez had died.

The letter Stanley had read had gone out to the newspapers Monday, Receta y Precio had said. Méndez had gotten back to Mexico City from Veracruz on the Saturday before and had been killed that night. Paz put it together. If Méndez was a careful scientist, he would have wanted proof that the codex was fake, just as he had that it was real. Once he got it, he would have talked to the baron before he left Veracruz. Then the first thing he would have done in Mexico City on Saturday was report to Maritza, his boss. Maritza called Receta y Precio, who got Katun on the afternoon flight to keep Méndez from taking what he'd found out any further. Katun was right for the job: he would work silently, and Méndez knew him. Maritza led Katun to Méndez's house, then hung back until there was a body for her to discover. But it was too late.

Méndez had had time to write his letters and get them into the mailbox for Monday's pickup. The whole dig was forever discredited, the whole strip mining of artifacts was shut down.

One more track, one more piece of sign, Paz thought, but he felt none of the old excitement. No one might ever know he'd found it this time.

He ripped the last picture up, slid the letter opener into his coat pocket, then struck a match from a matchbook he found on the desk and lit the pile of torn photographs. When he had made sure the pile was burning well, he sat down in the desk chair to watch it burn its way into the desk. Thinking, planning were no good now. You couldn't plan until you knew what was coming next. You held on, stayed alive. One big sensor nerve.

It was less than five minutes before he heard footsteps in the hallway — on the thick carpeting he couldn't tell whether they were a man's or a woman's — and the door to the room next to his opened and closed. Then silence again. He got up. As he did, the lock on the door from the adjoining room began slowly and quietly to turn. He tensed, took the letter opener out of his coat and flattened himself against the wall beside the door.

Just as slowly and quietly as the lock had turned, the door opened and Maritza stepped through it. Before she could say his name he was behind her, his arm wrapped around her face, muffling her, with the letter opener pushed against the soft flesh beneath her chin. She struggled instinctively at first, then slowly relaxed: he could feel her breath against his forearm calming, the way it had as she'd eased into sleep in her apartment in Mexico City. She wore no business suit tonight, but a pale lavender floor-length dress of some very soft, very thin material that hung as light as smoke on her. And the perfume, he noticed almost against his will as he held her, the perfume was still the same.

By increments he released the pressure of his arm and turned her to face him, keeping the letter opener firmly against her chin. Her eyes were filmed as she raised them to him. "There," she mouthed and, without attempting to move her head against the letter opener, pointed awkwardly behind her to the bedroom she'd come out of. It was at the end of the wing, and from it a sliding door opened onto the lawn. "Outside."

He gripped her arm and led her to the door, then forced her through it ahead of him. The rain was coming steadily now, rattling loud as hail on the roof and running like beaded ropes from the eaves. It hit the walkway in front of the door and sent tiny bits of liquid shrapnel onto their shoes. Maritza pointed to a storage building across the lawn at the edge of the jungle. They ran.

Under an overhang of the roof of the storage building she brushed her wet hair away from her eyes. The lavender dress clung to her now like an emanation from her skin. "Oh, Quint," she said rapidly, out of breath. "He's at Katun's village. I wanted desperately to tell you inside before. Baron von Hummel's at Salomón Katun's village."

"You're sure of that? How do you know?"

"Yes, I'm sure of it! He thought Katun was his friend — he thought that Katun would protect him after Méndez was killed."

"When?" Paz said. "How long has he been there?"

"Since he disappeared. All week."

"Is he all right? Where's Katun?"

"I don't *know*, Quint. I don't know. I just found out about it today. Carlos and Peter know he's there, too, but they don't care. They know that Katun will do the same thing they would have done to him."

Paz studied her face. The appeal he'd seen inside the house was still there, but marked more clearly by fear now. "Why are you telling me this, Maritza? What do you want?"

"I want it all to be over, Quint, just over. As soon as they're finished packing here, we're supposed to be leaving. We're going to Panama in your brother-in-law's airplane. I can't . . . do that, I can't just disappear forever with that man. Please, please get me away from him. I'll testify, anything, just — get me away from him."

"What's in Panama?" Paz said.

"Your brother-in-law just called home to have those two million dollars transferred to Carlos's bank there. Carlos and Peter are giving up, vanishing. As soon as we get to Panama and they pick up the money, they've told Stanley they'll let all of you go. They won't, Quint. I know they won't."

Stanley does, too, Paz thought. He said he would get what he could, and that was what he could get: a little time. Paz knew it was up to him to get more, much more. He had no idea if he could trust Maritza now, what her motives really were. Yesterday he'd thought he could kill her; tonight he'd been sure he could. But he was outside now, free, because of her. Maritza was what he could get. "What's the best way to leave here?"

"I know where the keys to the Land Rover are. You can meet me at the garage." She indicated the next building over, maybe twenty yards away, with her eyes. "Once we're into Papantla we can go to the police."

"No good," Paz said. "Receta y Precio probably owns the police in Papantla."

"We *have* to go, Quint. You can't do anything by yourself."

"Can you get me a gun? A pistol?"

She opened her small cocktail purse and handed Paz a snub-nosed .32. "Take it. It's Carlos's."

He made sure it was loaded, then slipped it into his shoulder holster. "Get the keys and wait for me in the garage. If I'm not there with the others in fifteen minutes, take the Land Rover and get out by yourself. Which rooms are the others in? Have they moved Teri?"

"Quint, there's no way you can — " Suddenly she pointed past his shoulder. "Look!"

He turned and caught the figure of the houseboy with a rifle in one hand and an umbrella in the other ducking through the rain toward the garage. "Move!" he said and pulled her into the darkness on the back side of the storage building.

She stood inches from him, only an outline, a warmth, and a scent, as they waited for the houseboy to fumble with the lock on the garage. They'd have to wait it out: the sound of gunfire would bring the whole household onto them.

They stood silently for a time, then Maritza said quietly, "You told me you were still married, Quint. You're not, are you?"

"No."

"Is she really your fiancée? The woman Peter brought up?"

"No."

"But she's with you."

"She's with me."

"Do you love her?"

"Why, Maritza?"

She moved closer and laid her hand lightly on the back of his neck, as if she needed the solidity of something. "There was always just you, Quint," she said, her voice barely above a whisper. "Not my husband, not Carlos. My God, not Carlos."

"Then what's between you? You and Receta y Precio?"

"I didn't lie to you about everything in Mexico City, Quint. You mattered so much even one lie hurt. That's why when we slept together at my apartment, I couldn't . . . *use* what we'd had. It was the truth that I've been afraid for so long, of so much. Ever since I started taking things from the museum for Collosini."

"Were you taking things even when we first met each other? That long ago?"

"No, Quint, oh, no. I didn't have any need to then. It's not that I *wanted* to get involved with these people. Please believe that. Ever since anyone quit being able to make money in Mexico, my husband's business has been dying. He's a good man, Quint. I told you I don't love him the way I loved you, and that's true. But he's tried to be good to me and I needed somebody to do that after you left. I told him the money I gave him was from government loans I could get because of my job — the loans you don't have to pay back if you know the right kinds of people here."

"And Lovinger got to you through Collosini, and Receta y Precio through Lovinger." Stanley might not have been right about Receta y Precio's being brilliant. But he was thorough, viciously thorough. He found a way to get an assistant director of the National Institute of Anthropology and History itself to front for his looting, and he used it. First Stanley, now Maritza.

"He threatened me first, told me he could make me lose my job, and then he told me that he could help my husband's business. He had all the connections, he said. He kept me so off balance, so afraid, that when he told me he wanted me to come up here with him one week, I did, I just . . . did. I didn't have anybody to go to, Quint. You're the first one I've been able to tell any of this to."

"I'm listening," he said.

"I've tried to get out, Quint, I truly have. When I thought the codex was real, I went to Collosini. I thought I might make enough all at once so that I could stop, perhaps even convince my husband to take me back to England." She took a step back from Paz and let her hand drop. "I thought I might not have to hurt him. I'm going to hurt him now, aren't I, Quint? He doesn't know about Carlos, about . . . oh, *God*, Quint, how did I let things get in such a horrible mess?"

"You had help with it," he said.

"Not with all of it. *I'm* responsible for part of it. I was the one who was responsible for getting you down here this time. Did you know that?"

"No."

"*Claro que no.* After Humboldt was killed, Carlos decided we should make it look as if the codex had been stolen. He didn't know about the letter then, and if the codex had been stolen, you see, he could say that we had to keep going with the dig, since there might be other things as important as the codex there — maybe even another codex. I said to him, you have got to make it look as if the codex has truly disappeared, haven't you? So we have got to bring this man down here, this Paz, and let him look for it and not find it. He trusts Baron von Hummel, and his own sister will tell him she has seen the codex, so he will not doubt that it existed, and he will not doubt me when I tell him it was real, too. Everyone knows his reputation. If he reports that the codex was real and that he can't find it, then we will have every excuse to keep digging, no? I wanted to see you, Quint. And I was even more afraid of things after Humboldt was killed. I thought you might . . . protect me, get me out of this nightmare. I'm sorry."

Was killed, Paz thought. Passive voice. He almost pitied her — almost, but not quite. "Was Katun your idea, too?"

"No. It was Carlos. He said to me, if Salomón Katun watches him, we will know just where he has been and who he has seen, so we can always be prepared for what he has found out when he comes to us. When Salomón protected you from Henningsen, he thought he was making sure the dig went on. All he knew was that the dig was the only way he had of getting Carlos to keep sending him his guns. He didn't know about the airline — any of that."

"Wait. Receta y Precio is sending Katun *guns?*" More tumblers slammed into place: what had the note Teri made on the computer printout said? A Customs rep had checked out the bank in Panama as part of an arms investigation? Mother of God, Paz thought. In Veracruz, he'd imagined himself finding more and more rot in an apple he was cutting open. Was there no apple left now? Was there nothing but rot?

"That's why Katun is helping him. Salomón would never loot that city for just money, Quint. He's an *indigenista*, an Indian separationist. He needs more than just money if he's going to start a rebellion."

"That's crazy. An *Indian* rebellion? Now?" Teodoro had told
him Katun was a separationist, but being a separationist and
actually starting a rebellion were not the same thing at all.

"You don't know how bad things have gotten since you left,
Quint. *Everything's* falling apart. There are Indians like Katun
all over the country. The Indians have always hated the
government, and now that everybody else does, too, they think
it's the right time to do something. They're starting to take
over municipal palaces, army garrisons — and they're accepting
guns from whoever will supply them, the Cubans, people like
Carlos, anybody. Katun's just one of them."

"The baron knew about the guns, too?"

"Oh, no! The guns are the reason the baron finally told
Humboldt the codex was faked. When the first shipment of
them came in to Katun last month, he knew he had to stop
everything. He could live with the looting — it was only
'collectors' junk' they were finding, he said. But he knew how
many Indians would get slaughtered if Katun got a rebellion
started. He's never gotten over the war, Quint. It was because
of the war that he began his work."

"Why did he fake the codex, Maritza? Why would he think
he had to?"

"He's so old, Quint, so weak now. He knew that if he didn't
find the codex on this dig, he'd never have the strength to
mount another one. He had to make sure somebody else would
carry on for him. So he made a false codex. He was going to
show it to a few people and pretend it was stolen so that
everybody would keep looking for another one — which is just
what Carlos would have wanted him to do. But the baron
didn't even tell Carlos about it. He didn't tell *anybody* what
he was doing."

"Not even you?"

"Not even me. I didn't know until . . . until Humboldt called
me. The baron was so *sure* that he was right, Quint. He'd
spent so much of his life trying to prove what he believed
about the Jews and Quetzalcoatl, and he thought he had. But

nobody would really believe him unless there were some kind of proof nobody could doubt. So he was going to create just enough doubt to keep people searching. It was a kind of greed, I think, except not for money. I don't think he could bear to think of everything he'd invested his life in just *stopping* when he died, as if he'd never even existed. Do you understand?"

Paz remembered the difference between understanding and excusing, and said, "Yes."

He took a step back so he could see around the edge of the building. The houseboy had gone inside the garage but had left the door open. He could come out at any moment. *Hurry, damn you*, Paz thought. How much longer could it take Receta y Precio and Lovinger to pack and then to come looking for him? Fifteen more minutes? Ten? He would give the houseboy five.

"What will they do to me, Quint?" Maritza said. "If I testify for you, and if you tell them I helped you find the baron, what will they do to me? I'm so afraid of that, too, now."

"They'll go easy," Paz lied. He reached out to touch her, but she turned her back on him and leaned against the wall of the building.

"No. I don't think they will," she said. "But I'm glad I told you everything, Quint. I'm glad I told you first."

The houseboy backed out of the garage dragging a trunk, then stopped to shove the door closed. In Mexico City, Paz remembered, he'd thought how simple this case was going to be: all he had to do was find out who the two people who'd gone to Collosini were, and he could put it all together. Now he knew who the two people were, and it didn't matter at all, not at all. He was sure that Collosini hadn't even died because of either of them. He'd died because he'd figured the connection between Stanley and Receta y Precio and Lovinger (that was why Stanley's name was on his desk), and had tried to cut himself in. Katun had done *that* job for Receta y Precio, too.

It had been just last Tuesday Paz had been in Mexico City. He'd told himself then that he was owed an easy one.

The houseboy disappeared into the main house with the trunk. Paz stepped into the light and held his hand out toward the darkness that still hid Maritza. "It's time to go," he said.

Wearily she pushed off the wall and turned to him. He still couldn't see her face when her body stiffened, when her arm flung itself out in the air uselessly toward him, when she screamed his name, "Quint! God, Quint!"

Instinctively he crouched and whirled. Even in his crouch, the machete hissed by only inches from his head. He tried to lunge for the shape in white pantaloons above him but lost his footing in the wet grass and went down on his side. Through the rain everything was indistinct. He saw the shape raise the machete again, then Maritza seemed to try to rush past, but she slipped and became a lavender blur between himself and the floodlight on the building. Then she screamed again and fell out of his line of vision. He shoved himself to his knees and saw the machete come down on Maritza's body beside him, saw the wet lavender staining dark, saw the machete rising high again and glistening in the floodlight, then starting to fall.

He fumbled the little .32 out and fired without aiming. The machete stopped. Katun's face froze, as if he were listening to something happening at a great distance. Then he shrieked, a high, angry wailing sound that seemed to fill the air so completely that it could have come from the dark line of trees as easily as from a single throat. He clutched at his side and, the machete dangling limply from his hand, leapt toward the darkness behind the storage building. Paz wrenched himself sideways and grabbed for Katun's leg. His fingers brushed wet cotton, but no more. Katun's shriek trailed away and was lost in the sound of a body crashing through underbrush.

Paz scrambled to his feet and ran toward the house. If he could get inside, find cover — he had the pistol now and that gave him a little room to maneuver. The rain slashed down as heavily and as warm as water from a bathroom shower and to keep it out of his eyes he had to duck as he ran. The lawn was a marsh, and his feet hit with great splats. He lost his footing, went down, and came back to his feet. His pants clung to him like thick canvas.

When he was twenty feet from the house, the houseboy stepped out of the door again, rifle raised this time. Paz threw himself into a dive to his right, just seconds before the flash of the rifle lit the houseboy's face. He rolled, hit his feet again, and made it to the garage as the second bullet ripped into the lawn behind him. Somewhere on the wet lawn was the pistol, too, where he'd dropped it. It would have to stay there.

He was free. Heading back to the house now would be suicidal. Lights were coming on in all of the rooms, and in a moment the doors would slam open and men with guns would come running through them.

He sprinted across the driveway in front of the garage, toward the road to the airstrip. The road, too, was lighted, but once he was beyond the first curve he would be hidden from the house. He would have to risk it, have to take the chance that Receta y Precio and Lovinger would be in too great a hurry, now that they knew he was free, to spend time running him to ground. He figured their best hope was to get into the air as quickly as they could, and they knew it.

As he made his way up the slippery road, half running, half walking to preserve what breath he could, he heard the cats threatening the rain. When he passed their cages, he saw that if they had been restless before, they were actively angry now. Surely they'd missed being fed tonight, surely those cages weren't always left open to the rain as they were now. He pitied them and understood them.

He crouched at the end of the road long enough to make sure no one was guarding the plane. The only light he had was from the last floodlamp on the road behind him, but it allowed him to see that the plane sat dark and solitary on the strip. Someone had come back for the Land Rover, and so the rain walked in unobstructed sheets across the open space. He listened. From the direction of the house he thought he heard a gunshot, but nothing from the road behind him, though he could have heard nothing less loud than the Land Rover through the noisy rain. He would have to assume — pray — that if they went after him at all, they would head along the road toward town. He sprinted again, this time toward the plane.

What he did beneath the cowling of each engine he had to do by touch: find a spark plug wire and jerk. He knew that he was tearing flesh off his knuckles as he groped over the engines, but he didn't care. He kept pulling until he had a fistful of wires, and then he splashed his way to the edge of the strip and flung them away down the hill into the brush.

Inside the plane he dried his hands quickly on paper towels, fumbling his way in the dark. In the cockpit he had to risk switching on a map light to find the radio. When he did, he realized he was utterly lost. Did you have to have a key to make the damned thing work? He wished now he'd spent less time with Ethelbert and more with the air support people. He tried the On switch and the instrument lights glowed. Fine, he thought. Step one. But how did you reach somebody? *Could you reach anybody from here?* What frequency? Blindly he picked up the mike and pressed the button. "*Aló,*" he said. "*Aló, Aló. Pido socorro, pido socorro, pido socorro.*"

He listened. Nothing. He switched to the next frequency and tried again. A hiss, nothing. He flipped to the next frequency, then the next. As he tried the next, lights flashed through the cockpit; he cut the map light and radio and dropped to the floor. The lights brightened, and he heard the granny-gear whine of the Land Rover just outside the plane, circling it, drawing up at the door, stopping.

Cautiously he risked a look outside the plane. One of the *pistoleros* was pulling suitcases from the rear of the Land Rover. The other, the earringed one, stood in a poncho holding Lovinger's sawed-off shotgun on Stanley as Stanley helped Mary Margaret and Teri, who held her left arm close to her as if it were in pain, out of the Land Rover. The skinny, red-haired pilot and Receta y Precio were the last to climb out. No Lovinger. Where was Lovinger? Was he coming just behind in another car? Paz wondered with a flash of panic. Christ, he couldn't handle two cars. But no, so many people wouldn't have stuffed themselves into the Land Rover if there were two cars. Then where the hell *was* Lovinger?

The pilot lowered his head against the rain and trotted for the door of the plane. Wherever Lovinger was, he was the *next* problem now. Paz put his back to the instrument panel and squatted so that he was ready to spring.

The pilot saw him as soon as he turned from the cabin toward the cockpit, and stopped short. Paz made a circling motion with his finger; the pilot looked puzzled a moment, stepped back, then pivoted to turn on the cabin lights. He left the cockpit dark. Good man, Paz thought.

The blue barrel of the shotgun preceded the earringed *pistolero* into the cabin, just as Paz had hoped: they would put one gunman inside the plane as they were loading and leave the other outside.

Paz sprang. He got both hands on the barrel and wrenched it, hard. The earringed *pistolero* had been using one hand to hold on to the railing; the shotgun popped easily from the other. Paz slammed the butt into the man's face and the man staggered backward, missed the step below, and went down into the mud at the foot of the steps. Paz had a clear shot at the other *pistolero* and he took it, the shotgun's noise filling the cabin and obliterating whatever was coming from Receta y Precio's open mouth as he seemed to shout some useless warning to the man, who was already spinning backward into the grill of the Land Rover, pieces of his chest flying away through the light like moths. Then the earringed *pistolero* was on his feet and starting up the stairs again, and Paz took that shot, too. His aim was too quick: low and to the side. But it caught part of the man's leg, and he crumpled.

Stanley moved more quickly than Paz would ever have thought him capable of doing. He first threw a hard shoulder block to knock Receta y Precio off balance as he fumbled with the flap on his holster. Receta y Precio lost his wind and sank down onto his knees. Then Stanley grabbed Mary Margaret and pulled her backward, out of the lights of the Land Rover and behind it for cover. Teri broke for the plane and for Paz, blocking any shot he might have at Receta y Precio.

She made it as far as the steps.

The earringed *pistolero* got a grip on only one of her ankles, but that was enough. Teri kicked at him with her free foot, but he held on and anchored himself to the steps with his body. Teri reached for Paz. "I can't, Quint," she said. "Help me, oh, Jesus, Quint!"

Paz moved out onto the first step, knowing he had to get both her and himself inside the cover of the plane before Receta y Precio recovered his balance and got to his pistol. He took her hand and pulled. He knew he couldn't chance another shot at the earringed *pistolero*, either, with the sawed-off shotgun at such close range. The thing's shot pattern was so wide half the pellets would ricochet off the steps and into Teri's legs. A bow and arrow would be more use to him now, he thought.

The pilot tried to push past Paz, panicking, looking for room to run. "Get the hell back!" Paz told him, fighting to keep his own balance on the narrow step.

Then Receta y Precio made the whole problem academic. He found his balance and his revolver, which he brought up to sight on Paz's face. Paz still had no shot he could take with Teri so close in front of him.

He shoved Teri backward, away from him and out of Receta y Precio's line of fire — but still not out of the shotgun's. Then he dove, dove as if the muddy airstrip to the side of the steps were water; he was somewhere in midair when he heard Receta y Precio's shot. When he hit, he was close enough to the fuselage that in three rolls he was under it, then in prone firing position, trying to find Receta y Precio to get a shot in. But Receta y Precio had been quicker. He was behind Teri, reaching up, his stubby arm tightly around her throat and the revolver pointed at her cheek. And sprawled halfway out of the plane, on the steps, only his shoulder visible from where Paz lay, was the pilot.

"Paz, get out here," Receta y Precio shouted, as if he were disciplining a dog. "Come out here into the light. Do you hear me? I want you out here. I want you out here *now*."

Paz started working his way toward the front of the plane, crawling on his elbows the way he might have moved beneath barbed wire in an obstacle course. He stayed just far enough back from the fuselage that Receta y Precio would have to kneel to get a shot at him, kneel and make himself a larger target. Or if Paz could get a side angle, figure maybe to catch Receta y Precio with just the edge of the shot pattern . . .

He was almost to the wing when Stanley crawled out from beneath the Land Rover, his eyes fixed on the dead *pistolero*'s gun a couple of yards ahead of him in the mud. His movement must have caught only Receta y Precio's peripheral vision, but Receta y Precio needed no more than that: he fired a single quick round and Stanley jerked, made an *uff* sound, and sank down in the mud.

"Stanley? Stanley!" Mary Margaret shouted from somewhere on the other side of the Land Rover.

"Stay there!" Paz answered her.

Confused, Receta y Precio whirled and fired beneath the fuselage in the general direction of Paz's voice. He tried to back away, out of the spill of light from the door of the cabin and toward the more total dark that began behind the Land Rover's headlights. But the *pistolero* held fast to Teri's ankle. "Señor," he said to Receta y Precio, his face a smear of blood from a cut the shotgun's butt had made. His voice was pleading. "Señor, help me to stand up, señor. You won't leave me here, señor. Señor."

"Let *go*," Receta y Precio ordered.

The man held fast. "Señor — "

"For the last time, let go!"

The *pistolero* managed only to raise his free hand in a kind of supplication before Receta y Precio shot him.

And then there was nothing Paz could do, nothing but watch Receta y Precio back away through the rain into the dark, the pistol again at Teri's cheek, Teri silently struggling and trying to keep her feet as he dragged her in front of him, the two of them moving as if they were locked together in some awkward, hated dance.

But they weren't moving toward the road that led back to Receta y Precio's compound; Receta y Precio was apparently taking her straight along the airstrip. What was there in that direction? Paz desperately tried to reconstruct the mental map he'd made of the area from the plane. He remembered only jungle and the slope of the hill at the end of the strip. Then something else, a path, a narrow path that cut through the valley and over the next hill. It had gone to Salomón Katun's village.

Stanley's collarbone was broken; Paz would bet on it. But that was good, since it meant the bullet had gone in too high to hit any organs. The greatest danger was that he would bleed to death, Paz knew as he helped Mary Margaret ease him into the back seat of the Land Rover. For Stanley's sake, Paz was glad the shock had caused him to lose consciousness, but it made getting him into the Land Rover viciously slow, and anything slow was an enemy now.

The pilot's wound was less clear. Receta y Precio's bullet had caught him in the chest, so there was no way of knowing what was going on inside his body. But he was still breathing evenly and his windpipe was clear. For him, too, time meant everything.

And time meant everything for Teri. And somewhere back down the road to the compound was Lovinger.

"They got out at those cages," Mary Margaret said to Paz, her breath labored and straining as she helped him lift the pilot's legs into the passenger's seat of the Land Rover. "He and Receta y Precio and the houseboy were hanging on to the running boards, then they jumped off and after a minute Receta y Precio came back, but that was the last I saw of Lovinger or the houseboy." She was black with mud and somewhere she'd lost her diamond necklace, but she was tearless and efficient as she worked, stanching first the bleeding from Stanley's wound with gauze from the Conquest's first aid kit, then the pilot's. "It was like Edward G. Robinson," she said abstractedly.

"Meg, listen," Paz said to her from beside the Land Rover. "I'm going down there first, through the woods. Wait for me to come back — Lovinger might have set up an ambush of some kind on the road. If you hear guns, get behind the wheel of this thing and go like a bat out of hell. Can you drive it?"

"Of course," she said, sounding a little offended.

"No matter what you see, or who, keep going. The road to Papantla should be the one to the right of the lake. Find the hospital."

"You'll come back, Quint," she said, article of faith in a big brother or statement of fact Paz couldn't tell. "And then what?"

He thought a moment. "Then I'll drive us into Papantla. Somebody needs to keep that bleeding down. That's you." He couldn't take the path Receta y Precio had taken with Teri in any case — not even Ethelbert would try it tonight. There were a thousand places for ambushes, there would be a score of turnings where you could get lost, and even if he made it to Katun's village, the path would be the direction they'd be expecting him to come from. If he remembered, the trail up to there from Papantla was no longer than the path from this airstrip. With the Land Rover to get them into Papantla, he might even make better time going that way.

After they got past Lovinger.

He carried with him both the shotgun and the dead *pistolero*'s .45. He stayed on the road until he was close enough to the first floodlight to be a visible target. The surface of the road was layered with a thin mud that was as slick as motor oil, so that he could only walk now, walk or skate when the slope grew sharp. The rain in the forest around him hissed with a sound like a radio without a station; nothing but the shree of the cicadas cut through it.

Making his way through the underbrush was even slower than moving over the mud of the road. The trees broke the force of the rain but not the blinding volume of it, and he knew that if this hadn't been new growth, he wouldn't have made it at all without a machete.

As he approached the floodlit clearing where the cages were, he stayed low, blinking away the water that filled his eyes again as soon as he did. From here the hedges hid the bottom four feet of the cages, which had roofs but were open to the blowing rain on the sides. So he could see nothing but the still, gray upper portions of the cages, no movement but that of the rain-heavy branches in the wind. He crouched closer through the underbrush. Something scuttled away from him low on the ground, and he jumped back and struck at it with the pistol. He hit weeds, a fern, mud.

At the clearing, he broke for the hedges, the noise of his running covered by the sound of the rain. When he reached the hedges he waited again, still crouched, listening. He heard a faint thumping noise, but none of the complaining he'd heard from the cats on the way up. He inched his way to the edge of the neatly trimmed foliage and tried a snapshot look at the nearest of the cages. They were open and empty.

Afrimex, he thought. That was what Receta y Precio had made Lovinger and the houseboy stop off with him for, then, making it clear that Lovinger was no more than a houseboy now that his connections meant nothing. The people in cages and the animals free. Even in the warm rain Paz felt a chill of fear as he thought of what was around him in this dark underbrush now.

But where were Lovinger and the houseboy? They'd had more than enough time to have emptied all the cages and made it up the hill to the plane.

Paz thought he knew. He stood and stepped into the clearing.

The houseboy's legs protruded from behind the hedges on the far side of the clearing. The hindquarters of a jaguar were straddling the legs, the jaguar's tail slowly swishing.

The male lion lay at ease still in his cage, his jaw hanging open in a slow pant. He looked at Paz with little interest. One of his huge paws rested across Lovinger's body as if the lion were a house cat holding a catnip mouse down. The blowing rain had left the bottom of the cage wet, so that Lovinger's blood had spread over the floor, diluted, a weak red film. His face had deep claw marks on it, and one of his eyes hung loose from its socket like an egg on a string. The lion had begun with his back. Most of it was missing.

Excess baggage for the flight south, Paz thought. Receta y Precio would have a use for *pistoleros,* but not for these two. And he had made sure that if either was identified, no one could ever be sure of the exact cause of death.

The lion lowered his head, took Lovinger's shoulder in his mouth and lifted it. When the flesh tore away, Lovinger's body dropped limply with the thump Paz had heard from behind the hedges. Paz thought of Maritza's waiting body on the floodlit lawn below, then of the two dead men on the airstrip.

With the shotgun, he drew a bead on the jaguar first. The lion would have to disentangle himself from Lovinger, then try to maneuver his way out of the cage. Paz would have more time for the lion.

ELEVEN

THE NARROW ROAD that twisted through the hills into Papantla seemed to exist only to provide the dozens of vanilla and coffee bean merchants some frontage for their businesses. It clearly hadn't been designed for cars. The Land Rover lurched through potholes and between parked cars with inches to spare, while Mary Margaret tried to cushion Stanley in the back seat and Paz used one hand to hold the pilot more or less upright in the seat beside him.

The rain had eased into an intermittent drizzle as they'd slid down the muddy road from Receta y Precio's. But once they were on the pavement, its function of slowing them seemed to have been taken over by a deluge of people. Even before they hit the edge of town, the shoulders of the highway had been filled with them: women in elaborate lace dresses like brides, men in the white pantaloons and smocks that made them all look like versions of Katun, all walking toward Papantla. Now, as Paz tried to maneuver the hilly, clogged medieval streets of the town itself, he realized the task was hopeless.

"What is it, Meg?" he asked. "What festival?"

Mary Margaret seemed to consult some half-forgotten mental calendar of holy days for a moment. "June? Corpus Christi."

"Then it'll go on all night," he said and swung the Land Rover off the pavement and, lurching, onto the tiled sidewalk. "Look," he said. "We'll never make it this way. I'll get a cop. Are you still all right to drive?"

"I think so. Quint, don't go up to that village. For God's sake, not by yourself."

"Stay here," he said. "I'll find a cop."

He got out and pushed through the crowds toward the lights of what he took to be the *zocalo* ahead. At the next intersection he found a tan-uniformed local traffic cop. Shouting over the noise of a record store's loudspeaker blasting out some weepy song about lacerated hearts, the cop told him the Seguro Social hospital was less than three blocks away. Paz gave him a short-term lie about an automobile accident, and, for five thousand pesos, the cop was only too glad to give up trying to direct the stalled traffic and make a way for the señor's car to the hospital.

Mary Margaret was already behind the wheel when they got to the Land Rover. Paz knew he'd have to leave the shotgun behind now, but he had the .45 and that would have to do. He leaned into the Land Rover and dug a flashlight out of the glove compartment while the cop stood in front of the Land Rover and examined the license plate.

"Tell them anything you want at the hospital," Paz told Mary Margaret while he shoved the shotgun out of sight beneath the seat. "But before you talk to any kind of cop, get a call through to the embassy. Tell them to get Gallagher. Explain to them what's happened. Remember the name Teodoro Alcalde, too, at Mexican customs in Veracruz. He's your second call."

"Quint, *please* go to the police first."

He straightened up. "I do that and everybody in that village could be dead or in Guatemala by the time I get through explaining all this," he said and touched her arm. "Good luck."

Through the windshield Paz saw the cop's face suddenly

harden, and knew that he had recognized the license number. Of course, he thought. Receta y Precio's plates would be memorized by every cop in town.

The cop stepped to the side of the Land Rover. "I assume you will come with us to the hospital, señor," he said to Paz, his hand resting on the hilt of his revolver.

"*Cómo no?*" Paz said. "Why not?" The cop was trying to peer into the Land Rover now. Paz stepped back as if to give him a better view. Even a local traffic cop, he thought, would recognize the bullet hole in the pilot's shirt. The cop leaned in the window. Paz elbowed a drunk out of the way and shoved into the crowds again, looking for an alley.

The cop would get to the first phone, Paz knew: his head start was small. He would have to move fast in territory he didn't know. But at least he thought he could count on the cop to see that the well-dressed gringos got to the hospital. The man wouldn't want to buy into the trouble not doing that could bring him.

The trail to Katun's village had begun somewhere behind the cathedral, Paz remembered. He checked to make sure the cop had stayed on the block behind with Mary Margaret instead of following him into the piss-smelling alley, then flowed into the crowds again, heading uphill.

At the *zocalo*, the crowds were even thicker — and there were more cops. There was more light here, too; strings of bare bulbs swung between huge hardwood trees to light the food stalls, which sent smoke from roasting meat and boiling porkskins up toward the cathedral like incense. In a shop window he saw himself, muddy and European among the clean white clothes and dark faces of the Indians. He knew a cop would see that, too. He knew what cops saw.

He was halfway across the *zocalo* when he picked up on the two of them working him. Not coming after him, just sending eye signals and pacing him through the crowds, which meant they hadn't gotten the word on him yet. They were as easy for him to keep in sight as he was for them among the small Totonacs. He slowed, stopped at a stall to buy a sweet potato *camote*, feeling in the throbbing of his blood the seconds passing as he forced the thick candy down.

The cops stopped, too.

Receta y Precio had headed for Katun's village, Paz figured, because Katun was the last man he had any hold over: Receta y Precio was Katun's last link to an arms supply, and Receta y Precio would buy what he could with that promise. He would want Katun to help him get out of the country, or at least to the temporary safety of Mexico City. And once they were under way, Teri would only slow him down. She would stay alive only as long as Receta y Precio was in Katun's village.

Paz eased back into the crowd, smiling, knowing that until he had a bath and change of clothes, nothing would make him look normal. With the .45 in his shoulder holster, he couldn't even afford to take off his filthy coat.

As he moved toward the cathedral, the music changed. Here there were no record store loudspeakers, but street bands that played in circles of yellow light thrown by kerosene lanterns or burning oil drums. The music was drums, flutes, harps that joined in wailing, repetitive songs whose words were in a language Paz didn't understand but recognized. It was the language that he had thought might be the one birds would speak when he'd heard Salomón Katun speaking it. He stopped again. The two cops moved just ahead of him, closing in, and stopped, too.

Paz checked what he had in front of him before he could make it to the darkness behind the cathedral. The only way up seemed to be by way of a long stone stairway rising to the cathedral beside a high retaining wall that kept the church from sliding down into the *zocalo*. The entire wall was covered by a block-long mural that had something to do, as best he could tell, with the history of Mexico, or of the world, or of the universe. To get to those steps, he had to fight his way through the most dense crowd of all, the one surrounding the storeys-high pole of the *voladores*, the fliers, who were already on their four-cornered platform at the top of the pole.

Paz had to make the steps, then, before the cops did. He pushed forward, heading toward the *voladores*. As he did, he saw a third cop edge through the crowd toward the first two, hook up with one, signal to the other, and start moving toward him. Mary Margaret's cop had found his phone.

Paz was almost relieved that the coyness was over, the waiting and pretending. It was a race, and everybody in it knew it was now. Paz squeezed between people when he could, used his hands and his shoulders when he couldn't. His one advantage was that the cops had to vector toward him through the crowd along the legs of a triangle. Their distance to the steps was longer.

As he fought forward, he watched the high platform of the *voladores* as if it were a lighthouse to steer by. They were getting ready to fly, he knew. He'd seen them a dozen times on tour in Mexico City. The leader stood in the middle of the four men who waited for his signal at the corners of the platform. He held a wooden flute and a drum that he played faster and louder as Paz approached, crescendoing toward the moment when they would launch. Like the others, he was a bird, with his feathered headdress that described the plane of a broken circle over him, like an aura.

Paz reached the steps just as the leader gave the signal to the four *voladores*. The men leapt out into the air while the crowd's cheers rose, fireworks exploded, and skyrockets arced and flashed in the night sky beyond the *voladores'* spotlights. Ten feet behind Paz the first of the cops looked up at the *volador*, and Paz rammed his way among the bodies that packed the steps.

The noise and cheering covered the curses of the people who fell away behind Paz. By the time he was twenty feet up the steps, all three of the cops were behind him, picking their way among the people who had lost their footing and fallen as Paz had forced them out of the way. One of the cops had his gun out, though Paz knew he wouldn't use it, not yet, not until he was clear of the crowd. Paz pushed harder. A boy about Craig's age lost his balance as Paz shoved, and leapt into space from the edge of the steps. Paz saw that he landed on his feet, laughing, on a pile of street vendor's blankets. From the corner of his eye, he saw the *voladores* circling outward, their feet tied to ropes that unwound from the pole like long Maypole ribbons, sending them farther and farther out into the air, bright birds, becoming for a few seconds the oldest dream of all.

Then he was at the top of the stairs, with the stone courtyard of the cathedral spreading out before him toward the dark street that would lead to the trail to Katun's village. The courtyard was nearly empty compared to the *zocalo* below, and he threw himself forward into a run across it.

He knew he would have somehow to reach the jungle ahead of the cops. Odds were that they were younger than he was, faster, and they knew these streets. Only someplace where there *were* no streets would he lose them.

He kept his speed up as best he could, running on slippery stone with dress shoes, as he hit the street behind the cathedral. The lights from the festival didn't reach here, and the street was nearly deserted, its wet cobbles reflecting the dim streetlights as if they were only torches. From below, the sound of the music and the crowds seemed to be coming to him from beneath a thick blanket. Only the weak light of a cantina, from which arguments and boozy singing spilled into the street, broke the patterns of stone wall, wooden balconies, and dark overhangs of tile roof as he ran. It seemed to him that he was somehow running backward in time, too.

As the houses grew sparser along the street, he passed small groups of Indians, late stragglers, heading for the festival.

Katun's people, Paz thought, as they turned with silent curi-
osity to watch him. A pistol fired behind him; he swerved and
kept running.

Then the street simply ended: a last house, then a few final
cobbles beside a corn field, and it was done. Here the trail
began, sloping away in two rutted tracks wide enough for a
cart or a pickup down the mountainside into the jungle. Paz
crashed ahead into the corn field, switching on the flashlight
as he did so that the cops would see him.

He stayed among the cornrows, slanting in what he judged
was the general direction of the village, for maybe a hundred
yards, then picked up the trail. He looked behind him to see
if he could see flashlights following, but there were none.
Without them, the cops would thrash around blindly in the
corn field for a while, then head back for reinforcements and
lights. They wouldn't chance the trail in the dark with a man
ahead of them who might be armed, might not even chance it
at all until morning. He stopped, took his coat off and threw
it into the bushes, and drank the air until the trembling in his
muscles subsided.

The rain's intensity had picked up again, not to the monsoon
strength it had had before but to a steady downpour. As Paz
started up the trail, the insect noises became as loud as a rail
yard, and he could hear the calls of hunting night birds above
the hiss of the rain. Human sounds had ceased: not even the
music from the festival reached here.

He used the flashlight only in brief flicks to check the area
ahead of him, then moved on from memory. When he had
gone what he guessed should be most of the way toward
Katun's village, he stepped off the trail and into the relatively
open space of a coffee planting, the coffee bushes growing in
even rows beneath banana trees that protected them from the
sun. He didn't use the flashlight at all here; the rows of bushes
kept him from getting lost. Sooner or later, he knew there had
to be a side trail that would lead into the village.

He found the side trail by the lights. To his right, as he came to the end of the coffee planting, he saw dim but steady sheets of light from open doors and windows, light broken into odd shapes by the tree trunks, shimmering through the rain. And angling off toward those lights was a path. He took it, feeling the wet branches of the underbrush slap at him like hands.

Near the first lighted hut he drew up to listen and watch. It was after ten by now; those who were going to the festival were already there. The rest of the villagers were inside, away from the rain, either in bed or getting ready for it. Still, he skirted the edge of the huts when he began to move again, heading toward the temple mound that he'd seen at the head of the widened trail from the plane.

The mound was much larger than it had seemed from the air. It had been cleared of trees so that its pyramid shape was recognizable against the low gray clouds. Brush and grasses still covered some of it, but the side that faced the village had been cleaned and, as best Paz could tell in the reflected light from the houses, roughly restored: the staircase that had once led to the temple on top was a wide ramp running straight up the side again. The pyramid rose in tiers, maybe a dozen of them, adding up to the height of a four-storey building. The excavations had been done from the side fronting on the main street, too, and the dirt taken from the tunnel had been piled to either side of the entrance in long mounds. Beside one of these sat an apparently homemade bank of floodlights on a wooden cart.

But it was less the mound than the large, round, white-plastered hut next to it that Paz knew had to concern him now. The *cacique*'s hut, Katun's hut. When Paz had seen it from the plane he'd remembered the sensation he had felt as he had looked up at the puma's cave high above him in a cliff in the Andes. And now he had come here, just as he'd finally made it to the cave. This sensation was different, purer, the way it had been when he'd begun to crawl into the cave itself: no anticipation, no excitement, only fear.

The hut was lighted, and through the open door Paz could see a man passing back and forth, back and forth, as if he were walking a baby or carrying things from one place to another. He couldn't get a look at the man's face, but from his size and clothing he knew it was Receta y Precio. Nothing else was moving inside the hut. Paz took out the .45, released the safety. Using the wooden store for cover, he sprinted for the nearest mound of dirt in front of the pyramid, staying low. He counted to twenty, waiting to see whether he'd been spotted, then moved out from behind the dirt toward the hut itself.

He'd only gone a few paces when he caught the movement outside the hut. It was a flash of white, an arm moving up to touch a face or adjust a collar. For a moment he froze, then cut sharply to his left and behind the cart with the homemade bank of floodlights, where he almost tripped over the power wire. He caught himself on a wheel of the cart, cursing twenty-peso electricians who ran power wires directly up to overhead lines and left them hot during the rainy season.

The movement came again, and this time Paz could see what it was as the man stepped into the light that spilled from the hut's door. It was a hand adjusting the strap on an AR–15 automatic rifle.

No, Paz thought, he hadn't been owed an easy one. He was expected.

The man with the rifle was dressed *jarocho* style, as Katun had been, but was easily half again as large as Katun. He stood a moment, looking up and down the muddy street, then leaned into the hut and said something to someone inside. He apparently got a reply, stretched, and walked toward the bushes at the rear of the hut, fumbling with his fly. Paz had only as long as it took a man to piss to get inside the hut. There was no time for strategies, for subtlety. He could cover the distance to the hut by short hops from dirt mound to clump of bushes to trees, or he could risk seventy or so yards of open ground. He pushed himself off the cart into the molassesy mud of the open ground.

At the hut, he decided to go in low: the thing was round, with no blind corners. He could make himself a bad target and still sweep the room. He squatted beside the door, gripped the .45 with both hands, and threw himself sideways into the door.

"Freeze! Police!" he yelled, habit and fear taking over. If there was a gang of Totonacs in the room with Receta y Precio, who would understand him?

But there was only one: Katun. He lay in a hammock, shirtless, with a wide cotton bandage around his waist and an AR–15 across his lap. Receta y Precio spun to face Paz from beside the room's only table, a jade fertility goddess the size of a bar of bath soap in his hand.

"Quint, oh, Jesus," Teri said as she stood up from a roughly made ladder-back chair beside the table. As she did she winced, and Paz could see that her right forearm was swollen and yellow. It was the arm he'd seen Lovinger hit with the shotgun at Receta y Precio's.

"Can you get the rifle? You've got to get the rifle," Paz said. He kept the .45 trained steadily on Katun's skeletal face.

"I can get it." Teri's face was drained, grayish, as she moved around the hut's center post so she could take the rifle by its butt. She cradled it lightly against her side with her left arm.

"Point it at the back of Katun's head," Paz said. "Let him feel it." He steadied himself against the door frame and pushed to his feet, the pistol trained on Receta y Precio now. "Lie down on the floor. Keep your hands on your goddamned head. Where's your pistol?"

"On the table," Receta y Precio said. He did as Paz had told him. "You'll never extradite me, Paz. You know that."

"Your choice," Paz said. "A drug charge in the States or an arms charge here. I know which one I'd choose."

The table was covered with artifacts — jade, clay, turquoise and gold, obsidian. There were fetishes, painted bowls, figurines, pendants, earrings, gold pins. As Paz picked up Receta y Precio's pistol, his eyes fell on a plate with a stylized plumed serpent design along the edges. In the middle of the plate was a black Star of David.

An open jute bag stood on the opposite side of the room so that Katun had a clear view of what went in it. Negotiating, Paz thought. Receta y Precio needed travel money and Katun got promises.

"Can you cover them? Both of them?" Paz asked.

"If I can sit down," Teri said.

"Is it broken?"

"Probably. The bastards wouldn't make me a sling. It's starting to hurt like hell, Quint."

"We'll get out as quick as we can." Paz slid the chair over to her, lobbed her Receta y Precio's pistol, then faced Katun and said in Spanish, "Make a sound and she'll kill you." Katun gave no sign of having understood. His sunken eyes met Paz's. There was no expression at all in them, no hate, fear, comprehension, nothing.

Paz squatted again by the door, on the inside this time. In seconds, the sound of a man splashing through mud and rain puddles came from the side of the hut, and then the guard he'd seen before was in the doorway. The man looked puzzled, then angry, as if he'd caught someone in bed with his wife, and began to raise the AR–15. Paz slammed the .45 upwards into the crotch of his white pantaloons, and he doubled over with a sharp grunt. As he did, Paz brought the pistol up again, this time into the man's face. The man toppled sideways. Paz was on his feet and gave him a last chop to the back of his head as he was going down. The man lay still. Paz worked the AR–15 off his shoulder and leaned it beside the door.

Katun had watched impassively, as if the man had been a character in a book that didn't particularly interest him. Paz knelt beside him and pointed the .45 at his face. Even now, he felt the sense of being in a charged space when he was this close to the man. Katun almost imperceptibly shrank back from Paz's closeness, and Paz smelled an odor from him that reminded him vaguely of wet earth.

"Where's Baron von Hummel?" Paz asked him.

"I don't think he speaks Spanish, Quint," Teri said. "They've been using something I've never heard."

"Yes, he does. He *won't* speak Spanish. But he's got to understand it. He's the *cacique.*" He moved the .45 closer to Katun's face. "Don't you?" This was the man who had tried to kill me, and saved my life, Paz thought. Had either of those things meant anything to Katun? Paz tried to see something behind the black eyes that would give him a clue, something that might tell him how the man had felt when he was bringing his machete down on Maritza. He couldn't; he remembered now the last thing he'd thought when he finally came upon the puma at the back of the shallow cave just before he shot it. He'd thought the puma had looked at him the same way it would have looked at a stone.

"Do we understand each other?" he asked Katun. "If you don't tell me where Baron von Hummel is, I'll kill you and I'll kill your man over there on the floor, then I'll go through this village killing every living thing I can find."

"Paz — " Receta y Precio said.

Without taking his eyes from Katun's, Paz said to Receta y Precio, "And I'll kill you, too, you son of a bitch."

He cocked the .45. He had thought of himself as king of the borders, all the borders you could cross. And this one? "Where is he?"

"*Está allá,*" Katun said, and motioned faintly toward the pyramid with his chin.

"Show me," Paz said. He stood up, stepped back. Painfully, unsteadily Katun eased himself out of the hammock. On his feet, he swayed a moment, then seemed to get his balance.

Paz said to Teri, "You'll be all right here?"

"For a while," Teri said. Her voice was weak, strained.

From the dirt floor, Receta y Precio said in English, "You're being stupid, Paz. Do you actually think you're going to get out of this village towing an old man and a woman with a broken arm?"

"One way or the other, yes."

"Katun needs me, Paz. He'll let you go if I tell him to. Leave me behind with those artifacts and I'll make sure you get out."

"Christ almighty, man. It's busted," Paz said. "I know that and Katun knows that. If he kills us, he knows somebody will still come here looking for us. If he lets us go, he's got to figure I'll carry the word on him. You're no good to him now."

"He won't think that way," Receta y Precio said, talking rapidly, selling. "He just knows I'm the only one who can get him what he wants. He's like an animal, Paz — I've trained him. He'll do what I tell him."

"The only thing you could do for him now is to slow him down, if he could figure out some way to run. He'd kill you in a minute, you ass. And so will that woman in the chair, if you move." Paz flicked the .45 toward the door. "You first," he said to Katun.

Katun took a couple of wobbly steps, hesitated, then his legs folded and he began to fall toward the door. On instinct, Paz reached for him. As he did, he took one of his hands off the .45 and spread his arms, the way he might have to catch a child who had lost its balance on a bicycle.

By the time he brought them back together, Katun had the AR–15 Paz had left leaning against the wall. Paz kicked, and the rifle flew from Katun's hands and out the door. But with the incredible quickness that Katun had shown at Collosini's, he rolled through the door and fell on it again before Paz could get to him. Paz took a step toward him, then whirled and threw himself on Teri. She screamed as the chair splintered beneath them, and Paz knew she had landed on her broken arm.

But it had worked. Paz had knocked them far enough to the side of the door that Katun had no shot — or at least not at them. During the confusion Receta y Precio had clambered to his feet and gone for the sack of artifacts. Now he grabbed it and ran for the door. Paz let him go: he would be a screen, something between them and Katun.

Receta y Precio got as far as the door and stopped. Paz rolled off Teri onto his stomach and aimed at the darkness beyond the door. "The window," he said to Teri. "Can you cover the window?"

"Yes," Teri said, the one word low, through teeth clenched against her pain.

From the darkness came a burst of sentences in Katun's language. Receta y Precio answered and held up the bag of artifacts. Katun said something else, his voice rising and his speech growing more rapid. Receta y Precio slowly lowered the bag of artifacts to the ground. Katun's voice was calmer when he spoke again, but Receta y Precio wagged his finger and took a steady step toward the darkness. He held his hand in front of him as if he were approaching an unfamiliar dog, then took another step, all the while speaking in a low, steady voice.

"Receta!" Paz said, "Get down, you damn fool!"

"He's mine, Paz," Receta y Precio said without turning. "He's *mine.*"

Katun said one short word. Receta y Precio took another step and snapped his fingers on his outstretched hand, as if he were commanding Katun to give him something. Katun said the short word again. Receta y Precio took another step.

Katun fired on full automatic and caught Receta y Precio solidly in his midsection. Receta y Precio jerked backward into the room like a man who'd had a hard tackle thrown on him, and four fist-sized holes appeared in his back as suddenly as they might have in a grotesque animated cartoon. Paz raised his hand against the splattering blood, but it did little good. He felt it warm as the rain water against his face.

He got off three quick blind shots through the door as Receta y Precio was going down, then rushed it. Stupidly rushed it, he thought, if Katun hadn't disappeared completely by the time he got there.

Teri was trying to get to her feet. Paz turned back to the room and lifted her to the hammock. She was breathing in quick gasps, trying to control the pain in her arm. "Oh, God, Quint. Oh, *God*," she said.

"It's over," he said. "Can you walk?"

"You don't have Baron von Hummel yet. Go."

"Teri — "

"Look. You're too close now not to finish, so *go*, damn you." She shoved him away from her with her good arm. "And take the rifle — leave me the pistol. It's better at close range." She held out her hand for the .45.

He gave it to her.

Katun had indicated the pyramid; that was all Paz had to go on. He understood that Katun could be setting a trap, but he didn't think so. It would be too obvious a one, and Paz would be prepared for it. Katun would know that. And he would know that his only hope for surviving was escape. He would need time to organize his people to slip away into the jungle with the arms he'd bought for them with their dead city, and there was no more time.

Nevertheless, Paz stayed to the shadows as he dragged Receta y Precio's body outside the hut, then started for the pyramid. Down along the village street, a dozen or so people who had been drawn out of their huts by the gunfire huddled in the rain. But they were old people and children; the young were still at the festival. He stepped back into a stand of trees to give himself some cover in case Katun was still watching, and fired a short warning burst over their heads. "*Policía!*" he shouted. "*Regresen a sus casas!*"

That would be enough for them to understand. Police and gunfire. Stay home, it meant. Cover your head. Keep out of it and wait till it goes away. They knew.

At the mouth of the tunnel into the pyramid, he took the

flashlight from his pocket and, keeping his body to the side of the entrance, swept the tunnel with it. What he saw was a small mine shaft, timbered and braced with logs; its dark earth walls reflected no light. It seemed to go back roughly a hundred feet and stop, and there were several smaller side tunnels off it.

"Baron von Hummel!" he shouted. Only a muffled, faint echo came back to him from the soft earth of the tunnel's walls; it was as if the pyramid had swallowed the sound, as it did the light. "Baron Frederick von Hummel!"

He stepped into the tunnel and walked a dozen paces. It was cooler here, and, without the sound of the rain, silent. The damp earth smell was as pungent as the deep coal cellar's at his grandfather's house had been. "Baron von Hummel, it's Quintus Paz!" A king snake flickered by him toward the mouth of the tunnel.

At each of the side tunnels he used the same technique: first sweep it with the flashlight while he kept himself out of the way, in case there was any fire to draw. Then quick-check it with a bob of his head before stepping past it. None of them proved to be more than fifteen feet deep, and each of them was empty. If anything had been found in them, he knew it was now in a dealer's gallery in Los Angeles or Tokyo or London.

The room at the end of the tunnel wasn't empty. It wasn't big, no larger than a bedroom in a tract house. But it was big enough to hold the crates of weapons that were stacked around its walls, obscuring bright murals of what seemed to be kings and captives, processions, feathered dignitaries, human sacrifices. The descriptions of what was in the crates were cleanly stenciled in English — model numbers, military requisition numbers, type of weapon or ammunition, company and place of manufacture.

And it was big enough to hold the baron, who after all was, as Mary Margaret had said, a frail little man. Six or seven crates had been shoved together and stacked in the center of the room to make a kind of platform; he lay on it looking upward, feet together and hands at his sides as if he were at attention. The wood of the crates was stained with blood, which had run down their sides to be soaked up by the dark earth.

Paz approached the platform, loosely covering the lens of the flashlight with his fingers to soften the harsh light. He was surprised to see how sparse the baron's hair had gotten, with only a few gray wisps left on the sides. He had several days' growth of beard on his thin face, which meant Katun had brought him in here only recently, maybe not even until today. His pale blue eyes were still open, and he was naked to the waist. His face was rigid in an expression that could have been either fear or revulsion, as if he had been visited at the last by the horror he had set out half a century before to flee from.

As Paz drew closer he saw the clean incision just below his rib cage, encrusted with blood that had dried and cracked like spilled paint. It had been made in a place from which you could reach inside to pull a man's heart out.

He stepped back. On a crate he hadn't noticed against the wall he saw a crudely carved wooden statue of the reclining god Chac-Mool, receiver of sacrifices, his hands cupped on his stomach to make a bowl. The statue stared blankly at the crates of guns and, behind these, the feathered kings who marched in their frozen procession around the walls. Paz knew, but didn't want to know, what the shapeless mound in the bowl was. He looked away from it, feeling a burst of nausea in the back of his throat.

He tried to associate the shrunken body on the platform with the man who had rummaged with such energy through the antiques shop in Quito once, and who had brought a few days of lucidity and peace to Paz's father's life (and Paz's) now and again through those rootless years of his childhood. His mind told him there was no connection, but his gut said that was a lie. He put the flashlight down and unstrapped his shoulder holster, and in the close, cool silence, took his shirt off and carefully spread it over the baron's face and naked chest, stretching it wide as if there were much more to cover than this one old man in this small, quiet room.

Paz paused at the mouth of the tunnel, breathing deeply the air from the wet jungle. He squeezed his eyes tightly shut for a minute or more, trying to block out what he had seen in the room behind him, in the week behind him.

The rain had almost stopped, and the noise of the insects had claimed the night again. Mist was beginning to rise from the jungle; the lighted windows at the end of the village street were blurring, losing their shape. Paz's wet pants hung on him as heavily now as if they were made of cement. He slung the rifle over his shoulder and stepped fully out of the mouth of the tunnel.

As he did, he felt the other rain.

It was the tail end of a small landslide, a trickle of loose pebbles that had begun much higher up on the pyramid and had had a clear run to the bottom down the ramp that had once been a stairway.

Anything could have started a landslide like that, Paz thought. A bobcat, an iguana, even a snake. Anything.

Even Salomón Katun.

What if Katun hadn't escaped, then? What if he had decided to stay and make a stand instead, had decided to go to the high ground, where he would have an unbroken field of fire the whole length of the village street. It was conceivable and, as Paz thought about it, even probable. Katun had been to Mexico City, had seen the scavengers, the beggars, the people from villages like his who lived in the bleak shantytowns. For a man like him, would staying here and making a fight be any worse than escaping to that?

He could have cut around to the side of the pyramid while Paz was heading for the tunnel, and climbed it when Paz was inside. He could be there now, in position, waiting.

Staying close to the mounds of dirt, Paz worked his way to a clear view of Katun's hut. Teri had put the lights out, and Paz was relieved. If Katun was a very good shot, he could hit anything in the hut he could see from where he was.

Teri had made the darkness her friend — but so had Katun. It was a friend Paz had to take away from him.

He looked back up at the pyramid. In the darkness, Katun could be lying on any one of the dozen tiers. But he wasn't, Paz knew. If he'd truly gone for the high ground, he would be at the very top, where he could control all the approaches. You'd be a fool to go after a man in a position like that, especially with mist rising.

If Katun was up there at all.

Would I be disappointed, Paz asked himself, if he wasn't?

He stuck with the mounds of dirt for cover until he worked himself as close as possible to the bank of floodlights on the cart. Then he made a dash across the twenty feet of open ground that remained between the mounds and the cart. Everything would depend on Katun's not seeing him, not knowing what was coming.

Once he got to the cart, he stayed very still for perhaps five minutes. If Katun had gotten only a glimpse of him, he still might not know where he'd gone. He began slowly to feel for the switch, grateful now for the twenty-peso electrician who'd been too lazy to disconnect the wire from the power line.

He found it and braced the rifle on the cart beside the switch. Then he flicked on the flashlight and pitched it like a hand grenade toward the open space in front of the pyramid. A burst of rifle fire from the pyramid sent geysers of mud up in its beam; it spun crazily a few feet along the deserted street and went out.

Now.

When the floodlights came on Katun was still standing, the rifle to his shoulder, aiming. As Paz had guessed, he was at the very top of the pyramid, where the temple had been. In another half hour, he would have been invisible in the mist. He swung the rifle toward the floodlights without lowering it and fired, sweeping the cart, the lights, the ground around them, blinded and striking without thinking at the thing blinding him.

As Paz pulled the trigger and held it, the rifle butt pounding his shoulder like an airhammer, he wondered what was in Katun's eyes now. Then Katun stopped firing and the rifle tumbled away down the side of the pyramid. He stood for the briefest of moments more, looking around him as if he were trying to find an escape from the light, before he fell forward into the misting air.

EPILOGUE

THE BITTERSWEET SMELL of the desert night after a rainy-season *chubasco* storm followed Paz into Teri's apartment. He crossed the living room, eased the door to her bedroom open, saw that the light was out, and started to close it again.

"Quint?" she said.

"Didn't mean to wake you," Paz said. "I'll stay at my place tonight. You need rest."

"It's OK. I was waiting for you. Where have you been?"

"Harmon sent me on a stakeout at the border. He didn't tell you?"

"I left early — had to get my cast checked. Where on the border?"

"Short Street in Nogales. Some kid pitching Baggies full of coke over the fence to another kid with a fielder's glove on a front porch on our side."

"Good pitching arm?"

"Didn't miss a one. Boring as watching bullpen practice."

"Back to normal, eh?"

"Back to normal."

"You don't have to keep standing in the door, you know."

He came into the room and sat on the edge of the bed, careful not to disturb her arm. Her loose hair spread over her pillow in the spill of light from the living room, catching points of it, shining.

"Sorry the Mexicans pulled your work permit?" she said and reached for his hand.

"I don't know that it matters. I talked to Mary Margaret today. By the time Stanley gets out of the hospital and finishes paying his fines and straightening out his legal and money messes, odds are there won't even *be* an airline."

"That wasn't what I was asking. Are you sorry?"

"Did I have a choice?"

"All along. Lots of them."

"Then no, I'm not sorry. Not for the choices."

"Me neither. Not for yours, not for mine."

He gently stretched his feet out on the bed. "Harmon get his report done before you left?"

"He was on the phone to Mexico all morning. Gallagher's agreed to swear he never got in touch with you in Veracruz to tell you you were off the case. The deal is that he gets credit for busting the thing up, though. Not you."

Paz made a face. "How about Teodoro?"

"He's claiming you checked in with him before you headed up to Papantla, so you're covered there. He's even saying it was the fault of one of *his* people for not following instructions to meet you at Receta y Precio's."

"And the Mexicans are buying that?"

"What can they do? He's hitting them with the argument that there would have been — as Harmon put it — this damned Custer's last stand Indian uprising, and that you and he stopped it."

"So I'm clear."

"Not yet. But Harmon thinks you will be. I saw him put the endangered lizard file on your desk."

"How about you?"

"If you're clear, I'm clear. I officially went down TDY under cover — as your sister's private secretary. I backdated the orders today."

"Harmon's taking some chances."

"I wave my cast at him. He knows he owes us."

"How is it?"

"Mending, the doctor says. It itches."

They sat in silence for a while, feeling the rise and fall of the pulpy breeze through the window. At length Paz said, "I got Craig to the driver's license bureau before I left today."

"He do OK?"

"Yep. I met Bess's fiancé when I picked him up. You want to go to the wedding?"

"She *invited* us?"

"*He* did. His ex-wife's coming. He's modern, Bess says."

"You're not going, are you?"

"Not me." He felt a jab of loss — though not regret — when he thought of the wedding. That would get easier, he knew. Not easy, but easier. Like the pain he felt because of Maritza and the baron. In time, easier.

"Take off your shoes and stay awhile," Teri said.

"In a little bit. I'm expecting company."

"*Now?*" Teri said.

The sound of a car or truck clunking to a stop came from outside the window, then the thud of a door closing.

"Right now," Paz said and got off the bed. "Be back."

Teri pushed herself upright with her good arm. "What is it, Quint? Who's out there?"

"Don't worry," Paz said. "It's a friendly."

Outside, just at the edge of the lights in the gravel parking lot, Ethelbert sat on the fender of his listing truck with the top of a beer can barely rising from between his log-size legs. He waved when Paz approached.

"You saw me," Ethelbert said.

"Picked you up getting in your truck in the parking lot at the federal building."

"That soon? I got to be more careful. Last time you were all the way home before you made me." He grinned his jack-o'-

lantern grin; behind him in the truck the front sight of his .38 glowed softly from the dashboard. He'd put fluorescent paint on it for night shooting, Paz knew. "You mind I'm here?"

"It's OK. I've been wanting to catch up on things with you."

Ethelbert reached into a paper bag beside him on the hood. "You want a beer?"

"No thanks. What's up?"

"You heard they got the guys that took Derek down?"

"I heard. In Hermosillo."

"Yeah. I want to go down there, Quint."

"Then go."

"Come with me. You got some pull in Mexico."

Paz shook his head and smiled. "I can't get away, Ethelbert. Believe me."

"Why not?"

Paz thought a moment, then lightly slapped Ethelbert's knee. "Endangered lizards," he said. "I've got a hot case about some endangered lizards I just can't let go."